# WHEN HE WAS A DUKE

## The Duke's Legacy
### Book 1

## Tess Thompson

## ARE YOU SIGNED UP FOR DRAGONBLADE'S BLOG?

You'll get the latest news and information on exclusive giveaways, exclusive excerpts, coming releases, sales, free books, cover reveals and more.

Check out our complete list of authors, too!

No spam, no junk. That's a promise!

### Sign Up Here

www.dragonbladepublishing.com

*Dearest Reader;*

*Thank you for your support of a small press. At Dragonblade Publishing, we strive to bring you the highest quality Historical Romance from some of the best authors in the business. Without your support, there is no 'us', so we sincerely hope you adore these stories and find some new favorite authors along the way.*

*Happy Reading!*

*CEO, Dragonblade Publishing*

# PROLOGUE

*Ashford Estate, one week before Christmas…*

BEFORE THE CLOCK struck nine that December evening, the Ashford children would find themselves quite alone in the world, though at half past eight they concerned themselves only with the likelihood of suitable sledding weather.

Snow adorned the topiaries in the garden beyond the tall windows of Ashford Manor's grand drawing room, where the scent of cinnamon biscuits lingered, mingling with the crackle of a warm fire. Sebastian lounged on the hearth rug, the rough weave scratching against his elbows as he balanced a book on his chest. Sophia lay beside him, half asleep, her silky hair tickling his arm as she shifted closer, one hand clutching the soft ear of her favorite stuffed rabbit.

James, always restless, stood at one of the drawing room's impressive windows, his breath fogging the glass as he peered out at the falling snow across the estate's vast grounds. "Think it'll stick enough for sledding tomorrow?"

"Only if it keeps falling," Sebastian said without looking up from his book.

Their father chuckled from his leather armchair, though Sebastian noticed him glance toward the window with a slight frown before returning to his newspaper. Papa had seemed distracted all evening, his usual easy laughter coming a beat too late, his fingers drumming against the chair's worn leather arm.

"You boys will find any excuse to ruin your trousers," Papa said.

"Ruin them gloriously," James replied with a grin.

This was their sanctuary—the one hour each evening when Papa set aside his duties to simply be with them. Other fathers of his station left their children entirely to nurses and governesses, but Papa had insisted upon this ritual ever since Mama's death. Sebastian had always felt safe here, surrounded by familiar warmth and the sound of Papa's voice reading aloud or answering their endless questions about everything from Latin conjugations to why stars shone.

Papa set down his newspaper and leaned forward, carefully adjusting Sophia's stuffed rabbit so its worn velvet ears lay just so against her cheek. "You'll catch a chill, poppet."

Sophia stirred, nuzzling deeper into the rabbit's fur. "M'not cold. Just sleepy."

"I'll put you to bed soon," Papa said, his voice soft as worn silk.

A sharp knock echoed through the manor's grand entrance hall. Then another. Louder, more insistent.

Papa's hand stilled on Sophia's hair. The drumming of his fingers against the chair arm stopped entirely.

The children all looked up at once. Mrs. Ellsworth appeared in the doorway, her face drained of color, her usually steady hands trembling as she clutched her apron.

"Your Grace," she said, her voice stretched thin as wire. "There are constables at the door. They say they must speak with you immediately."

Sebastian watched his father's face carefully. Papa's expression remained outwardly calm, but Sebastian caught the way his jaw tightened, the way his shoulders went rigid. As if he'd been expecting this.

"Did they say why?" Papa asked, though his tone suggested he already knew.

Mrs. Ellsworth shook her head. "Only that it's urgent, Your Grace."

Papa rose slowly, his movements deliberate and controlled.

He smoothed his waistcoat with hands that barely trembled, then looked at his children with eyes that held too much knowledge, too much sorrow.

"I'll return shortly," he said, but the words sounded hollow even to Sebastian's young ears.

The moment Papa stepped out, the peace of their evening shattered like ice on a pond. James pressed his palms against the cold window glass, his breath coming faster. Sophia curled tighter against Sebastian's side, her rabbit's fur growing damp with sudden tears she couldn't name.

Sebastian lay frozen on the hearth rug, his book forgotten, listening to the muffled voices from the entrance hall. Papa's voice, measured and careful. Other voices, harder, more demanding.

Then a clatter. A sharp, angry shout that made Sophia whimper.

The drawing room door burst open with such force that it struck the wall.

Their father stood in the doorway, flanked by two uniformed constables. His face was pale as the winter sky, his shoulders rigid with barely contained emotion. One constable held a piece of official parchment; the other kept his hand resting meaningfully on the hilt of his weapon.

"By order of the Crown," the first constable declared, his voice cutting through the room's warmth like a blade, "Edward Ashford, Duke of Ashford, you are under arrest for the murder of Lady Eleanor Wentworth."

It was as if ice water had been thrown in his face. Sophia bolted upright with a strangled cry that seemed to tear from her very soul. James spun from the window and stepped protectively in front of his siblings, his young face twisted with confusion and dawning rage.

Sebastian went utterly still, his book sliding forgotten to the floor with a dull thud. The fire's warmth no longer reached him. The scent of cinnamon biscuits turned sour in his mouth.

"There must be some mistake," Papa said, and Sebastian heard the careful control in his voice—the tone Papa used when he was furious but trying not to frighten them. "I barely knew Lady Wentworth. I certainly had no reason to harm her."

"The evidence says otherwise, Your Grace. A bloodied candlestick bearing your family crest was found on your property. Come peacefully. For the children's sake."

Papa's eyes found each of theirs in turn—James's fierce and frightened, Sophia's brimming with tears she didn't understand, Sebastian's wide with a horror that seemed to age him years in an instant.

"Listen to me," Papa said, his voice steady despite everything crumbling around them. "I am innocent of this charge. Remember that, no matter what anyone tells you. I love you. Be brave for each other."

And then the constables led him away, his footsteps echoing through the grand entrance hall until the manor's heavy door closed behind them with a sound like the sealing of a tomb.

Mrs. Ellsworth gathered Sophia into her arms, the little girl's sobs muffled against the housekeeper's shoulder. She motioned for the boys to come close, her own eyes bright with unshed tears.

"You'll stay with me tonight," she whispered. "We'll... we'll sort everything out in the morning."

But as Sebastian watched the fire begin to die in the grate, the flames sputtering lower while snow continued its relentless fall outside the manor's windows, he felt something cold and hard settle in his chest. The twelve-year-old boy who had lounged peacefully on the hearth rug just minutes before was already disappearing, replaced by someone who understood that the world was not safe, that peace could be shattered in an instant, that even dukes could be dragged from their homes in chains.

He would need to become stronger. Harder. Someone who could protect what remained of his family when the adults had failed them so completely.

The fire died to embers, and Sebastian Ashford began his transformation from boy to the man who would one day stand in the shadow of Newgate Prison, promising vengeance on those who had destroyed everything he loved.

Six months later, the thick, clammy fog that had settled over London seemed to seep into Sebastian's very bones as he led his siblings through the narrow, twisting streets toward Newgate Prison. Each cobblestone beneath his worn boots felt like a step deeper into a nightmare from which there would be no waking.

The boy who had once lounged by the fire with a book balanced on his chest was gone. In his place walked someone aged beyond his years, his hand clasped so tightly around Sophia's that he could no longer feel his fingers. The weight of responsibility sat on his narrow shoulders like a lead cloak. He was all they had now.

Sophia had grown thinner still, whittled down to little more than bird bones and enormous blue eyes. She stumbled beside him, her breath coming in short, frightened puffs that made small clouds in the bitter air. Her free hand clutched the same torn piece of lace—all that remained of the handkerchief Papa had given her on her last birthday, back when their world still made sense.

James walked three paces ahead, his shoulders rigid with a fury that seemed too large for his small frame. His boots struck the cobblestones with deliberate force, as if he could somehow pound his rage into the very stones of London. The boy who had once defended weaker classmates now carried a different kind of fire. One born of injustice and helpless anger.

The stench of coal smoke and the Thames wrapped around them like a burial shroud, mixing with the sour smell of un-washed bodies and rotting vegetables. As they drew closer to the prison, the crowd thickened—a writhing mass of humanity drawn by the promise of spectacle. Sebastian could hear their eager murmurs, the occasional cruel laugh, the betting on how long the condemned man would dance at the rope's end.

Their father. Their Papa, who had once lifted Sebastian onto his shoulders to see the Christmas pudding being lit. Who had taught James to fence in the long gallery. Who had called Sophia his "little poppet" and let her fall asleep in his study while he worked.

The day Papa was arrested still felt like a waking nightmare. They'd been having breakfast when one of the gardeners discovered a bloody candlestick hidden under a rosebush—not subtly concealed, mind you, but set at just the right angle to catch the morning light. Papa had sent for the police immediately. They'd arrived with news of Lady Eleanor Wentworth's murder. Someone had bludgeoned her to death in her own drawing room during the night.

Her husband, Viscount Wentworth, had been quick to name his enemy—the Duke of Ashford—as his wife's killer. A candlestick that had been in the Ashford family for generations had gone missing, and lo and behold, its match remained on the mantel of the Wentworth drawing room while its pair lay hidden in the Ashford rose garden.

The police might have investigated further. But they hadn't. They'd been quick to arrest, the courts quick to condemn. Almost as if Viscount Wentworth had undue influence upon the authorities.

He did. Sebastian knew it. Papa knew it too.

During their last visit to the cold, dark prison, Papa had explained the Viscount's hatred—an old rivalry that went back to their days at Cambridge.

"Your mother chose me, you see. Not the Viscount. He never forgave either of us for it. Emily had never wanted him, but he'd convinced himself otherwise. When she refused his proposal, telling him she loved me, he vowed to make us pay someday."

Papa's voice had been hoarse from the damp cell, his usually immaculate beard grown wild and shot through with new silver. "The candlestick, it was planted to entrap me. I'm certain of it. He killed his wife and had the evidence placed in our gardens."

"Why would he kill her?" James had asked.

"He was a man with little control over his emotions," Papa had said. "Spoiled. Privileged. Led to believe by his parents and the sycophants around him that he was better than others and therefore could do as he pleased. When we were at school together, he was known as a cheat and a liar. A petty brat who'd never heard the word no. I can only imagine what he would do if someone finally said it to him. Perhaps his wife disobeyed him or challenged him? Maybe they were fighting and he lost control of himself?"

Sebastian's stomach clenched so hard he thought he might be sick right there in the street. The taste of copper filled his mouth. Lord, he'd been biting his tongue without realizing it. But he couldn't stop. Couldn't falter. Papa had to see them. Had to know that whatever lies had condemned him, his children believed in his innocence.

"Sebastian." Sophia's voice was barely a whisper. "I cannot... I cannot breathe properly."

He stopped, pulling her into the shelter of a doorway while the crowd surged past them. Her face was pale as parchment, her lips tinged blue with cold and fear. He stripped off his own coat, threadbare now, but still warmer than her thin shawl and wrapped it around her trembling shoulders.

"Listen to me, Poppet," he said, using Papa's endearment. "We are Ashfords. We do not break. Not today."

She nodded, though tears leaked from the corners of her eyes.

They pushed forward again, and Sebastian spotted a familiar face in the mob—Susan, who had been their housemaid until they'd had to let her go along with most of the other servants. Her face was streaked with tears, her cap askew.

"Susan!" Sebastian called out.

She turned, and her expression crumpled when she saw them. Without hesitation, she began shouldering her way through the crowd, her voice rising above the din: "They're Lord Ashford's children! For God's sake, let them through!"

"Stay strong," she whispered in Sebastian's ear as the crowd parted. "We all know the truth. Someday everyone will too."

The path Susan had opened led them closer to Newgate's towering stone walls, blackened with soot and age. In the courtyard beyond the gates, a wooden scaffold stood like an altar of death. The black-draped cart waited nearby, and the hangman's noose swayed gently in the morning wind.

Sophia made a sound—not quite a sob, not quite a whimper. Something broken and small. James cursed under his breath, words he'd learned from the stable boys, his hands shaking now as well as clenching.

Then the prison gates groaned open.

Their father emerged into the gray morning light.

He was thinner than even Sebastian had feared, his clothes hanging loose on his frame. His skin had the pallor of a man who had not seen proper sunlight in months, his once-muscular figure now gaunt, his intelligent eyes hollow. But even with the heavy shackles around his wrists and ankles, even surrounded by guards, he carried himself like the duke he was. His head was high, his step steady.

When his eyes found his children in the crowd, his composure almost broke. Sebastian saw it—the way Papa's breath caught, the way his lips parted as if he might cry out. For just a moment, the Duke of Ashford was simply a father seeing his children for the last time.

"Papa!" Sebastian raised his hand, his voice carrying over the crowd's murmur. "We are here!"

Relief flooded their father's face, erasing years from his grizzled visage. For an instant, Sebastian could see the man who had taught him to ride, who had read him stories by the fire, who had promised that everything would always be all right.

Papa's gaze locked on Sebastian first, and a silent question passed between them: Will you take care of James and Sophia?

Sebastian nodded. "I shall do my best, Papa," he called out, his voice steady despite the tears streaming down his face. "I give you my word."

Next, the duke's gaze moved to his middle child. James lifted his chin, his eyes flashing with love that mirrored their father's. Papa had often said James was like their mother—fierce, loyal, and protective of those they loved. As the two communicated without words, it became obvious to Sebastian that his father was asking James to forgive, to live without bitterness.

And finally, he turned to his little Sophia. She broke away from Sebastian's grip and stumbled forward. "I love you, Papa!" she sobbed. "Please do not forget us!"

"I could never forget, Poppet!" Papa's voice carried clearly across the courtyard.

Then Sophia asked, in her sweet, high-pitched voice that somehow carried over the crowd's murmur, "Will you tell my mother I said hello? Does she know me, do you think?"

Papa's face softened impossibly. "She does, love. I'm sure of it. In fact, she visits me often in my dreams and tells me how proud she is of her pretty, smart daughter."

The clergyman stepped forward then, a thin man in black robes who began to murmur the familiar words of final prayers. Papa listened with bowed head, his lips moving silently. When the time came for his last words to the crowd, his voice was calm, measured, dignified.

"I am an innocent man," he said, his voice carrying over the hushed crowd. "Someday, God willing, the truth will be revealed. You need only look to Viscount Wentworth to see who really killed his wife."

Then his voice softened as he turned to his children. "Each of you has brought me more joy than a man deserves. You have blessed me beyond measure. Never forget how much I love you. And please, do not let my fate make you bitter. Live with truth and integrity. Let your hearts lead your decisions. Be happy, knowing I shall be watching you from heaven. So very proud."

The executioner stepped forward—a massive man whose face was hidden behind a black hood. His movements were swift and practiced, horrible in their efficiency. Sebastian found himself thinking, with strange detachment, that this was the man's job. Afterward, he would go home to his wife and children and forget that his actions had torn a family apart forever.

The noose went around Papa's neck with a sound like whispered death. The trapdoor yawned beneath his feet like the mouth of hell itself.

Sebastian's breath stopped in his chest. The world narrowed to this moment, this terrible, final moment. Beside him, Sophia whispered the Lord's Prayer through her tears, her small voice barely audible.

Without warning, Sophia tore away from Sebastian's grasp and ran toward the scaffold, screaming Papa's name. A guard caught her before she could reach the steps, his hands gentle but firm as he held her writhing, desperate form.

"My little love," Papa called to her, his voice impossibly tender. "It is all right. I am not afraid. Go to your brothers."

Sebastian gathered Sophia into his arms, feeling her small body shake with sobs that seemed too large for her fragile frame. James dropped to his knees on the cobblestones, his hands pressed flat against the stones as if he could somehow anchor himself to the earth.

Papa closed his eyes. His lips moved in silent communion with his God. Then he opened them once more and looked toward his children with a smile that was both heartbreaking and somehow, impossibly, peaceful.

"I love you," he mouthed one final time.

The executioner's hand moved to the lever.

Time stretched like spun glass, fragile and endless.

Then the lever fell.

The trapdoor beneath Papa's feet gave way, and the rope

snapped taut with a sound that would live in Sebastian's nightmares forever. For a moment, everything stopped. The Duke's body convulsed as the noose tightened, his final, grotesque jerk signaling the end.

Papa hung lifeless in the bitter wind.

James collapsed completely then, rocking back and forth on his knees, his shoulders heaving with silent, violent sobs. Sophia went limp in Sebastian's arms, as if her spirit had simply fled from a pain too great to bear.

But Sebastian remained standing, watching as the executioner cut the rope and Papa's lifeless body crumpled to the wet ground. His father—his guide, his hero—lay in the dirt like a discarded thing.

Several guards came forward with a stretcher. When they had Papa situated, they lifted him and headed toward the heavy prison doors. Sebastian half-expected James and Sophia to rush toward their father's body, but they remained by his side. Perhaps they knew, as he did, that Papa's soul was no longer there.

Around them, the crowd began to disperse, murmuring amongst themselves about the spectacle they'd witnessed, their bloodthirsty desires satisfied.

Damn them all.

Sebastian stood among the wreckage of their childhood, his heart a gaping wound. But something else was taking root there, something colder, more deliberate than simple grief. Not just vengeance, though that burned in him like Greek fire. It was purpose, sharp and clean as a blade.

He would not simply restore their name. He would destroy the man who had orchestrated this travesty. Viscount Wentworth would pay for every lie he had told, every piece of false evidence he had planted, every moment of suffering he had inflicted upon their family.

Sebastian would learn the art of patience. He would master the games of power and politics that had defeated his father. He would become everything he needed to see justice done. He would ensure his siblings lived full lives—ones that fulfilled their father's wishes. With opportunities and freedom. And love. That most of all.

And he would never, not for a single day of his life, forget the sound of that rope going taut, or the way his father had smiled at them even as death reached up to claim him.

The boy who had walked to Newgate Prison that morning was gone. The boy who had once read peacefully by the fire while snow fell beyond the windows was nothing but a memory.

In his place stood someone harder, colder, infinitely more dangerous.

Someone who would make the world remember the name Ashford—and tremble at it.

Someone who would make Viscount Wentworth suffer.

# CHAPTER ONE

O N A QUIET July evening, Sebastian Ashford stood at the edge of Brighton's Lower Town docks, watching the sun bleed gold and crimson across the English Channel. Twelve years of planning, and he was no closer to destroying the man who had murdered his father.

The visit to Ashford Hall that afternoon had left him raw. Weeds choked the circular drive where carriages had once delivered distinguished guests. The family crest on the rusted gates was barely visible beneath years of neglect and salt air. Everything they had been, everything they should have inherited, was rotting away while Viscount Wentworth lived in luxury built on lies.

Sebastian turned from the water, his jaw set with familiar resolve. Time to get back to work. James would need help at the tavern tonight, and Sebastian couldn't afford to lose himself in bitterness. Not when he still had a promise to keep.

The narrow streets leading back to the Stag & Anchor reeked of rotting kelp and despair. Sebastian passed the usual collection of drunks and whores, dice games and stolen goods changing hands in shadowed doorways. This was their world now, not by choice, but by the machinations of a man who should have hanged instead of Papa.

The tavern's sign creaked overhead as Sebastian pushed through the entrance. He breathed in the familiar scents of spilled ale, woodsmoke, and damp, salty sea air that had seeped into the bones of the place. Pipe smoke curled from the mouths of men, drifting up to linger against the soot-darkened beams. Lanterns swung from the ceiling, their golden glow flickering against stone walls that had witnessed decades of Brighton's rougher trade.

The scrape of chairs on uneven floorboards and the occasional burst of raucous laughter filled the air. No matter the evening, it was always the same here. Sebastian might have found solace in the familiarity of it all, but he most decidedly did not. Although he respected the men who frequented establishments like this, he could not help but feel misplaced. He'd been meant to be a lord, not one of these roughnecks. His family's estate was only miles from here, decaying in the briny air with nothing but ghosts to roam the hallways. Yet here he was.

Tonight, as most evenings, the establishment hosted men who worked with their hands and bodies. A table of sailors played a loud game of dice, their coins clinking against the crude wooden table. Hands calloused and scarred from rope work lifted pints or tumblers of rum. Gamblers and rogues sat in the shadows at the far end of the room, well-dressed in fine waistcoats that didn't necessarily match their station. Thievery was as common as gambling here.

A barmaid dressed in a skirt hitched slightly higher than was proper balanced a tray of drinks while sidestepping a man's attempt to slap her bottom. Sebastian caught the glint of a dagger tucked into her garter. Smart girl.

James stood behind the scarred mahogany bar, sleeves rolled up, golden curls falling over his forehead as he poured drinks with practiced efficiency. At twenty-two, he'd grown into his strength, but Sebastian could still see the furious ten-year-old who had wanted to fight the whole world on that terrible morning at Newgate.

Sebastian still found it hard to believe that James had won this place in a poker game. How a man could gamble away his livelihood in such a manner was beyond Sebastian's comprehension. If he could have his old life back, he would never risk losing it again. But James had lucked into a way to make a living when their options were so limited. Out of nowhere, his brother had a business and they could live in the rough rooms above the tavern.

It had been twelve years since they'd watched their father hang. A lot had transpired in those years, none of which had been good.

They'd been sent to live with Eugenia Langston, a distant cousin of their mother's. Living with the Langston's had not been as they'd hoped. Far from it. Sophia, at only eight years old, had been banished downstairs to live with the servants and work as a scullery maid. Sebastian had been sent out to work with the gardeners, living in the bunkhouse with the rest of the outdoor staff. James had been ordered to live with the horses, forced to muck out stalls, clean hooves, and haul heavy buckets of water in exchange for meager meals. Somehow James had kept up with the work, despite being so young. By the time James was fourteen, he was as strong as most men.

By then, both brothers shared scars on their backs from regular whippings. Baron Langston was a mean, vicious man who enjoyed hurting helpless boys. At least those brutal years had taught Sebastian something useful about gardening.

"You're late," James said without looking up, sliding a pint across the bar to a waiting sailor.

"Went to see the estate." Sebastian grabbed an apron and tied it around his waist. "Our estate."

James's hands stilled for just a moment. "How bad?"

"Bad enough." Sebastian began wiping down glasses, the familiar routine helping to settle his nerves. "But not our concern tonight."

They fell into their usual rhythm of pouring drinks, breaking up the occasional fight, keeping the peace among Brighton's rougher elements. Sebastian had learned to appreciate these men, even if this wasn't the life he'd been born to live. They were honest in their appetites, their anger, their loyalties. Unlike the aristocrats who smiled while they plotted one's destruction.

Near midnight, as the crowd began to thin, Sebastian found himself serving two young men at the far end of the bar. Their accents marked them as local workers, and they were deep in their cups, complaining loudly about their troubles.

"Bloody Thorncroft," the first was saying, a thin man with dirt permanently embedded under his fingernails. "Two years I've worked those gardens, and he tosses me out like rubbish."

His companion, clearly the worse for drink, squinted at him. "Who's Thorncroft again?"

"Head gardener at Wentworth Manor, you great fool. Been telling you for an hour." The thin man took a long pull of ale. "Says the aphids on the roses are my fault. Like I can control every bug in Sussex."

The name Wentworth chilled Sebastian's blood. He forced himself to continue his work, ears sharpening to catch every word.

"Wentworth Manor," the drunk one repeated slowly. "That's the place where the lady got murdered, innit?"

"Aye. And now his lordship's decided to throw a ball. First one since it happened. Masquerade, they're calling it." The thin man's voice turned bitter. "Thorncroft's beside himself, needing everything perfect. That's why he sacked me. Needs proper hands before the fancy folk arrive."

Sebastian set down the glass carefully, his pulse quickening. A ball at Wentworth Manor. The first since Lady Wentworth's murder. And they needed a gardener.

"When's this ball, then?" the drunk asked.

"Three weeks, near enough."

Sebastian glanced toward James, who was occupied with a group of sailors at the other end of the bar. His brother hadn't heard the conversation, hadn't caught the name that still had the power to turn Sebastian's blood to ice.

Wentworth.

The man who had framed their father. Who had stood in

court and wept crocodile tears over his murdered wife while sending an innocent man to the gallows. Who had destroyed their family and stolen their future.

And now Sebastian had a way inside his house.

He knew about aphids. Ladybugs were their natural predator, and a mixture of soap and ash could clear them from rose bushes within days. Simple enough knowledge for any country-bred gentleman's son who'd spent years working in the Langston gardens. Knowledge that could get him past Wentworth's gates.

The two men finished their drinks and stumbled out into the night, their complaints fading into the general noise of the street. Sebastian continued his work mechanically, his mind racing with possibilities.

A masquerade ball. Dozens of guests, servants running everywhere, the chaos of a grand social event. And Sebastian would be there, tending the gardens, invisible as all servants were to their betters. Close enough to watch. To learn. To find the evidence that would finally prove what he'd always known.

That Viscount Wentworth had murdered his wife and framed Lord Ashford.

"You've got that look," James said quietly, appearing beside him with empty glasses to wash.

"What look?"

"The one you get when you're planning something dangerous." James's voice was carefully neutral, but Sebastian heard the worry underneath. "What is it?"

Sebastian glanced around the tavern, making sure no one was listening. "Wentworth's looking for a gardener. And he's throwing a ball in three weeks."

James went very still. For a moment, Sebastian saw his brother as he'd been at ten, all fury and helpless rage, wanting to strike back at a world that had torn their family apart. But now there was something else in his eyes. Understanding. Resolution.

"This is it, then," James said quietly. "The chance we've been waiting for."

"I think so. I can get inside his house, learn his habits, maybe find evidence."

"Sebastian." James leaned forward, his voice intense but low. "I know you have to do this. We both know Papa's memory won't rest until justice is served. But promise me you'll be careful."

Sebastian felt the tension in his chest loosen. He'd expected arguments, pleas to abandon his mission. Instead, James understood what this meant.

"You're not going to try to stop me?"

James's mouth twisted in a bitter smile. "Stop you from finally getting the chance to clear Papa's name? To prove what we've always known?" He shook his head. "I've watched you carry this burden for twelve years. I've seen how it eats at you, knowing the truth and being powerless to act on it."

"Then you understand why I have to try."

"I do. But that doesn't mean I'm not terrified." James's voice roughened. "Wentworth destroyed Papa. He could destroy you too if he discovers what you're really doing there."

"He won't. I'll be just another servant to him. Invisible."

"See that you stay that way." James gripped Sebastian's forearm. "Get the evidence we need, but don't take unnecessary risks. We've lost enough already."

Sebastian nodded, already running through the possibilities in his mind. After twelve years of waiting, of planning, of carrying the weight of Papa's memory, finally he had his chance.

"Tomorrow morning, I'll ride out to Wentworth Manor and apply for the position."

"And I'll be here, keeping things running, waiting for word from you." James's eyes were fierce with the same protective instinct that had once driven him to defend weaker boys at school. "Just come back to me, Sebastian. Come back with the truth, but come back alive."

Sebastian felt the weight of his brother's faith, his trust, his shared need for justice. "I will. I promise."

Viscount Wentworth had no idea what was coming for him. But he would learn.

Soon.

THE BARMAIDS HAD nearly finished washing up the tables and were now asking for their pay, so Sebastian excused himself to take care of them.

Sebastian paid the women and sent them on their way. "You're walking together, isn't that right? There are all kinds of riffraff on the streets this time of night."

They agreed, giving him cheeky grins and promising to return tomorrow evening. He walked with them to the door, planning on locking it behind them so he could start closing up. Besides one last poker table, the tavern had emptied out.

He'd just seen off the barmaids when, out of the corner of his eye, he saw a dark figure approaching. Someone slight. Definitely female. Limping? She wore a cloak with a hood that covered her face. When she stepped into the light shed from the streetlamp, she pulled back her hood.

He gasped. It was his sister.

"Sophia? Is it you?" He blinked, sure his eyes were playing tricks on him. But no, it was Sophia. His darling sister. There was no mistaking her fair, heart-shaped face and golden hair and those big blue eyes that had captured his heart the moment she was born.

"Sebastian, thank God I found the right place."

They rushed toward each other, embracing tightly. "What in the world are you doing here?" He glanced around, eyeing a gang of rough-looking men across the street. "Never mind. Let's go inside." He rushed her through the door and locked it behind them.

"Sophia? I cannot believe it's you." He held her at arm's

length, taking in every detail. He'd not seen her in three years and had hoped to make a trip to Bristol where she'd been working, but hadn't yet had the opportunity. She was as pretty as ever, but a dark bruise under her left eye looked fresh. Her eyes were red and swollen, as if she'd been crying for hours.

"I've had to leave my position." Sophia's eyes filled with tears. He reached into his pocket for a handkerchief and handed it to her. She dabbed at her eyes, then slumped against him. "I've not eaten since yesterday. Do you have any scraps left in the kitchen?"

There was obviously more to the story, but she seemed too weak to tell him now. "Yes. Come sit. I'll get you something warm to drink and eat." He led her over to a table in the corner.

"Stay here. I'll find you something from the kitchen," Sebastian said.

"Where's James?" Sophia asked, unbuttoning her cloak. "I'm dying to see him."

"He's back in the poker room. I'm sure he'll be out in a minute."

Sebastian hustled into the kitchen. The cook had put everything away for the night, but he managed to find a loaf of bread, a few slices of ham, and some butter. Upon his return, he found Sophia sitting with her face in her hands. She looked up at him, giving him a thin smile.

"Here, eat. Then you can tell me what's happened. Do you want a sherry or whiskey? Ale?"

"An ale would be nice, thank you," Sophia said, already tearing off a chunk of bread.

He went behind the bar to pour a pint and returned just as the poker game broke up. A half dozen disgruntled men filed out of the back room and headed toward the front entrance. James came out last, quickly moving to unlock the door and bid them all goodnight.

"Someone's going to shoot you one of these days," one of them growled on his way out.

"Now then, don't be such a sore loser," James said, shutting and locking the door behind them.

James turned slowly and then stopped, paling at the sight of their sister sitting there. "Sophia? Is it you?"

"Yes, James, it is me." Sophia stood, holding out her arms.

James rushed over to hug her, pulling her off her feet and holding her tight before setting her down and searching her face. "You've been hurt?"

She briefly touched the bruise on her cheek. "Yes. I've had some difficulties. I've lost my position."

"How did you know where to find us?"

"It's a long story," Sophia said.

"Sit and eat. Then tell us everything." James held Sophia's chair for her, then took a seat himself. Sebastian joined them at the table.

"What has brought you to us?" James asked. "Something's happened."

Sophia blushed and her eyes filled with fresh tears. "It's mortifying to have to tell you. The man I was working for... he assaulted me."

Sebastian's fists immediately clenched. "What did he do?"

"I ran away before he could do much harm," Sophia said hastily. "But he managed to bruise me pretty badly. He underestimated my strength, however. All those years working at the Langstons made me strong. We have them to thank for that, I suppose."

"You ran away and came here, then?" James asked, his voice low and dangerous.

"Yes. He was drunk and pulled me into his study when I was on my way up to bed. We fought, and I managed to get away. Perhaps I did some damage to his manhood with the heel of my boot." She smiled wickedly, even as tears gathered at the corners of her eyes. "It wasn't the first time he'd tried, but I couldn't stay any longer. I thought maybe I could live here with you and find work as a governess somewhere in Brighton."

"Of course you can stay with us," James said immediately. "We'll figure out the sleeping arrangements. The apartment's not large, but we'll make it work."

"I hate to put you out," Sophia said.

"Don't be ridiculous. You're our sister," Sebastian said. "We only have one another."

"I feel better already, being here with you." Sophia wiped her eyes. "I'm so very weary of it all. All this trying and trying and trying."

Sebastian reached across the table and squeezed her hand. "You're safe now. That's what matters."

"Actually," Sophia said, sitting up a bit straighter, "I may have already found a new position. On my way here, I stopped at an inn in Arundel for the night. The innkeeper mentioned that a gentleman there was desperately seeking a governess. His sister and brother-in-law were killed in a carriage accident, and he's been left guardian to their two-year-old daughter."

"You spoke with him?" Sebastian asked.

"Briefly. He seemed quite decent—overwhelmed, really. The poor man has no idea how to care for a small child, and his housekeeper is too old to manage a toddler. He offered me the position on the spot when he learned of my experience." Sophia managed a small smile. "It would mean leaving Brighton again, but the wages are generous, and he seemed genuinely kind."

"Where is his estate?" James asked.

"Rosemere Hall, near the coast. It's not too far from here, so I could visit more often."

Sebastian felt a surge of relief. His sister would be safe, well-paid, and close enough that they could see each other regularly. "That sounds ideal. When would you start?"

"He's returning to Rosemere tomorrow. I'm to follow in a few days, once I've had time to rest and gather myself." She looked between her brothers. "Is it all right if I stay here until then?"

"As long as you need," James said firmly. "And if this man

gives you any trouble, any at all, you come straight back to us."

"I will." Sophia reached for both their hands. "I've missed you both so much. I know we've all had to make our own way in the world, but being apart from you… it's been the hardest part of everything we've endured."

Sebastian squeezed her hand, then exchanged a meaningful look with James. His brother nodded slightly.

"Sophia," Sebastian said carefully, "there's something else. Something important we need to tell you about Papa."

She looked up sharply, her blue eyes widening. "What do you mean?"

"We've found our chance," James said quietly. "The chance we've been waiting for all these years."

"To prove Papa's innocence?" Sophia's voice was barely a whisper.

Sebastian nodded. "Wentworth is looking for a gardener. And he's throwing a masquerade ball in three weeks. The first one since he murdered Lady Wentworth."

Sophia went very still. For a moment, she looked exactly as she had at eight years old, standing in the shadow of Newgate Prison with tears streaming down her face. Then something hardened in her expression—the same steel that had helped her survive the Langstons, that had given her the strength to fight off her attacker.

"You're going to work for him." It wasn't a question.

"I am. I'll get inside his house, learn his habits, find evidence of what he really did." Sebastian leaned forward. "Sophia, this could be it. This could be how we finally clear Papa's name."

Tears spilled down Sophia's cheeks, but she was smiling. "After all these years, do you think we might finally get justice?"

"I can only try my best," Sebastian said. "Like Papa taught us."

"What do you need from me?" Sophia asked.

"Just be safe," Sebastian said. "Stay close enough that we can reach you if needed, but far enough away that you won't be connected to whatever happens."

"This gentleman you're going to work for, what's his name?" James asked.

"Henry Montrose. Why?"

Sebastian and James exchanged another look. The timing was almost too perfect. Sophia would be safely settled with a new employer just as Sebastian began the most dangerous mission of his life.

"Just curious," Sebastian said. "It sounds like a good situation for you."

Sophia studied their faces. "You really believe we can bring him down?"

"I have to believe it," Sebastian said simply. "Papa deserves justice. We all do."

"Then Godspeed, brother." Sophia squeezed both their hands tightly. "Bring that monster to his knees."

"We're family," Sebastian said, looking at both his siblings. "That will never change, no matter where life takes us. And soon, God willing, we'll have our name back."

# CHAPTER TWO

ROSE WENTWORTH WAS dreaming.

She was eight years old again, standing in Papa's study on the night of the masquerade ball. The fire had burned low in the hearth, casting strange shadows that made the furniture look like crouching beasts. She clutched her cloth doll to her chest, breathing in the lingering scent of jasmine, Mummy's favorite perfume.

But there was something else. The metallic smell of blood. And burning candle wax.

"Mummy," she called out, her voice small in the vast room.

Her mother stood by the window in her ball gown, the pale silk shimmering in the firelight. She wore a mask, and her hair hung loose down her back. But when she turned, her beautiful face was wrong. Twisted, caved in on one side. Dark liquid pooled at her feet, spreading across the Persian rug like spilled ink.

"Run, Rose," Mummy whispered. But it wasn't her voice anymore. It was the voice of something else, something that made Rose's skin crawl with terror.

She tried to move, tried to scream, but her feet were rooted to the floor. Behind her, she felt eyes watching. A presence that made her want to disappear entirely.

Rose woke with a gasp, her heart hammering against her ribs. Sunlight streamed through the gaps in her bedroom curtains, chasing away the nightmare's chill. She clutched the delicate lace-trimmed coverlet to her chest, her skin damp with perspiration. Twelve years, and the dream still came to her. Always the same. Always leaving her hollow and shaken.

The door opened quietly, and Prudence appeared with the morning tea tray, her kind face immediately creased with concern. "My lady? I heard you scream. Was it the dream?"

"Yes. The same as always." Rose pushed herself upright, accepting the cup of tea Prudence offered. The warmth helped steady her hands. She shook away the dream. It was of no consequence. Just a silly nightmare that had followed her into adulthood.

But she wasn't fine, and they both knew it. How could she be when she'd never remembered what really happened that night? The doctors said it was natural for a child to forget trauma, but Rose sometimes wondered if the not-knowing was worse than the truth.

Despite twelve years passing, Rose still found it impossible to understand how anyone could murder a mother, leaving a little girl orphaned. Taking away a little girl's mother over a petty rivalry was unconscionable. Lord Ashford had paid for it with his life. Rose took small comfort in that, even though she'd heard the man had left three children behind. Two sons and a daughter who had already lost their mother, leaving them orphans. Her naturally sympathetic nature made it impossible to think ill of them. They'd been as much victims as Rose. She sometimes wondered what had become of them but would never have asked her father. He forbade her to speak of her mother's death.

Prudence moved to the French doors that opened onto the balcony, pulling back the heavy blue brocade curtains and tying them with silken cords, but leaving the sheer inner curtains loose to flutter in the summer air. "The sun's quite cheerful today. That should help."

Rose smiled despite herself. Prudence had a way of assigning moods to the weather that never failed to amuse her. "You're right, as always."

This was the south of England, after all. There were many ways to describe rain, mist, and clouds. Not today, however. July brought sunshine and warm weather. And all the lovely roses.

Rose threw back the coverlet and slipped from beneath the linen sheets. She pushed aside the pale blue silk drapes from her carved wooden four-poster bed. Prudence helped her into her robe before Rose crossed the room, the powder-blue Aubusson rug soft under her feet.

She walked out to the balcony and gazed out at the rolling Sussex countryside, sighing with pleasure. Golden fields of wheat and barley and clusters of ancient oaks and elms lay beyond the manicured gardens of the estate, with paths that wove between lush rose beds and ivory trellises. A narrow lane wound past the estate toward the village, where the only hint of life was distant smoke from the chimneys of early risers.

Sounds of birdsong and the humming of bees in lavender pots replaced any lingering effects of her bad dream. Breezes brought scents of freshly cut grass and honeysuckle growing on her balcony walls.

How she loved summertime.

Rose let out a contented sigh. "I'm awfully glad to be home. The Season exhausted me. I'm afraid the city's not for me."

The Season had been mortifying in every way. She'd not anticipated being a wallflower, but night after night she'd sat alone, wishing someone would fill in her dance card. But it was like she was poison, the way the eligible men stayed away. Or worse, whispered about her when they thought she couldn't hear.

That's the Wentworth girl. You know, the one whose mother…

Her father's reputation is hardly pristine…

I'd not go near her. Not with what I know of her father…

"It is nice to be home, my lady," Prudence said sympathetically. As always, Rose's lady's maid was immaculate in a simple navy dress, her golden blond hair pinned neatly under her starched cotton cap.

Movement caught Rose's eye. A lone man on horseback traveled up the road toward Wentworth Manor. Who could it be this time of morning? Perhaps someone inquiring about work. Prudence had mentioned that Mr. Thorncroft, their head gardener, had dismissed a lad the day before. Mr. Thorncroft was beside himself about the aphids on the roses, and the boy had been an unworthy opponent to the tiny, terrorizing bugs.

The man halted his horse in the driveway. He dismounted gracefully and handed the reins to a stable boy, rolling his shoulders as if he had come a long way. Although leanly built, his shoulders and chest were substantial. He was tall too; she guessed him to be over six feet. He plucked a flat cap from his head and ran fingers through dark, thick hair as he turned in a full circle, clearly taking in the grounds.

There was something rugged and untamed about him, yet elegant and proud too. His face seemed skillfully carved from a piece of driftwood—high cheekbones, deep-set eyes, and a long, thin nose all perfectly symmetrical. She could not see the color of his eyes. If she hadn't known better, she would think he'd been raised as a nobleman. It was the proud jut of his chin and straight posture, perhaps, that gave her such an impression.

However, he wore only a loose linen shirt, rolled up over his thick forearms, and a dark brown, fitted waistcoat that emphasized his muscular frame. As did his dark, fitted trousers that clung to muscular legs. His worn riding boots were covered with a coat of dust. A plain leather satchel hung across his chest.

Goodness. The morning was warm already. She set aside her hot tea but continued to watch the stranger who had arrived on horseback.

Mr. Thorncroft appeared from behind one of the manicured hedges to greet him, holding out his weather-worn hand.

Ah, yes, he was here about the gardening position.

Why had the palms of her hands dampened and her pulse

raced? Was she really so starved for the sight of a handsome man that she'd immediately seized upon the unsuspecting gardener? She was disgraceful.

"Do you think he's here about the gardening position?" Rose asked, gesturing toward Thorncroft and the visitor, who now walked beside the head gardener with his hands folded behind his back, nodding his head to whatever was being said.

"I suspect so," Prudence said.

"I hope he knows what to do about the aphids."

Prudence smiled. "For his sake, I hope so too."

Rose nodded, but she couldn't look away from the stranger. There was something about him that seemed at odds with his rough clothing. The confident way he moved, the proud tilt of his head. He looked like a man with an intriguing past.

"He carries himself well for a common gardener," Rose said. "Do you not agree?"

"Perhaps he's not so common. These days, many gentlemen have fallen on hard times."

Rose returned her gaze to the man who made her stomach flutter. In her young life, that had never happened when she'd looked at a man of any type, common or noble. She felt a strange desire to get closer, to see him better. But why? Perhaps it was simply that he was the first interesting thing to happen since her return from London.

Or perhaps it was the way he'd paused in the drive, looking up at the house as if he were assessing it. As if he had plans for the estate.

"Come, Prudence," Rose said, stepping back into her chamber. "Help me dress. It is time for me to start my day."

After breakfast with her father, she would head out for her morning stroll. Perhaps she would get a better view of this large, seemingly inquisitive man. What harm could come from that?

THIRTY MINUTES LATER, Rose stood before the tall, gilded mirror as Prudence finished buttoning her gown. The dusty blue muslin was one of her favorites, with delicate embroidered vines trailing across the sheer overlay and an ivory satin ribbon cinched just beneath her bust. Prudence had arranged her dark hair in a neat chignon, and her bonnet and gloves waited on the dressing table.

"You're pretty as a picture, Lady Rose. The blue contrasts nicely with your green eyes."

"Thank you, Prudence." Rose smoothed her skirts, steeling herself for the day ahead. "I suppose I must go downstairs before Father grows cross with me. He's already irritated enough about my failed Season."

"Mrs. Blythe will be ready to meet with you after breakfast about the summer house party." Prudence hesitated, her fair cheeks flushing pink. "But there's something I need to tell you first."

Rose's stomach clenched. Prudence had been with the family since before Rose's birth, first as head maid, then promoted to lady's maid when Rose turned sixteen. She was loyal, protective, and privy to all the household gossip. When Prudence looked worried, there was usually good reason.

"What is it?"

"Your father has asked Mrs. Blythe to send an invitation to Baron White. For the house party."

The words sent ice through Rose's veins. She sank onto the edge of her bed, memories flooding back unbidden. Baron White at that dreadful London ball, following her into the garden. His sweaty hands, his brandy-soaked breath hot against her neck as he whispered things that made her skin crawl. The way her father had looked at her afterward, tired and resigned, when she'd told him what happened.

*"I told him where to find you."*

Her father's words still echoed in her mind. He'd practically served her up to that horrid man, all because she'd failed to attract a better offer during two full Seasons.

"Oh, Lady Rose." Prudence sat beside her, taking her trembling hands. "What can I do to help you?"

Rose forced herself to breathe slowly. She wouldn't fall apart. Even if it nearly killed her trying, she would be brave. Face whatever came for her. What choice did she have? "Does Father truly think so little of me that Baron White is the best I can hope for?"

"Lady Blackwell has been whispering in his ear again," Prudence said. "She's made it clear she won't marry him until you're... settled elsewhere."

Of course. Honoria Blackwell, her father's widowed mistress, who'd been circling like a vulture ever since her own husband died and left her in reduced circumstances. The woman wanted Rose gone so she could finally become the new Lady Wentworth.

"Prudence, I'm afraid for what is to come," Rose said.

"As am I, my lady. I tremble to think what will happen to the staff if he marries Lady Blackwell," Prudence said.

"You are all so dear to me. Yet, I'm powerless to protect you. She has her claws into him, and I don't anticipate her releasing him anytime soon. I'm afraid I'm doomed to marry Baron White." She clamped her teeth shut to keep her lips from quivering like a child.

"If only you could find a love match." Prudence looked up at the ceiling dreamily, as if she could conjure one from the heavens. "A handsome duke who is very, very rich and will agree to take us all with you when you marry."

"Wouldn't that be wonderful?" Rose asked, smiling at the idea, before lowering her voice. "But not Hargrave. He must stay with them."

Prudence giggled. "Yes, please."

Hargrave had been the family's butler since her father had been in his teens. The staff and Rose despised the man, although none of them would say it out loud. Hargrave was not someone to make an enemy.

Rose stood abruptly, moving to the window. She pressed her

forehead against the cool glass, watching the new gardener walking alongside Mr. Thorncroft in the distance. Even from here, she could see his confident movements, the way he carried himself with dignity despite his rough clothes. A former soldier? She felt sure suddenly. The square of his shoulders and straight back—a military man. He'd fought in the wars, only to return to tend gardens.

Would it be so bad? She enjoyed being in the gardens more than anywhere else, other than curled up with a book. However, she didn't have to dirty her hands as this man would.

Soon, she might not have that privilege. If she was forced to marry Baron White, she would move away to his home. Away from her mother's rose garden. The one thing she'd left to Rose that thus far no one had been able to take from her.

There were only three days before the house party and Baron White's arrival. Three days before she'd have to smile and play the gracious hostess to the man who'd tried to assault her. Three days before her father would expect her to accept Baron White's renewed advances with gratitude.

"What if I told Father I won't marry him?" Rose asked.

Prudence's silence was answer enough. They both knew what would happen. Rose would be cut off entirely, left with nothing and nowhere to go. And her father would simply arrange the marriage anyway. After all, she had no legal right to refuse.

"I feel like I'm suffocating." Rose pressed her palms against the window. "Like the walls are closing in and there's no air left to breathe."

"Oh, my lady," Prudence said, her voice thick with sympathy.

Rose straightened, squaring her shoulders. She couldn't change what was coming, but she wouldn't spend the next three days cowering in her room either.

"After breakfast, I'll take a walk. I need air." She reached for her bonnet. "Some time in Mummy's rose garden before I meet with Mrs. Blythe might help clear my head."

"That's a good idea. The rose garden always soothes you."

Rose tied her bonnet strings with fingers that trembled only slightly. "Will you tell Mrs. Blythe I'll meet with her in an hour?"

"Of course, my lady."

Rose paused at the door. "Prudence? Thank you. For always looking out for me. I don't know what I'd do without you."

"We'll find a way for you to be happy," Prudence said softly. "Somehow. We simply must."

Rose nodded, though she couldn't see how. As she made her way downstairs, she felt like a condemned prisoner walking to the gallows. The only difference was that her execution would be a slow one, played out over decades of marriage to a man who revolted her.

But for now, she could still breathe free air and walk in her mother's garden. For now, she could pretend that three days was nearly enough time to figure out a miracle.

Even though she knew it wasn't.

ROSE MADE HER way downstairs, her thoughts churning with equal parts dread and determination. The grand hall stretched before her, sunlight filtering through the arched windows to illuminate the portraits of her ancestors. She paused before the painting of her mother, commissioned just months before her death.

Lady Eleanor Wentworth sat in her beloved rose garden, forever frozen in a butter-yellow silk gown, pearls at her throat, a pink rose in her delicate hand. Her smile was sweet but tinged with sadness, as if she'd somehow known what was coming.

"Give me strength, Mummy," Rose whispered.

She straightened her shoulders and continued down the sweeping oak staircase. With each step toward the breakfast room, her resolve hardened. She would not simply accept whatever fate her father had planned for her. Even if it meant running away.

The footman opened the door with a bow, and she stepped inside. The room smelled of coffee and bacon, but her stomach was too knotted to appreciate it.

Her father sat reading his newspaper, his posture rigid in his perfectly tailored maroon coat, silver hair combed neatly off his forehead. He didn't look up when she entered, merely grunted an acknowledgment. The gold chain of his pocket watch glinted as he turned a page. No doubt he'd be checking it frequently, as if her presence were an inconvenience to be endured.

"Good morning, Father." She bobbed her head before helping herself to a modest portion from the elaborate sideboard.

"Good morning, my dear." His tone was measured, cold. When he finally looked up, his thin-lipped smile conveyed nothing but disinterest. His sharp features and ice-blue eyes had always reminded her of a predator evaluating prey.

Had her mother loved him? Or had she merely endured him?

"I'll be meeting with Mrs. Blythe this morning about the house party. Is there anything in particular you wish me to do?" Rose settled into her chair.

"Excellent. You have much to prepare for. I've asked her to include Baron White as our special guest." He folded his newspaper with crisp precision. "I trust you'll make a better impression this time. I have high hopes for your marriage."

Rose's fork stilled halfway to her mouth. So it was to be stated as fact, not discussed. "May I know who else will be attending?"

"Mrs. Blythe has the complete list. I've included your friend, Lady Daphne." His tone suggested he'd granted her an enormous favor.

At least there was that. Daphne would be a comfort, and perhaps her shy friend might finally find someone who could see past her nervousness to her wit and kindness.

"You're also to plan the theme for the masquerade ball," her father said. "I expect it to be the finest of the summer."

"The ball? We're having a ball?" She stared at him, flabbergasted. They had not had a ball since her mother's death.

He nodded, as if he'd included her in his plans all along. "Your mother excelled at such things. The last ball we held was her celestial theme—a thousand stars, she called it. She had the ballroom ceiling painted like the night sky."

Rose leaned forward, hungry for any detail about her mother. "She loved the stars?"

For a split second, what could be regret flickered across his face before he said, "She did. She wore silver that night, like starlight herself." His voice softened, then hardened again. "By midnight, she was dead."

By midnight, she was dead and Rose was left without a mother. Rose remembered sneaking from the nursery that night, watching her mother glide down the hallway in that shimmering gown, beautiful as an angel.

"Why are we having the ball again now?" she asked quietly.

"Honoria wishes me to announce our engagement sooner rather than later. She has grown rather impatient." He picked up his coffee cup, his movements precise and controlled. "It is time I remarried."

"I see." Rose forced herself to keep eating, though the berries now tasted like ash. "And when is this to happen?"

"Our engagement will be announced at the ball. As will yours."

Rose's cup rattled against its saucer as she set it down. "Mine?"

"Baron White has asked for your hand. I've accepted." Her father's blue eyes were as cold as the winter sky. "You'll be married within the month after that."

The room seemed to tilt. Rose gripped the edge of the table, her carefully constructed composure cracking. "You've already accepted? Without speaking to me?" This was even worse than she'd anticipated.

"Dearest, you had two Seasons to secure a better match and

failed. Baron White is willing to overlook… certain circumstances. It's more than generous, considering."

"Considering what?" The words came out sharper than she intended. "What circumstances?"

He gave her a withering look. "Considering how awkward you are. As much as it pains me to say it, you embarrassed me. Seeing how you faltered and stumbled brought shame to our reputation. I would have thought you to have more charm and wit, given the education provided you. Alas, it is not so. Instead, you made a fool of yourself at every turn."

She flushed with shame. It was true. Her dance card had remained empty. She had sat with the other wallflowers at every ball. There was no other explanation. She was undesirable to men, despite her healthy dowry. There was no worse failure for a young woman of her class. If only she could understand what she was doing wrong. Or was she so unattractive that men would pass her over, even though her father was rich?

"Your choices are clearly lacking. Perhaps Baron White does not seem the right choice, but in time, you'll grow to care for him. He will look after you, Rose. Which will give me peace of mind."

And Honoria in his bed.

She kept that thought to herself.

"Baron White arrives in three days for the house party. You'll be the perfect hostess, and by the time he leaves, the engagement will be settled."

Rose stood slowly, her breakfast barely touched. "If you'll excuse me, Father, I believe I'll walk in the gardens. The roses are particularly lovely this time of year."

"Those damned roses," Lord Wentworth muttered under his breath. "Always the roses."

Rose walked from the room with measured steps, her head high, but inside, her mind was racing. Three days. What would she do? She would have to run away. But to where? She had no one to turn to. No one to offer her a home or shelter.

As she stepped into the morning sunlight, she breathed in the scent of her mother's rose garden and closed her eyes for a moment, praying for a miracle. But as she'd learned very young, miracles were only in fairy tales. This was real life. Her life. Doomed to marry a disgusting old man because no one else would have her.

# CHAPTER THREE

SEBASTIAN LIKED THIS Amos Thorncroft. He looked a man straight in the eyes. With stark white hair and thick black eyebrows, he might have seemed intimidating, if not for his warm smile. Though not tall, he carried the weight of broad shoulders and hands worn rough by decades of work. The kind of hands Sebastian could respect.

"Right then, Doyle, let me show you the grounds properly," Thorncroft said, adjusting his cap.

Sebastian nodded, grateful for the deeper tour. The brief interview earlier had secured him the position, but now he needed to understand the layout. If he was going to complete the real reason he was here, every detail mattered.

"I appreciate that, sir. I want to do the work justice." Justice, yes. Not the kind Thorncroft expected though.

Thorncroft's gray eyes assessed him again, just as they had earlier. "Good. A man who takes pride in his work is worth keeping."

Sebastian followed him down the gravel path, eyes alert. Every hedge, path, and outbuilding was a clue. This was enemy territory, and he couldn't afford to overlook a single detail. He studied sight lines to the house, servant paths, and back entrances.

They stopped at the edge of the rose garden, and Sebastian felt his breath catch. It was stunning—rows of vibrant blooms, trellises heavy with climbing roses, and a marble fountain murmuring at the center.

"Lady Wentworth planned this herself," Thorncroft said, his voice softer now. "She and I planted it together when she came here as a bride. Had a particular love for roses."

Sebastian nodded, though his chest tightened. This garden had been his mother's rival's creation, the woman his father was accused of murdering. He pushed the thought aside.

"They're beautiful," he said.

"Beautiful, but demanding. These roses are finicky creatures. We've got blackspot, and the aphids are driving me mad." Thorncroft gestured to a struggling bush. "What do you see, and what would you do about it?"

Sebastian crouched beside it, grateful for the hours he'd spent with the Langston's head gardener as his primary teacher. "Aphids. Left alone, they'll drain the sap and weaken the plant. That mildew is a byproduct."

"And the remedy?"

"Soap and water wash. Mild lye soap mixed in, brushed on every leaf, especially underneath. The soap breaks down their outer shells."

Thorncroft raised a brow. "A brush?"

"Like an artist's. Dip and paint until each leaf is coated." Sebastian offered a slight smile. "If there's no soap, I'll squeeze them off by hand and pray for ladybugs."

Thorncroft snorted his approval. "Fine, then." He turned, continuing down the path. "Come on. Plenty more to see."

Sebastian smiled to himself. It seemed he had passed the first test.

They continued down the pathway, passing through a wrought-iron gate that led to a more practical area of the estate. An apple orchard, its trees laden with green-tinged fruits, and beyond, a vegetable garden. Rows of neatly tilled earth showcased a variety of crops—carrots, cabbages, and beans. A scattering of sunflowers and marigolds added pops of color.

The scent of freshly turned soil, earthy and rich, mingled with the sweetness of ripening vegetables. The scent of life. Of growth. Renewal. To Sebastian, there could be no better smell in the world.

They walked on, the path winding toward a pond nestled among weeping willows. Sunlight dappled through branches and reflected upon the water where ducks paddled lazily across the surface, avoiding lily pads that floated in clusters.

From there, Thorncroft led him to the apple orchard. The trees stood in rows, their branches heavy with fruit glistening in the sunlight. A soft breeze rustled the leaves, carrying the scent of ripening apples.

"We've got Codling apples here in this first row. They're good for pies and preserves and whatever other delicious things our cook, Mrs. Carter, comes up with. The lady's a magician." He gestured toward the next row. "Them's the Golden Pippin. Real princess of a fruit, that one. Lady Rose loves them." They walked farther into the orchard, with Amos pointing out the small, sweet, and nutty Russet variety as well as a large cooking apple called a Kentish Fillbasket. "And finally, we've got the Redstreak, which makes a tasty cider."

"Do you press them here?"

"That's right. Just enough for our use. Any additional, we send down to the village for the children."

Amos took him to the last row. "And these here are our White Joaneting. They ripen the earliest. We'll harvest them next week. They won't keep long, though, so Mrs. Carter will make applesauce and put it away for the winter."

Thorncroft guided him toward the sweeping lawn near the manor. The grass was a vivid green, bordered by colorful flowerbeds. A pergola covered in wisteria stood to one side, providing shade and a picturesque spot for tea or quiet reflection. "Lady Rose likes to come out here to read, but more often she sits in the swing in the rose garden. You're not to disturb her, should you come upon her."

"Yes, sir."

"During the summer party, this is where the guests will gather for their croquet and games. And just over there, beyond the hedges, is our maze. We keep it trimmed at all times."

Sebastian's gaze swept across the expanse, taking in the grandeur of the estate. "How many gardeners do you employ?"

"Six to eight. Your priority will be the roses, as it seems you know what you're doing. Like I said, they're important to the family."

"I can do whatever you need. I'm strong and I grew up working in gardens."

Thorncroft continued to inspect him, as if he were suspicious of his intentions. Or was that simply a result of Sebastian's paranoia? Given that he did have dishonest reasons for being here, he worried his charade needed more refining.

"Don't take this the wrong way, but you talk kind of fancy for a gardener," Thorncroft said.

"My mother was educated but was forced out of Society." He'd prepared that answer should it come up. Hopefully, it was a good enough explanation for his new employer. "But she educated me herself."

"That so?" Thorncroft nodded, as if he'd like him to elaborate.

"I assure you, I can do the work and be thankful for it, regardless of the extent of my vocabulary. I'll be proud to tend to the roses and whatever else needs doing."

"Very good. Lady Rose spends a great deal of time outside. My aim is to surround her with beauty." Thorncroft's voice warmed. "Finest young woman you'll ever meet. Lost her mother young. Staff here would do anything for her."

Sebastian kept his expression unreadable. Lady Rose, beloved and sheltered, while Sophia had grown up under cruelty. The contrast stung. A fire lit in his belly. He would make this right. Even if he died trying.

They were nearing the rose garden again when Thorncroft stopped abruptly. A slim figure stood by one of the trellises, her dark hair twisted into a knot, bonnet dangling down her back.

"That's Lady Rose," Thorncroft said. "Best give her a moment."

It was then Sebastian noticed she was crying. Not admiring the roses at all, but dabbing her eyes with a lace handkerchief, her shoulders trembling.

She must have heard them, because she straightened and quickly restored her composure.

"Mr. Thorncroft. Good morning." Her voice was graceful and melodic, though Sebastian caught the strain and sadness beneath it.

"My lady, apologies for intruding." Thorncroft bowed, removing his cap.

Sebastian followed suit, heart thudding unexpectedly. She was beautiful. Dewy skin, expressive mouth, and striking green eyes that shimmered with pain.

"Are you quite all right, my lady?" Thorncroft asked gently.

"Oh yes. Quite well." She hesitated, then added, "The gardens are especially lovely today. You must extend my gratitude to your staff. You've all done such a remarkable job."

Thorncroft seemed to grow several inches. "Thank you, Lady Rose." He gestured toward Sebastian. "This is Sebastian Doyle, our new gardener. I'm showing him the grounds."

Her gaze shifted to Sebastian. For a moment they locked eyes. A thrill went through him, almost like one would experience when seeing a long-lost friend. Or lover? Someone familiar at any rate. He lowered his eyes.

"Mr. Doyle. I saw your arrival this morning. I hope you find the work to your liking."

"Thank you, my lady. I'm honored by the opportunity."

"I'm quite fond of our gardens. They were my mother's sanctuary, as they are mine." Her tone held the weariness of grief that remained after the loss of a parent. He understood it only too well.

"I'll do my best to meet Mr. Thorncroft's standards," Sebastian said quietly. He glanced up and found her eyes once again. They were the green of a mountain stream, impossibly clear.

She gave a small nod, sighing. "I must return inside. Much to prepare for the house party."

"We'll have everything perfect for your guests," Thorncroft said.

"I know you will, dear Mr. Thorncroft. You always do."

Rose turned and walked away, her blue skirts trailing across the gravel. Sebastian noted the slight tension in her posture, the way she carried an invisible but heavy weight.

"Poor lass," Thorncroft said. "Not been herself since returning from London. Something's troubling her."

Sebastian filed it away. Whatever pained Wentworth's daughter might prove useful.

"Come along," Thorncroft said. "Let's get you settled in the bunkhouse."

Sebastian tried to shove away the image of her tear-streaked face. He'd expected her to be haughty or cold. Instead, she inspired loyalty from the staff. And something else tugged at his heart. One he couldn't quite identify. A sense of protectiveness? Impossible. She was an extension of his enemy.

As they walked toward the stone building, Thorncroft gave him more details of where he was to sleep and take his meals. Sebastian was to sleep in the groundskeepers' bunkhouse with the other gardeners and eat with them. "The lads are a good lot, if not occasionally a little rowdy for my taste. You'll know no unkindness. I do not tolerate hazing or tomfoolery."

"Of course, sir."

"I have my own cottage not far from the bunkhouse, but I take my meals with the lads. Mrs. Carter and her helpers are fine cooks. You'll eat well here."

Typical hours would start in the early morning and go into the late afternoon, but with breaks and meals to break up the day. He was to earn a modest weekly wage. Much less than he could make working for his brother, but money was not his reason for being here.

"The estate provides all your tools but not clothes," Thorncroft said. "You'll need sturdy ones. We'll supply you with gloves and boots."

"Thank you, sir."

"This upcoming party's going to be a madhouse. Mrs. Blythe says at least a dozen guests will be arriving for a fortnight stay, which means we'll have to stay on our toes, anticipating needs, arranging tents and chairs for picnics, cutting flowers for Lady Rose's arrangements. You'll need to keep a steady head."

"Whatever you need, I shall do."

"This will be a trial, you understand. I'll assess your work in a few weeks and decide if you're worth keeping."

"I'll do my best to please you."

"All right, then. Let's get you settled in the bunkhouse. It's nearly time for our midday meal. We'll get you to work after that." Thorncroft paused when they reached the door to the bunkhouse, turning to Sebastian. "One last thing. I assume you know to keep your distance from Lady Rose and Lord Wentworth. We should remain invisible to them."

"Of course, sir."

"This house party will bring chaos. Guests everywhere. Best keep your head down."

Sebastian nodded. Inwardly, his pulse quickened. Chaos meant opportunity. He would observe, listen, and learn.

"I won't disappoint you, sir."

But as Thorncroft began outlining his duties, Sebastian couldn't quite banish the memory of Rose Wentworth's face. Elegant, sad, and haunting.

He reminded himself of the mission. The vow he'd made so long ago. The reason he was here.

And yet, her eyes stayed with him.

BETWEEN THE SNORING of the other men in the bunkhouse and his own restless thoughts, Sebastian couldn't sleep. His first day at Wentworth Manor had gone well, but now his mind churned with plans and possibilities. Every creak of the building and shift from a bunkmate only heightened his alertness.

At last, he gave up. Moonlight poured through the small window, silver and sharp. Maybe fresh air would quiet his thoughts.

He dressed in silence, boots in hand to avoid waking anyone. Outside, the night air was cool on his skin, carrying the damp scent of earth and hay. Overhead, stars glittered across the sky like diamonds. He had seen them from trenches in France, from the deck of Channel-crossing ships, and from the window of his childhood room at Ashford Hall.

He meant only to walk the grounds, perhaps check on his horse, Tempest. But as he neared the stables, something caught his eye. A distant glow where no light should be.

Instinct took over, honed by years of war. He doused his lantern and melted into the shadows beside the stable wall.

Far off, near the disused storehouse at the edge of the property, a faint glow spilled from partially open doors. A wagon stood outside, its wheels thick with dried mud. The horses stamped and tossed their heads, restless. Men moved in and out with speed and purpose, hefting wooden boxes with practiced ease.

Whatever they were doing, it wasn't sanctioned. Not at this hour and not with that level of secrecy.

Sebastian crept forward, keeping to the cover of hedges and outbuildings. His training came back to him. The art of silence. Of watching without being seen. As he drew nearer, a rich, unmistakable scent hit him.

French brandy.

Smugglers on Wentworth's estate.

Three men handled the crates while a fourth stood apart, overseeing the operation. Even in the dim light, it was clear this one was different. Stocky and well-dressed despite the late hour, he carried himself like a man used to command. A riding crop flexed between his gloved hands.

Sebastian went still. That small, casual motion chilled him to the bone. It reminded him of his childhood. Of Baron Langston. The whippings he and James had endured for any small or innocent infraction.

One of the laborers muttered, the words too low to catch. The overseer's head snapped up, and even from across the clearing, Sebastian felt the weight of that stare. The man said nothing. He didn't have to. The worker lowered his head and kept moving.

Sebastian etched every detail into memory. The French lettering stamped on the crates. The overseer's florid face, puffy and red, his hair dark and slicked back. The crispness of the operation suggested experience. This was not their first shipment.

This was what Sebastian had hoped for. Proof of Wentworth's crimes, laid out in front of him. If he could document this, tie it to the viscount…

A horse behind him let out a quiet whinny, and his heart leapt. He had moved too close to the wagon team. One of the men looked up sharply.

"What was that?"

Flattening against the storehouse wall, Sebastian held his breath.

The man with the crop stepped forward, eyes sweeping the dark. The tip of the whip tapped his thigh in a slow, steady rhythm.

"Probably nothing. These old buildings creak like bones in a graveyard." His voice was refined but worn, like a gentleman too long among criminals. "Finish up. We need to be gone before dawn."

Sebastian stayed frozen until the last hoofbeat faded. Only

then did he ease back toward the bunkhouse, every limb wired tight with adrenaline.

His hands trembled, not with fear but with something close to exhilaration. He had seen it. Real evidence. Wentworth wasn't just corrupt. He was running an operation on his estate, hidden in plain sight.

Inside, the others still snored. Sebastian slid into bed, but his thoughts raced. How could he document what he had witnessed? Who was that man with the riding crop? How often did these shipments occur?

He stared up at the low ceiling. For the first time in twelve years, he felt something like hope. He had found the viscount's vulnerability. Now he had to exploit it.

But first, he needed to identify the man with the crop. Something about him had seemed familiar, though he couldn't imagine they had ever crossed paths.

# CHAPTER FOUR

AFTER HER HUMILIATION of being caught crying by Mr. Thorncroft and the handsome gardener, Rose made her way to the kitchen to meet with Mrs. Blythe. When she entered, she was greeted by the usual bustle of the kitchen staff. They all stopped at the sight of the lady of the house to bow and curtsy.

"I'm sorry to interrupt. Please don't stop your work." Rose breathed in delightful smells of freshly baked bread, simmering stews and roasted meats, and the fresh herbs one of the kitchen maids was chopping at the butcher block in the corner. "I'm only here to speak with Mrs. Blythe. Is she in her office?" She plucked her bonnet from her head, instantly warm in the hot, steamy kitchen.

"Yes, Lady Rose." Their head cook, Mrs. Eliza Carter, stepped out from behind the stove. "She asked me to send you in when you were ready."

Rose had always felt more at home in the kitchen than in her father's formal dining room. Mrs. Carter had been with the family since before Rose was born, coming with Lady Wentworth when she'd married. Between her and Mrs. Blythe, they'd practically raised Rose after her mother died, filling the cold manor with warmth and affection her father never provided.

Eliza Carter had thick hair that had turned a lovely shade of silver, which she wore in a twisted braid on top of her head, though tendrils always escaped, clinging to her damp skin. She possessed a rosy pink complexion and bright, expressive blue eyes. Her jolly sense of humor permeated the kitchen and the food she made.

"Thank you. I've been out for a stroll in the gardens. It's such a lovely day."

"I hope you had your bonnet on." Mrs. Carter was always on her about her bonnet. God forbid Rose got any more freckles. But she didn't actually mind the woman's fussing. She'd spent many days down here as a child, doing her schoolwork or reading while the competent staff prepared meal after meal. They'd all doted on Rose, making her feel loved. Even if her father was cold and distant, she had never felt unwanted or in the way. Not in the kitchen anyway.

"I did indeed wear my bonnet," Rose said. "Most of the time."

"Dear me, child. Those freckles. And the ball coming up now? You must protect your skin."

"I will be wearing a mask at the ball." She gave Mrs. Carter a cheeky grin.

"Dear me, I suppose that's true, isn't it?" Mrs. Carter laughed, a bubbling gurgle of a sound that warmed Rose's heart.

The kitchen returned to its lively routine, with kitchen maids chopping vegetables and kneading dough. An errand boy ran in and out, collecting a basket to take to the village. Scullery maids positioned at the wash area scrubbed dishes while gossiping quietly to each other.

Pots, pans, and utensils hung on hooks along the walls, their polished surfaces catching the light. Pewter serving dishes were stacked on open shelves, ready to carry meals upstairs. A dedicated corner of the kitchen was reserved for baking, with rolling boards, bins of flour, and racks of cooling tarts, cakes, and loaves of bread piled high upon the counter.

Adjacent to the kitchen, the larder, kept cool by thick stone walls, housed hanging cured meats, cheese wheels, and baskets of root vegetables. Rose didn't care for it in there. The hanging flesh of animals did not appeal to her whatsoever. In fact, she couldn't stand the thought that they'd once been living creatures. It was simply too sad to think of.

She bade them farewell and headed down the narrow hallway to Mrs. Blythe's office. At the doorway, she paused, observing Mrs. Blythe at her perfectly polished desk. The room had only one small window, but it let in lovely light this time of morning, which illuminated the gold streaks in the housekeeper's light brown hair. Rose wasn't entirely sure why, but the space smelled of lemons, a scent she associated with the woman who ran their household with love and attention to detail.

Her desk was always neatly organized, with a leather writing pad and inkstand, quill pens, blotting paper, and ledgers. Small drawers contained account books, receipts, schedules, and notes. Floor-to-ceiling shelves held rows of leather-bound ledgers, inventory books, and manuals for household management. A board on the wall displayed the staff rota, menus for the week, and lists of duties for each servant. Small pins or hooks held keys to storerooms and other secured areas, labeled with brass tags.

When she was small and her governess had required a break, she would stay with Mrs. Blythe in her office. To keep Rose occupied, Mrs. Blythe would let her look through books with depictions of flowers and herbs, which the housekeeper had drawn herself and labeled. It was only a hobby, Mrs. Blythe had told her and served no real purpose, but Rose had adored each and every one regardless.

Now, Rose knocked softly, and Mrs. Blythe looked up from her sums. "Oh, dear me, I didn't hear you."

"I'm sorry to startle you. I've come to go over the party details. And the ball."

Mrs. Blythe nodded, shutting her ledger and placing it inside a lockable cabinet beneath the desk, where she kept payroll records and other sensitive documents. "Of course, Lady Rose. May I get you a cup of tea?" She gestured toward the small tray with a teapot, teacup, and a tin of tea leaves on a side table.

"No, thank you."

"Have you thought about a theme for the ball?" Mrs. Blythe asked, settling into her cushioned chair behind the desk. "I had no idea your father would bring it back and am worried about time to plan properly. We shall have to be clever."

"Yes, it was a surprise to me as well. Do you think a prison theme would go over well?"

Immediately sympathetic, Mrs. Blythe cocked her head and gazed at her kindly. "What's troubling you, my lady?"

Rose sighed, looking down at her hands. "Father's upset with me about my failure during the Season, and he's arranged for me to marry Baron White."

"What? No."

"Father wishes to marry Mrs. Blackwell. But she will not agree unless I'm out of the way."

Dead silence, followed by a draining of all color from Mrs. Blythe's cheeks. "We feared as much."

"Yes. It's unfortunate." Rose flapped her hands in front of her face, trying not to cry. The last few months had been so difficult. If only the Season had gone better.

"He's much too old for you." Mrs. Blythe flinched. "I'm sorry. Please forgive me for saying so."

"It's all right. The truth is the truth. No one else wants me. As you know, I sat alone at every ball."

Mrs. Blythe opened her mouth as if to share something but seemed to think better of it. Instead, she pursed her lips and shook her head.

"Baron White cornered me one night in Mayfair's garden. If it had not been for my quickness and a sharp nudge of my elbow into his ribcage, I may have been ruined. When I told Father what had happened, he didn't care. In fact, he told me he'd sent Baron White out to find me. I should have known then that it was Baron White he'd chosen for me to marry. I'll be engaged by the end of the summer."

"I shall ask Thorncroft to put the gardeners on high alert," Mrs. Blythe said. "The servants inside will keep close watch on you as well."

"I appreciate it, but it doesn't matter one way or the other. I'm to be married to him by the end of the year. I shall have to move away to live with him. It will break my heart to leave all of you."

"I'll be praying for a miracle, Lady Rose."

They left that subject alone and dove into the plans for the party and ball. They spoke at some length about the activities and menu for the weeks they would have a full house, then moved onto the masquerade ball.

"Your father wants invitations sent out to roughly a hundred guests from London and the surrounding areas here in the countryside. It's shorter notice than I'd like, but since it's the end of the summer, hopefully people will be delighted at the prospect of getting out of the city."

"Father told me my mother was good at choosing themes."

Mrs. Blythe's voice softened as she shared her memories. "Oh, yes. Lady Wentworth was the most inspiring hostess. There was the Moonlit Sea Soiree—guests were encouraged to wear sapphire or aquamarine. The women were all so lovely. Then one year we had a Venetian Carnival. Your mother hired harlequin dancers for the entertainment, and Mr. Thorncroft put together candlelit gondola rides on the pond."

"How marvelous."

"Yes, it was. She had a Harvest Masquerade one year and The Emerald Court Ball another."

"What about the last one? Do you remember much of that night? Father said the theme was a night of a thousand stars."

Mrs. Blythe didn't answer for a moment, clearly gathering herself, the pain of grief obvious in her eyes. "Your mother adored the constellations. She was forever looking up at them through her telescope."

"I remember Mummy's dress. It was silver and lavender, right?"

"That's correct. Her lady's maid, Lizzie, spent a month on it, working long hours. It was a masterpiece."

"My governess let me look just for a moment from the banister. Mummy looked like a princess."

"She was the most beautiful one there," Mrs. Blythe said.

"What else do you remember about that night?" In the years since Lady Wentworth's death, Rose had not felt comfortable asking about her mother's last hours. The questions were there, stuck in the back of her throat. But it was an unspoken command from Father that she not ask any of the staff about that night. Now, though, facing a marriage with Baron White, Rose no longer cared about pleasing her father or abiding by his wishes. A compulsion to know more drove her to ask Mrs. Blythe for further details. "Did you see her right before she was killed?"

Mrs. Blythe looked down at the desk, moving a stack of correspondence from one side to the other. "The guests all left around midnight. The carriages lined up for a mile. Prudence, Mrs. Carter, Lizzie and I were in the kitchen, having a cup of tea and a piece of the cake leftover from the party when Finch came running in." Her voice grew husky with obvious emotion. "He'd found her in your father's study and had been told to go into the village to wake the constable. We were all so shaken we didn't know what to do. Mary had been sent up to start the fire in your mother's room but came running in not long after Finch left for the stables."

"How old was Mary then?"

"She was only thirteen at the time. We'd only hired her the month before."

A fuzzy memory floated through Rose's mind of a young Mary Bright, her face thin and peaked. She'd sometimes been asked to look after Rose when the governess was needed elsewhere. They'd played together in the nursery. Hadn't they?

Now, Mary was their head maid. All grown up, tall and pretty, with a sweet but shy demeanor. Yet, there was a quality in Mary that Rose could never quite pinpoint. A lack of trust perhaps? She never quite looked in Rose's eyes.

"Poor Finch," Rose said. "Having to see her like that."

"He's never been the same, poor lad. We all loved your mother. Worshipped her. She was such a gentle, kind mistress to us. The house was never the same after we lost her."

"Were you surprised that it was Lord Ashford who killed her?" Rose asked.

Mrs. Blythe's lips pursed again. She picked up a glass paperweight in the shape of a bird, staring at it for a moment. "In truth, I never fully believed it was him."

Rose stared at her in shock. "But why?"

"It never added up to me. Nothing pointed to him whatsoever. He and your mother were on friendly terms. The night of the ball, I noticed them sitting together for some time, chatting in the drawing room, clearly enjoying their conversation."

She hadn't heard that before.

Mrs. Blythe continued. "For another thing, Prudence and I both thought we'd seen him leave early, right after his time with Lady Wentworth in the library. Just after the masks came off. But no one else could pinpoint exactly when. According to Hargrave anyway. Lord Ashford was a widower and had the reputation for being devoted to his children, leaving little time for social events. He and his wife were a great love match. According to my friend, he was devastated by her death."

"How did she die?"

"Childbirth, I believe it was. Anyway, Lord Ashford was known as a benevolent, decent man. His staff respected him for his kindness and generosity. Their housekeeper was a friend of mine. She was heartbroken for the children."

"How sad."

"Yes, it was. I didn't go to the hanging but I knew some who did. They said the children were beside themselves. The little girl begged them to spare his life. Lord Ashford claimed his innocence until the very end."

"I wonder what happened to his children?"

"They were sent away to live with some distant cousin. The

crown stripped the family of everything. Titles. Wealth. The manor was shuttered. Tenant farmers were left with nothing, not to mention all the people employed at Ashford Hall. It was a terrible thing."

"But if Lord Ashford didn't do it, then who did?"

"I've no idea. There were a hundred guests at the ball. It could have been any one of them." Mrs. Blythe paused, gazing toward the window. "They never found her mask. We all found that odd. Lizzie scoured the lady's quarters, but it was nowhere." She tilted her head, looking at Rose intently. "Why are you asking? Has something brought it up?"

"This unexpected ball, I suppose. I cannot understand why Father wants to bring it back. It seems sudden and strange."

"I agree, Lady Rose." Mrs. Blythe clicked her tongue sympathetically. "Regardless, we will plan a night that will stun our guests, as we did back in your mother's time."

"I wish I could go back in time and see her just once more." Rose glanced toward the window, where a robin had come to rest on the sill.

"She adored you. I believe she loved being a mother more than anything in her life. Lady Wentworth told Lizzie how much she longed for another child but it never came to pass."

"I'd have liked a brother or sister very much." Maybe then she wouldn't have felt so alone. "Was my mother's life anything but tragic?"

"You, my lady, were her joy."

Rose nodded, afraid she might cry. To hide her emotion, she suggested they return to planning the ball. "I did have an idea for a theme, but it might be silly. What do you think about A Midsummer Night's Dream?"

Mrs. Blythe's expression changed from sorrow to delight. "How enchanting. It's splendid."

Happy that Mrs. Blythe agreed, she spilled over with her ideas. "The women could wear gossamer gowns in soft pastels or moonlit silvers, like Titania and her fairies. They might like to wear floral headpieces or crowns. Masks could be butterflies or leaves or flowers, but of course, that would be up to the guests. Maybe even some will wear subtle fairy wings." She went on to say the gentlemen could wear sashes or cloaks inspired by Oberon and masks of satyrs or owls. "We'll transform the ballroom into an enchanted woodland, with hanging lanterns and floating candles. A depiction of a night sky could be painted on the ballroom floor. Lush floral arrangements, of course." She suggested the music be a string quartet, a harpsichord for quieter moments, and flutes and violins for spirited dances. "And maybe Shakespearean-inspired madrigals to perform?" She warmed, overflowing with ideas. "Is it too much?"

"Not at all, Lady Rose. We shall have to hustle, but I'm sure we can do it."

They narrowed in on a few other details. Mrs. Blythe suggested glazed fruits and berries served in golden goblets. Roasted pheasant, honeyed ham, and stuffed quail. Herb-infused breads, cheeses, and fresh honeycombs. Sugared violets, candied roses, and lavender shortbread biscuits. "We'll have to discuss it with Mrs. Carter, of course, but I'm quite certain she can come up with a delectable menu. Perhaps for drinks, we can serve a light, floral elderflower and champagne cocktail—a fairy nectar?" Mrs. Blythe's eyes twinkled at the idea. "Won't that be fun?"

"Yes, wonderful," Rose said.

Mrs. Blythe picked up a piece of paper from a neat stack. "Here's your father's guest list for both the summer house party and masquerade ball."

Rose took them in hand. The first two made her inwardly sigh. Two weeks of trying to avoid Baron White while managing Honoria Blackwell's conniving ways made her want to curl up in her bed and never come out.

Rose scanned the rest of the list, fingers tracing over each name. The gathering would be an eclectic one, and possibly very entertaining. Some were familiar acquaintances from the Season. Lady Daphne Merriweather, sweet and naive, had befriended

Rose during the previous Season. Lady Arabella Kingsley, the fashionable and wealthy widow, would be there as well, along with Miss Lydia Norbury, a woman of quiet strength who had inherited a fortune but never sought a husband.

Among the gentlemen, Viscount Edmund Gresham was expected—a man of intelligence and reserve, known for his impeccable manners and reticent nature. Then there was Sir Philip Easton, a charming baronet with a rakish reputation and a precarious financial situation, though he remained one of the most entertaining men of the ton. And, of course, Lord Jonathan Ellsworth, the talented musician whose love of gambling had landed him in dire straits. Rose suspected he had only accepted the invitation out of necessity.

The only name on the list she did not recognize was that of Lady Violet Stratton. "Do you know this young woman?" Rose asked Mrs. Blythe.

"I believe she is the young cousin of Mrs. Blackwell. From what I know, she's been sent from up north to live with Mrs. Blackwell, perhaps in the hopes of a good match."

"I certainly hope she has a more pleasant personality than that of Mrs. Blackwell," Rose said before she could stop herself.

Mrs. Blythe didn't respond, but Rose caught a slight twitch at the corner of her mouth.

A firm knock sounded at the door, followed by the quiet creak of its hinges. Tobias Hale appeared, dipping into a shallow bow. "My lady, Mrs. Blythe. My apologies for interrupting."

"Mr. Hale, I didn't expect you back so soon. What can I do for you?" Mrs. Blythe asked, smiling at him. The two were old friends and frequently collaborated.

Tobias Hale had been a presence in Wentworth Manor for years. He was lean and well-built, his frame hinting at a life spent in action rather than idleness. A strong jaw and slightly crooked nose made him rugged rather than classically handsome. His salt-and-pepper hair, more brown than gray, was kept neatly trimmed. His eyes were a deep, warm brown.

As their loyal steward, he handled estate business with efficiency, overseeing the tenants, managing accounts, and ensuring debts were paid. From what Rose had observed, he was a patient and soft-spoken man. A man one could rely on to behave with integrity. Rose often had the impression that he and her father had a somewhat distant relationship. Hargrave was her father's confidant. Hale was simply a man who worked for him.

"Business was settled sooner than expected," Hale said. "I figured I'd best return as soon as I could, given all that's coming our way in the next few weeks."

Mrs. Blythe gave a knowing nod. "I suspect things will be lively indeed."

"Please do not hesitate to ask for whatever you need," Hale said. "I've hired additional hands from some of the lads in the village. Whatever Lady Rose decides to do for the ball, we are at your service."

"Thank you, Hale. That's reassuring," Rose said.

"And now, I must be off. Mr. Thorncroft has asked me to meet the new gardener. He wants my opinion. He seems to think there's something the lad's hiding."

"Really?" Rose's eyebrows raised. "Is it because he seems educated?"

"I believe so. Thorncroft said something about how he talked real pretty." Hale smiled.

"I too have noticed it," Rose said. The handsome gardener had made an impression on her. Too much so.

"I'm sure there's nothing to worry about," Mrs. Blythe said. "His circumstances changed, and now he needs to work for a living. That's what Thorncroft told me anyway."

Rose wished to know more but knew better than to ask and give herself away. "I shall feel relieved to know your opinion," Rose said to Mr. Hale. "You have excellent judgment."

"You're too kind, my lady. I shall report in if I discover anything untoward."

As Hale left, Rose observed Mrs. Blythe's gaze following him out the door with an expression in her eyes that, if pressed, Rose would have to describe as lovelorn. How strange. They'd known each other for a long time. Hale had been engaged to Lizzie at the time of Rose's mother's death. Lizzie, who had been her mother's loyal lady's maid, had died just days after Lady Wentworth. Her horse had been spooked by something—no one knew what. From what Mrs. Blythe had told Rose, Hale had been devastated by the loss. In her words, "He's never been the same."

But that was a long time ago. Twelve years had passed. Was that enough time to heal a heart? Could he fall in love again?

"He's a good man," Rose said to Mrs. Blythe. "Handsome too."

"I suppose one could say so. Lizzie was my dear friend. The love of his life, that she was."

Rose wanted to pry further but didn't want to offend Mrs. Blythe. "I must be off. Thank you."

"Anything for you, my lady."

The women exchanged loving smiles before Rose got up and hustled out of the office before poor Mrs. Blythe saw the emotion brewing in Rose's chest. She had a sinking feeling that the ball might be the last fun she ever had.

Honoria Blackwell would be happy. Rose would not.

# CHAPTER FIVE

THE FIRST SEVERAL days of Sebastian's new position passed without incident. He found genuine satisfaction in impressing Amos Thorncroft with his knowledge of plants and flowers. Those brutal years with the Langstons had taught him something useful, at least.

On his third morning, he was tending to the roses in the garden's most secluded corner, carefully applying his soap mixture to rid the bushes of aphids. The work was methodical, almost meditative. And such beauty everywhere he looked.

The rose garden was breathtaking. Climbing roses cascaded over wooden trellises in waterfalls of pink and white blooms. Beneath one particularly elaborate archway hung a wooden swing, its seat polished smooth by years of use. Sebastian could easily imagine Lady Eleanor Wentworth sitting there with a book, perhaps with her small daughter playing at her feet.

The thought brought an unexpected ache to his chest. That innocent child had become the young woman he'd met just days ago—the enemy's daughter who looked at him with curious green eyes and spoke with genuine kindness to the servants.

"Good morning, Sebastian."

He spun around, nearly dropping his brush. Lady Rose stood at the garden's entrance, framed by climbing roses, her dark hair catching the morning sunlight like spun silk.

"Lady Rose." He quickly removed his cap and bobbed his

head. "I didn't hear you approach."

"I'm told my footsteps are too light. I'm always startling people." She moved closer, her dress rustling softly. "How are the roses faring?"

"Much better, my lady. The aphids are retreating."

"I'm glad to hear it." She paused beside one of the larger bushes, inhaling deeply. "This garden was my mother's pride. She and Mr. Thorncroft planted most of these roses together when she was first married."

Sebastian kept his eyes carefully lowered, as Thorncroft had instructed, though he found it increasingly difficult with her standing so close. "Mr. Thorncroft mentioned that to me. Someone close to me once told me that the best one can hope for their life is to leave something beautiful behind."

"That is a wonderful way to think about our legacy, isn't it?" Rose's voice grew wistful as she settled onto the swing. "Mummy named me after this garden, actually. Sometimes I come here to feel close to her."

"Understandable, my lady."

When he glanced up, she was gazing around the garden with such obvious love and longing that something twisted in his chest. This wasn't the spoiled aristocrat he'd expected to find.

"I admit to being curious about you. Where were you before you joined our staff?" Rose smiled, and Sebastian felt his heart skip against his ribs. The expression transformed her entire face, making her eyes sparkle.

Sebastian's pulse quickened, though whether from her smile or the danger of her questions, he couldn't say. "I served in the military from the time I was of age."

"Were you educated before that? You speak with such re-finement."

"My mother was born into a good family but she fell from grace. However, she managed to teach me letters and numbers and the art of elocution."

"What did she do?" Rose looked at him with wide eyes. "To

fall, that is."

"In the usual way." He left it at that, hoping she would fill in whatever she thought that meant.

"I see. Leaving her alone with a baby." Rose's voice was gentle, understanding rather than judgmental. "It must have been difficult for her. I can't imagine being cast aside. Or, rather, I can. And it would be terrifying."

"We managed." He returned to his work, hoping to discourage further questions, but also moved by her compassion.

"Is she passed now?"

"Yes, just before I joined the military." He thought of his papa as he said, "I miss her every day."

"I lost my mother when I was eight." Rose's voice grew soft, heavy with a grief that seemed to echo in the garden around them. "I, too, miss her every day. Sometimes I wonder what advice she might give me now."

The raw pain in her tone made Sebastian look up despite his intentions otherwise. She looked so young sitting there—so lost—that for a moment he forgot she was Wentworth's daughter. He saw only a girl who'd grown up without the one person who'd loved her most. Just like him and his siblings.

"I'm sorry for your loss, my lady. It is a terrible thing to lose a parent. Especially so young."

"Thank you." She was quiet for a moment, then seemed to shake herself. "I shouldn't be keeping you from your work. Mr. Thorncroft will be displeased if the roses suffer because of my curiosity about you."

Sebastian managed a small smile. "I think you're safe from Mr. Thorncroft's wrath, Lady Rose."

She laughed—a genuine, bubbly sound that felt like a soft tickle in his chest. "You might be surprised. He's quite protective of his gardens."

"Not above you, Lady Rose. From what I can tell, the staff's quite fond of you."

"And I of them. After my mother's death, I spent most of my

time with them. Father was away a lot and even when he was here, he had little interest in me. When we were in London, he was always at his club. Here in the country, he's mostly managing the affairs of the estate."

*And illegal brandy,* Sebastian thought grimly.

Rose stood from the swing, moving toward a particularly beautiful pink rose in full bloom. "My mother would have loved seeing how the garden has flourished. Mr. Thorncroft says these pink ones were her favorites."

She leaned forward to inhale the flower's fragrance, but her foot caught on an uneven stone in the path. Sebastian saw her stumble and reacted instinctively, dropping his brush and catching her around the waist before she could fall.

For a moment, they were frozen—her hands pressed against his chest, his arms around her slender form, their faces mere inches apart. He could smell the delicate scent of lavender in her hair, could see the flecks of gold in her green eyes, could feel the rapid flutter of her pulse at her throat.

"I am sorry for my clumsiness." Her cheeks flushed as pink as the roses.

Sebastian's heart hammered so hard he was certain she could feel it through his shirt. This close, he could see the gentle curve of her lips, the way her lashes cast shadows on her cheeks. She was beautiful—achingly, dangerously beautiful—and for one mad moment he forgot who they both were.

"Are you hurt?" he asked.

"No, I... thank you." But she made no move to step away, and neither did he.

The moment stretched between them, fragile and electric, until the sound of approaching footsteps broke the spell. Sebastian quickly steadied her and stepped back, his hands falling to his sides just as Hargrave appeared around the corner of the garden path.

"Lady Rose." The butler's cold eyes took in the scene with obvious disapproval. "Your father wishes to see you about the final preparations for tomorrow's arrivals."

"Of course." Rose smoothed her skirts, though Sebastian noticed her hands trembled slightly. "Thank you for... preventing my fall, Sebastian."

"Of course, my lady."

She walked away with Hargrave, but not before casting one last glance over her shoulder that made Sebastian's breath catch all over again.

He stood there long after they'd disappeared, his heart still racing, knowing that everything had just become infinitely more complicated. He couldn't afford to feel sympathy for her. Not when his father's memory demanded justice. Not when his siblings' futures depended on him succeeding in his mission.

But as he worked among the roses her mother had planted, Sebastian found that righteous anger was harder to maintain than he'd expected.

BEFORE SEBASTIAN KNEW it, Sunday arrived, bringing a day off for some of the staff. He decided to walk to the village. Perhaps he might overhear something useful about the Wentworth family?

As he set out, three house servants fell into step beside him. Mary Bright, the head maid; Prudence, Rose's lady's maid; Thomas Finch, a footman.

Prudence, tall and slender, had golden hair and wide-set blue eyes, her reserved nature softened by a quiet sweetness that reminded Sebastian of his sister. Mary, in contrast, had a thick head of brown hair and dove-gray eyes, her expression keen and observant. Finch, with his wavy blond hair, ice-blue eyes, and athletic build, carried himself with the easy confidence of a man accustomed to admiration—likely a favorite among the maids, Sebastian suspected.

Dust stirred beneath his boots on the dirt road, well-worn by carts and hooves. They wound past fields of golden wheat, rippling in the summer breeze, and pastures peppered with sheep and grazing cattle. Tenant farms dotted the landscape, their cottages made of modest stone with thatched roofs. Small kitchen gardens brimmed with cabbages, leeks, carrots, and herbs.

Farmers and workers in sweat-stained shirts glanced up as they walked by, waving or offering nods. Mary and Finch called out to some of them. On one farm, children, barefoot and sun-kissed, chased each other near the fences, while farmhands moved methodically through the fields, scythes in hand. A merchant's cart loaded with sacks of grain and bushels of apples came around a corner, forcing them to step aside to let it lumber past.

"You from around here?" Finch asked.

"I was living in Brighton. I've come home from the war only recently. Why do you ask?"

"You're drinking up the sights," Finch said. "I've lived here all my life and I forget to really look around me."

"Yes, it's easy to become complacent."

"What now?" Finch asked.

"It's easy to take it for granted," Sebastian said. "When you see something all the time."

"Aye. We were lucky, Mary and me," Finch said. "Only a few get a chance to get to work up at the big house. No better positions around here."

Mary turned her head to look at him, a grin lighting up her wan face. "I was only a wee girl when Mrs. Blythe hired me as a scullery maid. A good wind would've knocked me over back then."

"Might now too," Finch said, grinning.

"Me mum said I was getting fat last time I saw her," Mary said. "I didn't take offense though. She doesn't mean anything by it."

"She should be kinder," Prudence said. "Since you send all your wages to her and your little sister."

"I have no choice," Mary said. "What with my sister's troubles."

Prudence looked back to give Finch a pretty smile. He smiled right back at her. Was there something romantic between them? How nice it must be to have the freedom to fall in love. He could not lose focus on his purpose. Maybe later, after he'd proved his father's innocence he could entertain the idea of love.

Lady Rose's face came to mind. He shoved the vision aside.

They crested a gentle hill. The village unfolded before them, a cluster of whitewashed cottages with ivy crawling up the sides of the buildings and a church spire rising from the center. Paved with uneven cobblestones, the village square was quiet that day, other than a few wooden stalls and carts that lingered from the morning market, their owners finishing up sales before closing.

Children splashed their fingers in the cool water of the square's fountain, while their mothers gossiped nearby. Scents of fresh bread, roasted meats, and sun-warmed lavender tickled Sebastian's nose, mingling with the muted tang of horse manure and damp earth. A few stray chickens pecked at the ground near a wooden crate of apples left outside the greengrocer's shop.

Prudence kept her head held high, perhaps aware that she was a lady's maid and must hold herself to high standards. The other two, however, called out to friends, shouting across the square. Soon, they arrived at The Fox & Thistle. Finch bounded ahead to open the heavy oak door for the ladies and Sebastian. Inside, the air was thick with pipe smoke and the yeasty tang of ale, along with roasting meat and onions. Dried herbs hung from rafters in the low-beamed ceiling, darkened from age.

Finch took an exaggerated breath in through his nose. "Ah, yes, the scent of my childhood."

They settled at a corner table with bread, cheese, and ale. Sebastian listened as his companions chatted about household gossip, searching for an opening to learn more about the family he was meant to serve.

"I've heard the manor's had its share of troubles over the

years," Sebastian said, tearing off a piece of bread casually.

The three servants exchanged glances. Mary looked down at her hands.

"You mean Lady Wentworth," Prudence said quietly. "That was before your time, of course, but it changed everything."

"I heard she was murdered," Sebastian said. "That must have been terrible for everyone who worked there."

"It was." Finch's usual cheerfulness faded. "I was the one who found her."

Sebastian kept his expression neutral, though his heart began racing. "How awful for you."

"Lord Wentworth had sent me to fetch a book from his study. The ball had just ended, all the guests had left or were leaving, and we were cleaning up." Finch stared into his ale. "There she was, lying on the floor. Blood everywhere."

"The poor woman," Prudence murmured. "She was so kind to all of us. Such a devoted mother to Lady Rose."

"Did they catch who did it?" Sebastian asked.

"They arrested Lord Ashford within days," Finch said. "Found the murder weapon buried in his garden."

"But none of us believed it was him," Prudence added, then glanced around nervously. "We probably shouldn't speak of such things."

"Why not?" Sebastian kept his voice casual.

Mary finally spoke up, her voice barely above a whisper. "Because there are those who don't like questions being asked."

The way she said it sent a chill through Sebastian. He noticed how her hands trembled slightly as she reached for her cider.

"Lord Ashford seemed like a good man from what I've heard in the village," Sebastian said carefully.

"He was," Finch said firmly. "Everyone who knew him said so. That's why it never made sense. No one had an unkind thing to say about him, and he had no business dealings with Lord Wentworth. No motive."

"And we all saw how Lord Wentworth treated his wife,"

Prudence said.

Mary shook her head. "Prudence, no. We shouldn't talk about this. It's not our place."

"It was impossible not to see the way he was with Lady Wentworth," Finch said.

"What do you mean?" Sebastian's chest tightened. He gripped his tankard to steady his hand.

"He was ghastly to her," Mary said woodenly. "Lizzie had to patch her sometimes."

"He hurt her?" Sebastian felt sick, even though he wasn't surprised.

"Broken arm one time," Finch said. "Isn't that right?"

"Yes. And then there's the smuggling," Prudence whispered. "French brandy mostly. All illegal. That's how he made his fortune back."

Back?

"So we figured it was one of the lord's enemies that did it," Finch said. "As revenge. Or something like that."

"Was this Lord Ashford involved in the smuggling?" It hurt Sebastian to say his father's name in this context, but he had to pretend he didn't know anything about the Ashford family.

"Not Lord Ashford," Prudence said. "In fact, Hargrave told us that Lord Wentworth and Lord Ashford were old rivals. They hated each other, from what we heard."

"Aye, Lord Wentworth was keen to make sure we all knew about that story," Finch said. "He told the constable and anyone else who would listen—after Lady Wentworth's death."

"We mustn't speak about this," Mary blurted out.

All three of them turned toward her.

"Why?" Prudence asked softly.

"Do you know something you haven't told us?" Finch asked Mary.

Mary spoke so softly that Sebastian found himself leaning closer. "I didn't hear anything. Other than they were arguing about Lord Wentworth's business."

"Mary, you heard them well enough to know that?" Prudence had gone very still, and her cheeks and neck were splotched with red. "How come you never told anyone?"

"It ain't my place to talk about it." Mary cast a wary glance around the tavern. "And like Finch said, no one ever asked me."

"What else did you hear, Mary?" Prudence asked.

Mary glanced up, tears in her eyes. "It were Miss Rose I felt sorry for. Poor thing."

"Mary, what did you hear?" Finch asked. "You can tell us."

"She found out about his shady business. At the ball. Lord Ashford told her what he knew about the smuggling." Mary drained her cider and raised her hand for another. "Lady Wentworth confronted Lord Wentworth about it and they fought."

"Lady Wentworth didn't know before that night?" Sebastian asked.

"I don't think so," Mary said quietly. "From what I heard, Lady Wentworth was not happy. Said something about her father turning over in his grave. Said something about how it would kill her father if he weren't already dead to know what Lord Wentworth had done with her dowry."

"Right. It was her money," Finch said to Sebastian. "She brought it into the marriage. Saved the estate from ruin, from what we heard."

Sebastian had not known that. Finally, he was getting somewhere.

"What happened after you found the body?" Sebastian asked Finch.

Finch scratched the back of his neck. "I ran back to tell Lord Wentworth. He was in the library with Hargrave—they looked like they'd been having some intense discussion. When I told them what I'd found, his lordship seemed properly shocked. Collapsed beside her body, weeping and carrying on."

"And then?"

"Hargrave sent me to fetch the constable from the village.

Told me to ride hard." Finch took a long drink. "But here's the strange thing—when I went to saddle my horse, Thorncroft told me Hargrave had just taken another horse and ridden off in the opposite direction from the village."

Sebastian's pulse quickened, but he kept his voice level. "Perhaps he had other business to attend to?"

"At one in the morning? After a murder?" Finch shook his head. "Thorncroft said he was gone for hours. Didn't return until well after sunrise."

Prudence nodded. "I remember that. I was up with Lizzie—she was Lady Wentworth's maid, and she was beside herself with grief. We were in the kitchen trying to comfort her when Hargrave came back. He looked like he'd been riding hard, and when he heard us talking about what might have happened, he flew into a rage. Threatened to dismiss us all if we didn't keep our mouths shut."

Sebastian's mind raced. Hours. Plenty of time to ride to Ashford Hall and plant the murder weapon.

"What happened to Lizzie?" Sebastian asked.

Another glance between Finch and Prudence.

"She was killed not long after Lady Wentworth," Prudence said. "Thrown from her horse."

Murdered. That's the word she should have used.

Sebastian drew in a deep breath. Should he say it? Yes, he had to act boldly or he would never find the answers he needed. "You all think Lord Wentworth murdered her."

Mary gasped. Prudence and Finch exchanged another look.

"We have no way of knowing what really happened that night," Prudence said finally.

"That's right. None whatsoever," Mary said, a little too quickly.

"But that's what some of us believe," Prudence said. "Including me."

"And me," Finch said.

Sebastian covertly watched Mary while pretending to focus

on lifting his tankard to his mouth. A shimmer of perspiration on her forehead told him she was nervous.

She knew more than she was saying. Had she been outside the door when Lord Wentworth had brought the candlestick down on his wife's head? Like she'd mentioned, no one noticed her. She could have been there, invisible.

Before he could ask further questions, his companions quieted, glancing nervously toward the door. Sebastian turned to see Hargrave had entered the tavern.

"Don't say anything about this to him," Finch whispered. "He'll punish us if he knows we told you so much."

"Please?" Prudence's eyes widened with obvious fear.

"Nary a word, I promise," Sebastian whispered back.

The butler surveyed the room before his pale eyes settled on their table. He approached with measured steps, uninvited.

"Good afternoon," he said, settling into an empty chair. "Enjoying your day off?"

They all nodded mutely. Sebastian noticed how differently his companions behaved around the butler—shoulders tense, eyes downcast.

"So, Doyle," he said, voice smooth and sharp, "I trust you're finding our little corner of the countryside satisfactory?"

Sebastian set down his tankard. "Yes, sir. It's good, honest work."

"Hmm." Hargrave's gaze flicked over him. "Thorncroft speaks well of you. But I always like to form my own impressions."

Sebastian said nothing, letting the silence stretch. The fire crackled.

Hargrave tilted his head slightly. "Something about you doesn't sit right with me, Doyle. Can't quite figure out why."

Sebastian held his stare. "I just tend the gardens, sir."

"Let's keep it that way," Hargrave said mildly, though the steel beneath his words was unmistakable. "The Wentworths value discretion. I assume Thorncroft explained that."

"He did."

"Excellent." Hargrave gave a single nod, then turned to address the table at large. "Early start tomorrow, ladies and gents. Best not let the ale do your thinking for you."

He left without another glance, his shadow lingering long after he'd gone.

For a few moments, no one spoke. Then Prudence muttered, "He really knows how to ruin a person's day off."

"Indeed," Finch said.

"We should go back," Prudence said. "And Sebastian? It might be best if you didn't ask too many questions about the past. Some people have long memories."

As they prepared to leave, Sebastian spotted Hargrave outside, speaking with a stocky man in a constable's uniform.

"Who's that with Hargrave?" he asked Finch quietly.

"Constable Stephens. He replaced Pritchard a few years back. They say he's honest, but…" Finch shrugged. "Honest men don't tend to last long around here."

"Meaning Wentworth pays them to do his bidding?" Sebastian asked.

"That's right," Finch said. "An honest constable doesn't stand a chance."

The walk back to the manor was subdued. Sebastian's mind raced with everything he'd learned. The servants suspected Wentworth was guilty; Hargrave had mysteriously disappeared for hours after the murder; and Mary clearly knew something she was too frightened to share.

Most importantly, he now had a clear picture of what had happened that night. Lady Wentworth had discovered her husband's smuggling operation—funded by her own dowry—and confronted him about it. In his rage, the man who had already been abusing her physically had finally killed her.

And then he'd framed an innocent man to cover his crimes.

How could he get Mary to tell him what she'd really seen that night? And how could he prove what he now knew to be true?

# CHAPTER SIX

ROSE STOOD AT her bedroom window, watching Sebastian cross the lawn toward the rose garden. Observing him from afar like some lovesick schoolgirl had become a habit she could not seem to break. The way he moved captivated her. Long, confident strides. Head high. His flat cap pulled low to shield his eyes from the morning sun.

For three days now, she'd found excuses to position herself where she might catch glimpses of him working. What was it about this man that intrigued her so? He was a gardener, for heaven's sake. A decent man, no doubt, but hardly appropriate company for the lady of the house.

She knew the rules. Knew her place. Knew his.

Yet here she was, fingers twitching with anticipation, her pulse quickening at the sight of him.

Before she could think better of it, her feet were already carrying her out of the bedroom, down the stairs, and into the bright morning sunlight. She grabbed her bonnet on the way, tying it hastily beneath her chin as she crossed the dewy grass.

When she reached the rose garden, she hesitated at the entrance. Sebastian looked up from where he knelt beside a yellow rose bush, pruning shears in hand. He stood with easy grace and inclined his head.

"Lady Rose."

His voice, low and steady, stirred something deep in her chest.

"I've come to collect roses for an arrangement," she said, relieved at how steady her voice sounded. "For the drawing room."

"Of course, my lady." He gestured to a neat pile of freshly cut blooms on the grass. "These yellow ones might suit. Or perhaps the pink over there?"

She moved toward the pink rose bush, drawn less by the flowers and more by the man behind them. Kneeling beside the bush, she bent to inhale the delicate fragrance, the petals brushing her nose like a whisper. The scent was sweet, but it was not what made her dizzy.

She reached for one of the cut stems and winced as a thorn bit her finger. "Ouch!" Without thinking, she pressed the finger to her mouth.

When she looked up, Sebastian was watching her. Not politely, but with something darker. His gaze had gone molten, and she could see the pulse fluttering in his jaw. The space between them shimmered with a sudden, breathless tension.

"Let me see." He moved toward her, pulling a handkerchief from his pocket. His movements were purposeful, but not rushed.

She didn't pull away when he dropped to one knee beside her and gently took her hand. His fingers were warm and calloused—honest hands, capable hands—and the contact sent a jolt through her. The scent of leather and clean soap clung to him.

"It's nothing, really," she whispered, but her voice sounded unfamiliar. Low and husky.

"A hand as delicate as yours shouldn't meet with thorns." His thumb brushed across her skin as he wrapped the cloth around her finger. The touch was so gentle she could barely feel it, and yet it set her entire body alight.

Her eyes fell to his mouth, then to the hollow of his throat, where dark hair curled against damp skin. What would that skin taste like? She swallowed hard, horrified by her own thoughts and yet unable to stop them.

His eyes lifted to meet hers. For a moment, they stayed like that—silent, locked in a gaze that said far too much. His brown eyes held amber flecks she hadn't noticed before, and his lashes were far too thick for a man.

She pulled her hand away with effort. "Thank you. I'm fine. It was just a prick."

"I'll remove every thorn before you take them inside." He turned back to the flowers.

She stepped away, retreating to the swing beneath the rose arbor. The shade offered no relief. Not when heat pulsed through every inch of her. Not when she couldn't stop watching his large hands as he worked, flicking each thorn off the stem with quiet efficiency. Now she knew what that thumb felt like against her skin, and some foolish, reckless part of her craved the feeling again.

"It's really not necessary," she said. "I shall be more careful next time."

"It's no trouble, my lady." He looked up. "I won't have you pricking yourself again."

She flushed. No man had ever spoken to her that way before. So gently and with such care.

"A lady such as yourself should know only beauty, not pain."

Oh dear. That did it. She pressed the handkerchief still wrapped around her finger to her damp forehead. It carried his scent. Earth, leather, soap. She would keep it. He wouldn't want it back anyway. Not with the bloodstain.

She took a breath to collect herself. "Let me do something for you in return. What would you like? A treat from the kitchen?"

He hesitated. Then, quietly, "I don't suppose I might borrow a book from your library? The evenings in the bunkhouse are long. I'm not much for cards."

"You read?" It came out more surprised than she intended.

He chuckled, a warm sound that curled around her spine. "Does that surprise you?"

"A little."

"I enjoy poetry. Love stories. Shakespeare." His gaze was

steady, and something in it caught her off guard. "Anything, really."

"I'd be happy to find something for you," she said softly.

"There we are." He stood, cradling the roses in his arms as if they were fragile. "All safe now."

He stepped toward her. She reached out to take the flowers, and as he placed them in her arms, his fingers brushed hers again. Had he done it on purpose?

"Thank you," she said, her voice barely audible.

For a moment, they stood in the golden hush of morning. Bees hummed, birds called, but all she could hear was the thunder of her own heart.

Sebastian looked down at her lips, then stepped back.

"My pleasure, Lady Rose."

THAT EVENING, BEFORE supper, Rose slipped into the library. The room was warm and heavy with the familiar scents of tobacco and brandy. Her father had been there recently.

She found what she was looking for quickly—*A Midsummer Night's Dream*. Perfect for Sebastian, especially with the upcoming ball theme.

"Rose."

She nearly jumped out of her skin. Her father sat in the shadows of a high-backed chair, a brandy glass glinting in his hand.

"Father. You startled me."

"What are you doing?"

She hesitated, the play still in her hand. "Looking for something to read."

He took a slow sip of brandy, his pale eyes assessing. Then came the familiar condescension, coiled in civility.

"You must remember what a privileged life you've had Rose."

"What does that mean?"

"Access to books. An education. Sometimes I wonder if you truly appreciate all you've been given."

"But I do, Father. Especially my education. Books are one of my greatest joys."

"You'll have ample time to read once you're married. Baron White has assured me that you'll have whatever it is you wish for."

She gripped the book tighter. "What if my wish is to remain here. With you."

A snap of irritation sparked in his eyes. "We've been over this. This is what is best for you. A tidy marriage serves us both."

"But why?"

"You know the answer to that question," he said.

She did not, actually.

He got up from the chair and walked toward her, then held out his hand. "What have you chosen?" A slight smile played at his lips. "Ah, yes, preparing for the ball. Excellent."

"I am glad you approve." Her voice came out flat. The tone of someone who had given up. What else could she do?

"The work you've done to prepare for the ball has pleased me. I hope you will continue to do so. Please me, that is. By doing as I ask. You may not see it now, Rose, but I know what is best for you. I always have. You will have a good life with Baron White. Children. A home of your own."

She shuddered at the thought of Baron White's touch.

"You mustn't succumb to unhealthy thoughts," he said. "Your mother was not successful in doing so and it caused us both much unhappiness."

"What do you mean?" Rose held her breath, knowing her father's temper and his lack of patience when it came to her questions.

"I mean that your mother was prone to hysteria and melancholy. Most husbands would have had her committed to a place that could help her. Perhaps had I done so, she would still be here."

"How would that have kept her from being murdered?" The words were out before she could stop them.

He took hold of her upper right arm, crushing it in his strong grip. "You will not ask any further questions. You will do as I ask. Or there will be consequences. Perhaps the one I should have given your mother. Do you understand?" His grip tightened.

She nodded, tears blurring her vision so that her father's face distorted, making him even more menacing.

"Say the words," he said.

"I understand."

"That's my good girl." He let her go and charged from the room.

After he left, Rose stood frozen. He had threatened her. There was no mistaking what he'd meant. Marry Baron White or he would have her committed. She thought she might be sick.

But she gathered herself enough to escape to her room. Once there, she took out Sebastian's handkerchief and breathed in his scent. It had a strangely calming effect.

She slid it beneath her pillow. She had no idea why, other than it provided comfort.

THE NEXT MORNING, after breakfast and a meeting with Mrs. Blythe, Rose tucked *A Midsummer Night's Dream* into a basket and headed for the rose garden. Earlier, she'd spotted Sebastian with his leather satchel of tools headed in that direction.

She thought about bringing his handkerchief to him but decided against it. She wanted a little piece of him with her, nestled under the place where she rested her cheek during the night.

When she reached the garden, Sebastian was on his knees, his tool belt around his waist, peering closely at the leaves of one of the rose bushes. A spade and hoe were propped against one of the maple trees, and a basket with plant clippings beside them. His linen shirt clung to the muscles of his back, and she wondered what it would feel like to run her hands along the curves and planes of his shoulders. This, unfortunately, must be left to her imagination.

She called out to Sebastian, not wanting to startle him as she had the day before.

Upon hearing his name, he straightened, taking his cap off to wipe his brow. "Lady Rose."

"Good afternoon. I'm sorry to disturb your work, but I've brought a book."

"You have?" He grinned, transforming his serious visage into one of boyish glee. Was it the first time she'd seen him smile in such a way? She believed it must be, for it had a devastating effect, rendering her warm and floaty, as if she could dance without touching the ground.

"It's *A Midsummer Night's Dream*, and I shall tell you why I chose it, if it interests you."

"Yes, it interests me indeed."

She dug it out of her basket and looked around to see if they were being observed. Seeing no one, she reached her hand out to give it to him.

But he did not take it at first. Instead, he pulled out a handkerchief and wiped the dirt away from his hard-working hands. It was only when they were free of dirt that he took the book from her. "This is one of my favorites."

"I'm glad to hear that. Tuck it into your belt, so that no one sees," Rose said.

He did as she asked. "I enjoy the comedies. More so than the tragedies, I'm ashamed to say. The tragedies are so…"

"Tragic?"

He smiled, nodding slightly. "Yes. Too much like real life, perhaps? Man and his tragic flaw. The one that takes him down in the end."

"Do you think we all have a tragic flaw? One that will ultimately destroy us?" Rose asked.

His eyes glittered for a second or two before he answered. "I don't know about others, but I suspect it's true of myself."

"What could it possibly be?" She held her breath, feeling as if his answer was vitally important if she were to ever understand him. And she found she wanted desperately to do so.

His expression vacillated. She sensed his internal struggle—to speak the truth or not? Wasn't that the battle one faced every day, no matter what station one was born into? How much do we show others? What makes us choose to trust someone or not?

In the end, he appeared to come to a decision—to let her inside and show her a part of himself that he did not often share. At least that's what she presumed. "I'm a man fixated by the past. A harm inflicted upon my family that I've been unable to move on from. One that haunts my every moment."

"I'm sorry," Rose said. "Does it have to do with your mother's downfall? Perhaps the man who caused it?"

He placed his cap back on his head, shadowing his eyes. "Something of that nature, yes. Righting a wrong is an obsession. One that makes living rather difficult."

She drew in a sharp breath. "Like a circumstance from which a heroine cannot escape. A marriage decided upon by her father, for example."

"Is this one you find yourself in?" Sebastian's brow furrowed, and his eyes softened with obvious sympathy.

"My father's forcing me into marriage with a man I hardly know. A horrible man. He's as old as my father. If I do not do as Father asks, I'll be sent away to God knows where. Or maybe just cast aside, locked away from my home to perish on the streets. I've no mother to protect me. The staff who love me are powerless too." To her horror, tears pricked her eyes. "So, I too, must make a choice. To succumb to his wishes or run away. But I have nowhere to go. No skills or means to take care of myself." A tear slipped down her cheek and then another and another. Drat. How could she allow herself to cry in front of him? He had worries of his own without her begging him for attention like a spoiled child. "I'm sorry. Please forgive me."

He whipped out his handkerchief and unfolded it and refolded it so that the side he had wiped his dirty hands on no longer showed. "Take this."

She could have taken the hanky tucked inside her sleeve, the one embroidered with her own initials. But no. She would take his once again. Add it to her collection. She accepted it from his outstretched hand and dabbed at her wet cheeks. "But I cannot run. Of course, I can't. My urge for survival outweighs my disgust. How pathetic."

"Not at all, Lady Rose. We all have instincts from which we must call upon when threatened. That's all you're doing. I find you to be quite brave."

"I'm not though." Tears blurred her vision. She pressed the handkerchief against the hot flesh of her lids. "I'm weak. I'll do what I have to do so that I can continue to live in comfort. As Father made clear to me last night, it is not for me to decide my future or to be anything but a woman on a man's arm, planning his parties and running his household, bearing his children. And I'm supposed to be thankful for it. Count my luck and my blessings that I was born a lady instead of into a family where I would have been taught a trade or honed a skill like my staff. Isn't that funny? I envy them. As hard as they toil, surely it would not be as bad as lying with a man who smells of dirty feet." She giggled, feeling hysterical. "I'm sorry. I've said too much and embarrassed us both."

"Not at all. You mustn't fret." He stepped forward, reaching out to her but snapping back his hand at the last second. His brown eyes, the color of dirt after a rain, flickered with emotion. First anger, then sorrow, then something so sad and helpless that she could feel it in the depths of her stomach. The muscles in his jaw tensed as if holding in the words he wished to say.

Yet she heard them anyway.

*I would protect you if I could.*

She echoed back his sentiment, only out loud. "I would help you if I could."

"What would you do to help me?"

"To right whatever wrong has been done to you. If I had any power at all, I would offer it to you."

He let out a long sigh, his eyes darkening as they stared unflinchingly into hers. "Lady Rose, I quite believe you would. Alas, it cannot be done. We are twins in this way—powerless to decide our own fate."

Tears spilled from her eyes once more and she spoke with abandon, feeling reckless. "I shall remember this day. Later, when I'm trapped in Baron White's home. And his bed. I'll take comfort, knowing someone has understood me so very well."

"My mother used to say that one must never lose faith, even when the barriers to our happiness are stacked so thick and high they seem insurmountable. Can we agree on this anyway? To believe. To have hope?"

"For now, I suppose it's the only option afforded us," Rose said, patting away the new tears that flowed from her eyes.

"Tell me. What made you choose this play?" Sebastian patted the book he'd placed in his tool belt.

"It seems silly now, but I shall tell you anyway. The ball we're planning—I thought at first it was because it represents the beauty and magic of a fleeting summer night. But in hindsight, I suppose I wanted, for one night, to step into a world where love isn't dictated by duty. Where people follow their hearts. The lovers in the play are all at the mercy of forces outside of their control, yet it all works out in the end. They find true love. As you say, the comedies are decidedly better than the tragedies. Even if they are completely unrealistic."

"We have our books, Lady Rose. They'll never cease to be a comfort."

She smiled, wiping her eyes one last time. "Yes, this is true. Whatever happens, we can escape into them and forget our problems for a moment or two."

He patted his tool belt where the book lay hidden. "Thank you for this."

She nodded and then turned away, remembering the hand-kerchief balled up in her hand. She halted, then turned back toward him. He watched her intently, a worried crease between his brows. "I'm going to keep your handkerchief for the second day in a row." For the life of her, she couldn't begin to explain why she did what she did next. She reached into the sleeve of her dress and removed her own hanky. "But I'll leave you with mine. There's no need to return it."

She pressed it into his hand, lingering for a moment to feel the warmth of his skin, before she pulled away and nearly ran out of the rose garden and across the lawn to the house.

# CHAPTER SEVEN

FOR HIS MIDDAY break, Sebastian took his clandestine gift from Lady Rose, along with bread and cheese, to read under a chestnut tree near the herb garden, away from the others' chatter. He settled against the low stone wall, stretching his long legs out before him as he tore off a piece of crusty bread. The shade cast a welcome reprieve from the summer heat, its broad leaves rustling softly overhead. A perfect spot for a good read. However, instead of opening his book, his thoughts turned to Lady Rose. Her sudden appearance while he was working had befuddled him. Delighted him too. Which was dangerous.

He suspected she was as drawn to him as he was to her. Other than his family, he had not felt cared for in such a way by any other person. Not ever. The way she tilted her head when he spoke, clearly listening carefully to what he had to say, had moved him. When with Lady Rose, he felt like himself.

How strange.

And what was he to do with these feelings that seemed to have grabbed hold of his heart? He reached inside his pocket to feel the lace of her hanky, then pulled it out to draw in the scent of her perfume. She'd not returned his handkerchief from the day she pricked her finger but he'd thought nothing of it. But clearly she had kept it deliberately. The way his skin had warmed under her touch had unsettled him. So did the craving for more. What did it all mean?

He must set it aside for now. That was all there was to it.

He bowed his head and spoke to his father silently.

*I'll not give up on us, Papa. Nothing will deter me. Not even my own traitorous heart.*

He finished his chunk of bread, chasing it with a jar of cold water, then opened his book. However, he was distracted by voices coming from the other side of the stone wall.

"I can't for the life of me imagine why the lord wants to bring the ball back. After all these years? A masquerade, just like the night Lady Wentworth was killed seems in such poor taste." That was the voice of Mrs. Carter, the cook.

The other belonged to Mrs. Blythe, the housekeeper. "It's horrific. I'm desperately worried about Lady Rose. She'll be forced to marry that awful Baron White, and I'm afraid she'll find the same fate as her mother."

"Do you think he's violent?" Mrs. Carter asked.

"I feel certain of it. I've heard rumors," Mrs. Blythe said.

"What kind of rumors?"

"Of him hurting maids. One of them took her life after he…" She didn't finish but Sebastian knew to what she alluded. White was a rapist.

"Oh dear me, how can Lord Wentworth give her to him?" Mrs. Carter asked.

"He has his reasons. And her name is Honoria Blackwell."

"She'll be mistress of this house soon enough," Mrs. Carter said. "I don't know what's to become of any of us."

"I wish she could find a love match. Someone young and handsome. Someone who could take her far away from here," Mrs. Blythe said. "As much as it would hurt to lose her, I want her to be safe and happy."

"I felt sure she would have offers of marriage after the Season," Mrs. Carter said.

"No, it wasn't like that at all. She sat alone at the balls with an empty dance card."

"How is that possible? She's pretty and well-spoken," Mrs.

Carter said. "Perhaps more so than any other debutant this Season."

"We're not the only ones who hear the whispers about the lord's true business. My theory? No one wants to marry into this family because of it."

"Do you think so?"

"It's a dangerous business run by a dangerous man," Mrs. Blythe said.

"Baron White does not seem to mind. I wonder why?" Mrs. Carter asked.

"From what I've heard, he's as dishonorable as Lord Wentworth."

"Oh, poor Lady Rose," Mrs. Blythe said. "She'll be controlled by Baron White, just as her mother was in her marriage. I can't stand to see it. She's so lovely and pretty, and soon all the life will be sucked out of her. But she will be engaged to Baron White before the end of the summer. There's not a thing we can do about it either. We best keep our concerns to ourselves. Or we'll end up like poor Lizzie."

"God rest her soul," Mrs. Carter said. "All this talk of the ball has brought back too many memories of that night. I will never forget what Lizzie said to Hargrave the morning he returned from doing whatever it was he was sent to do."

"Yes, how could we forget? It was so bold and reckless—telling Hargrave she had no doubt it was the lord who killed his wife."

"And then questioned Hargrave about his whereabouts after she was killed," Mrs. Carter said. "Lizzie should never have said what she did to Hargrave. She might still be with us if not."

"Grief made her reckless."

Sebastian held his breath.

"You know as well as I—Lord Wentworth sent Hargrave off with that candlestick and planted it in Lord Ashford's garden," Mrs. Carter said.

"But how would anyone have ever proved it? Ashford had

been at the party. He and Lady Wentworth were old friends. Everyone saw them speaking together at the ball. Then, Lord Wentworth telling anyone who would listen that he and Ashford had a rivalry. The constable seemed to take that as gospel and didn't look further."

"He was in his pocket, you know," Mrs. Carter said. "It might be different should it have happened now, what with the new constable. He might not be for sale."

"Every man's for sale," Mrs. Blythe said. "Lord Wentworth can do whatever he chooses because he holds the purse strings."

"The rivalry was only one sided, anyway. They'd both vied for Lady Ashford's hand but she chose Lord Ashford. Lizzie told me Lady Wentworth used to speak of it occasionally—how she'd been Lord Wentworth's second choice—only chosen because of her money. She told Lizzie once that had she known the truth, she would never have married him. But you know what they say about snakes in the grass. You never see them coming."

They must have finished whatever task they'd come out to do because their voices faded away until he was left with only the sound of the bees and birdsong and the rustling of the chestnut tree and the pounding of his own heart.

AT THE END of the workday, the other gardeners headed off to a swimming hole at the edge of the grounds. Thus far, Sebastian had declined their invitations, preferring to spend time alone before they had their supper together in the bunkhouse. But today, having felt fire flow through his veins when Rose had touched him, he thought it might be best to cool off before he burst into flames.

He followed the others along a well-worn dirt path to a secluded wooded glade fed by a natural spring. The young gardeners, Thomas and Oliver, stripped off their shirts, pants, and stockings to wade into the water in their loose-fitting linen drawers. Jasper stripped down to his underwear as well, and then jumped into the water, whooping. Old Ned merely pulled off his stockings to put his feet in the water, puffing on his pipe. Sebastian, arms crossed, watched the others. If he were to take off his shirt in front of the others, they would see the scars from the beatings he'd endured at the Langstons.

But the heat of the day won out in the end. If the others noticed his scars, so be it. He peeled off his shirt, stockings and pants, tossing them aside, before wading into the water.

The men fell silent, staring at his back. Sebastian could only imagine what they thought when they saw the jagged and uneven scars from Baron Langston's riding crop. In addition, he had a long scar on his right side, just below the ribs, from a bayonet wound from fighting in the Peninsular War.

Sebastian shrugged off the stares and dove headfirst into the cool water. Nothing had ever felt as good. When he came to the surface, he noticed that Tobias Hale stood near the bank. His presence startled Sebastian, but the other didn't seem to mind.

They called out to him, respectfully, but in a way that told Sebastian it was not unusual for the steward to join them.

Sebastian treaded water in the middle of the pool, hoping to go unnoticed, but it was not to be.

"Doyle, may I have a word?" Hale asked.

"Of course, sir." His heart sank. What had he done wrong? He swam toward the bank and pulled himself up, water sluicing off his bare skin as he stood. He caught a flicker of something in Tobias's expression—perhaps the briefest moment of surprise and then sympathy as the older man took in his scars.

Sebastian reached for his shirt, pulling it over his wet skin and reached for his pants.

Hale motioned for him to follow. "I need to speak with you in private for a moment. Won't take long. No need to dress."

Sebastian felt the eyes of the other men on his back, only this time for different reasons than his scars. When one's boss's boss asks for a moment, it couldn't be good news.

Hale led him up to a grassy spot away from the others and sat on a thick, fallen log. "Sit, please."

Sebastian did so, careful to leave space between them, feeling like an idiot in nothing but a shirt and drawers. "Am I to be dismissed?"

"Thorncroft is pleased with your work. In fact, he says you're saving the roses."

"Thank you, sir." Sebastian smoothed his hair from his forehead, waiting.

"However, there's something I need to speak with you about." Hale paused, seeming to gather his thoughts. "I know who you are."

"What?"

"I know you're Sebastian Ashford."

"But how?" His heart raced, and despite his damp skin from the cool water, he began to sweat.

"Do you remember Mrs. Ellsworth? Your housekeeper? She was a good friend of my mother's. When I first met you, there seemed something familiar about you. Your eyes mostly. Also, you're clearly not the typical gardener—the way you hold yourself, the way you speak. I went to see Mrs. Ellsworth recently. She asked if you had any scars. I'd noticed the one on your hand."

Sebastian instinctually covered the scar between his thumb and index finger that was now stark white against his tanned skin. He'd gotten it when he was a child from breaking a wine goblet in his father's drawing room.

"She said you cut it when you were five. A wine goblet."

"Yes, that's right." He braced himself. "Shall I pack my things?"

"No. I have a vested interest in the truth. I initially came to work here to keep watch over Lady Rose—I promised her grandfather I would. But there's another reason. Lizzie was my fiancée."

Sebastian nearly fell off the log. "The lady's maid who was killed just after Lady Wentworth?"

"Yes. And I know without a doubt that she was killed by Lord Wentworth because she knew too much. Hargrave did it, I feel certain. So it was not only that I came here to keep watch over Lady Rose. I, too, have a thirst for justice."

"But it's been twelve years. Have you found nothing to support your theory?"

"Nothing I could go to the constable with, no. Our former constable was as crooked as they come, but the new one, Stephens, has told me himself he's interested in discovering what really happened. I've spoken to him, but he needs proof."

"How have you been able to work for Wentworth, knowing what you know?" Sebastian asked.

"Same as you, I suppose. My need for revenge outweighs logic or the wisdom to get as far away from here as possible." Hale loosened his cravat with a deft tug. "I can't rest until I've uncovered what really happened that night. It's not just for me, either. Lord Wentworth is forcing Rose to marry Baron White. Unless we can change the course of history, she will be doomed to a loveless, abusive marriage. Just like her mother."

Sebastian was at an utter loss for what to say next. Another man as keen to expose Wentworth as Sebastian? This scenario had never occurred to him.

"I saw you and Lady Rose today in the rose garden. I can see clearly what's beginning to happen between you. But you have to be careful. Lord Wentworth has eyes everywhere. Hargrave's sole purpose is to take care of the lord's interests. Which means that you are in danger if he were to catch you and Rose speaking with such intimacy as you were today."

Sebastian hung his head. "She has sought me out and I find that when I'm with her, all else seems to fade. Even my purpose."

"Which is?"

"To clear my father's name and restore the titles and wealth that were wrongfully stripped of us."

"Falling for Lady Rose would not serve you."

"No, it would not."

"I've been in the world a lot longer than you," Hale said. "And I have to tell you—falling in love is not something one chooses with one's mind. The heart is mysterious. Impractical."

"I'll not fall in love with her. She deserves better than a liar such as me."

"Yet, if you were to clear your father's name, she will lose everything. But you'll have recovered all you lost. If you were to have your title and fortune restored, you would be able to ask for Lady Rose's hand."

Sebastian couldn't believe what he was hearing. "Yes, but we're a long way from that."

Hale sighed. "Yes, we are."

"You won't tell my secret?"

"I have no intention of doing so. In fact, I believe we should become allies. Together, we might have a chance of finally sending Lord Wentworth and Hargrave to their rightful places in hell."

"But how?"

"I've no idea. But my mother used to tell me there was no problem I couldn't figure a way out of."

"What about Baron White?" Sebastian asked. "How can we save her from him?"

"I'd like you to keep a close watch on her after his arrival. As for me, I'm digging around, hoping to find something that will save her from him. I've hired a detective. Surely there's something scandalous in his past that will get him arrested. Or perhaps, with this new constable, we could prove the nature of White's and Wentworth's business partnership."

"Baron White is his partner? The illegal brandy?"

"You know about that already?"

"I saw the operation happening in the middle of the night." For a second, an image of the man with the riding whip came to mind. Was that White?

"What do you know about the smuggling?" Sebastian asked.

"I'm not allowed to see that side of his business. Lord Wentworth made it clear that should I poke around, I will pay for it with my life. When I went to the new constable, I got the feeling he was suspicious of what Wentworth is really doing. Unlike Pritchard, he isn't on Lord Wentworth's payroll. However, I feel certain Wentworth has threatened Constable Stephens, just as he has me."

Sebastian described the man he saw the night he'd witnessed the operation unfolding. "Is that Baron White?"

"Yes, that's him."

"That's who he wants to give Rose to?" Sebastian shuddered.

"It's security for him. If his partner is married to his daughter, there is less chance for betrayal."

"Right. Of course." It was all coming together in his mind. Sebastian stared at Hale, shaking his head. "You surprise me, Mr. Hale. A great deal."

"As do you, Sebastian Ashford."

Hearing his real name uttered made him want to weep. "This has defined my entire existence since I was twelve years old. Until today, I've felt no hope that I would be able to do what I set out to do."

"We're going to make this right. You've come this far, haven't you?"

"As have you."

"Please, keep close watch on Lady Rose. Once the houseguests and White appear, things will grow chaotic. Easier for White to compromise her in one way or another." Hale pulled his hat further down his forehead and stood. "Keep your eyes and ears open."

"I will."

Sebastian watched him walk away, stunned by this turn of events. Did he dare allow himself to hope?

# CHAPTER EIGHT

THE NEXT MORNING, Rose managed to sneak yet another book from the library and take it out to Sebastian before she had to prepare for the arrival of the houseguests. She'd chosen a popular romantic novel called *The Sorrows of Young Werther* by Goethe. She thought, however, as she crossed the lawn toward the rose garden, that perhaps it was too bold of a choice. After all, it was about a young man falling desperately in love with a woman he could never have.

No, she told herself. It was fine. They were not falling in love. She was simply being kind to the unusual gardener who desperately longed for reading material. It was nothing important. Nor was it strange that she'd kept his handkerchiefs and hidden them in her bedside table, pulling them out to put under her pillow before she fell asleep at night.

No, nothing untoward about that whatsoever.

He was currently watering the roses when she arrived. He straightened, giving her his usual greeting. "Lady Rose."

"Good morning. I've brought you something. I shan't be able to bring you anything else for the next few days. All the houseguests arrive today, and I'll be busy." She sighed, wishing it were not so.

"Will Baron White be one of them?"

"Yes. He will."

"I've been asked to keep a watch over you," Sebastian said.

Her breath caught, and she took a small step back. "What? By whom?"

"Mr. Hale. He's concerned for your safety. Given Baron White's reputation."

Stunned, she clutched the book to her chest as if to shield herself. "Oh. I didn't know Mr. Hale understood the danger." How had he known that White had nearly assaulted her?

"He doesn't want you compromised."

"It won't matter. I'll be forced to marry him regardless."

"Never give up hope, Lady Rose."

"We would need a miracle," Rose said.

"They've been known to happen."

She searched his face, tracing the contours of his cheeks and jawline with her eyes. "Do you have a dream? Something you wish for with all your heart? One that would require a miracle? Other than your fixation on revenge, that is."

He blinked. "I cannot think past that point to make room for any other dream."

"Then I shall pray for you to have one. And now I must go." She held out the book for him to take. "I hope you'll enjoy this one. You might find it overwrought."

"I shall report back. Thank you, Lady Rose." He glanced down at his feet. "No one has looked at me for a long time. Thank you for that."

"What do you mean?"

"I'm an invisible man to most. You've made me feel otherwise."

"Your station in life should not be all that anyone sees," Rose said.

"You know as well as I that it is and will always be so."

She bowed her head, her throat tightening. How she wished she could stay with him instead of going to greet Baron White and the rest of the guests. Worst of all, there was something else she dreaded even more.

"What is it, my lady?" Sebastian stepped closer.

She looked up and into his beautiful dark eyes, struggling to find the words. "My father's..." She stopped, swallowing hard. "My father's mistress will be coming today. He plans to marry her once he's rid of me."

"Is this why he's so anxious to marry you off?"

"Yes. She told him she would not marry him unless I was no longer here. She's had a series of misfortunes, leaving her without the funds to sustain the life she enjoys. Thus, she will marry my father." Rose shivered, despite the warmth of the morning. "She's horrid. She despises me, and the feeling is entirely mutual."

"I'm sorry to hear this, Lady Rose. If I could offer some comfort, I would."

"As I would for you." She smiled at him, then took a shaky breath. "I must go now."

She turned away quickly, walking with measured steps across the lawn, not trusting herself to look back lest he see the tears that had already begun to fall.

THE FIRST GUESTS to arrive were Viscount Gresham, Sir Philip Easton, and Lord Ellsworth. Rose stood beside her father on the front steps of the manor, greeting each in turn.

Lord Gresham was as Rose remembered. Polite and distinct, with an air of sadness in his striking blue eyes that made Rose curious about his past. What tragedies had befallen him? Regardless, Rose could almost feel the reluctance he felt at being there. Like her, he was expected to marry soon and produce an heir.

"Lady Rose, how well you look." Gresham took her gloved hand to brush his lips softly against her knuckles.

"Thank you, Lord Gresham, as do you. Welcome to Wentworth Manor."

Next, bowing politely, she welcomed Sir Philip Easton. He

grinned before kissing her hand. "Lady Rose, you're more ravishing with every day that passes."

"Thank you, Sir Philip. You're too kind." She smiled back at him, charmed by his obvious zest for life. His thick blond hair fell attractively over his forehead, framing light blue eyes that seemed to perpetually twinkle. If only it were someone like him that her father would consider. Although he had a rakish reputation, he was fun to be around, full of good humor and teasing. But with his precarious financial situation, her father would never consider him an appropriate match.

The last of the trio, Lord Jonathan Ellsworth, trailed behind the others, clearly distracted by the beauty of the estate. He lingered over a pot of flowers, leaning close to smell a foxglove. She noticed his cufflinks were slightly tarnished, and he fidgeted with them nervously—small signs of financial strain that tugged at her heart. He was of an artistic nature, an accomplished pianist who could be relied upon for entertainment, though his lack of ambition was well-known.

Rose's dear friend Lady Daphne Merriweather had become besotted with Lord Ellsworth during the Season. This worried Rose a great deal, but if her own fate was sealed, perhaps she could at least help her friends find happiness.

Hargrave showed the men inside, where there were drinks and refreshments waiting in the drawing room. Viscount Gresham and Lord Ellsworth had travelled with their valets, but Sir Philip Easton had none—not surprising, given his circumstances.

Her thoughts drifted briefly to Sebastian. How capable and strong he was. Thoughtful and protective too. Could these qualities only come to those forced into hardship? She certainly hoped not.

She was forced back to reality when another carriage arrived, this time carrying her three friends. Miss Lydia Norbury was the first one out of the carriage. Although old enough at eight and twenty to be considered a spinster, Lydia's beauty had not dimmed. She was slight and poised, and carried a maturity that came from years of caring for her ailing parents.

"Dearest, it's delightful to see you again." Rose took both her friends' hands. "You're looking very well."

"I'm not sure anyone could be after that carriage ride. I'm feeling rather queasy."

Lydia did look a little pale but still stunning in a muted lavender traveling dress. She'd never had a Season, which explained why Viscount Gresham's serious gaze lingered on her with curiosity.

"I'll have someone bring you something soothing for your stomach," Rose said.

"That would be much appreciated." Lydia lowered her voice. "How are you? Is all well?"

"I'm afraid not," Rose whispered back. "Baron White's on his way. I'll be engaged to him before the summer's end."

"Please, allow me to think of a way out," Lydia said. "I have money of my own now. Perhaps we can find a solution?"

Her kindness brought tears to Rose's eyes. "We'll speak later, yes."

Lady Arabella Kingsley smiled at the sight of Rose, taking her hands and kissing her cheek. "Darling Rose, how good to see you." She wore a striking burgundy day dress that made her green eyes pop. The dress was more daring than one might expect for a lady, but a widow had more social freedom.

"You as well. Was the ride terribly bumpy?"

"Not that I noticed. I was too busy looking out the window. I love to be out of London and breathe the fresh country air."

Rose drew close, speaking into Arabella's ear. "Father's arranged for Baron White and me to marry."

"And you don't want to?"

"I would rather poke my eyes out with a fork," Rose said, only half-joking.

"You poor thing. But perhaps you'll be like me and widowed after only a few years? This is the advantage of an older man, is it not?"

Rose giggled despite herself. "I'll try to see it that way."

"I promise I didn't poison him, if that's why you're looking at me that way."

"Don't even joke about such things," Rose said, laughing.

Finally, her friend Daphne Merriweather was beside her, clasping her hands. "Oh, Lady Rose, I'm so very happy to see you and to be invited to such a wonderful party."

Daphne wore a carriage gown in robin's egg blue that suited her bright red hair and alabaster skin. A wide-brimmed straw bonnet kept the sun off her delicate complexion.

A maid led all three women into the house, but not before Rose promised to meet them in the afternoon for lemonade.

Rose had just turned back when Honoria Blackwell's carriage appeared. Rose's father stepped forward as a footman helped Honoria down, though he restrained himself from showing too much familiarity.

Honoria stepped out as if she herself were the lady of the estate. Her crimson dress was slightly too tight, and her hat trimmed with rather gaudy feathers. But beneath her haughty expression, Rose caught a flicker of something else—anxiety, perhaps? The desperation of a woman who'd clawed her way up from nothing and was terrified of falling again.

Honoria's young cousin, Lady Violet Stratton, stepped out next. She wore an ivory muslin gown suitable for someone of only seventeen. She was petite and delicate with pale blond hair and large blue-gray eyes.

"Lady Rose, thank you for including me in your party."

"You're welcome, Lady Violet. I do hope you'll enjoy yourself."

"I imagine I will, although these events can be terribly awkward for those of us who are shy. My cousin's annoyed with me already, and we've only just arrived."

Rose bit her tongue to keep from making a rude comment. Violet thanked her again before following a footman inside.

Here came Honoria, looking down her long, thin nose at Rose.

"Lady Rose."

"It's a pleasure to see you again, Mrs. Blackwell."

"You're looking awfully wrung out, dear. Have you been ill?"

"As a matter of fact, I'm quite suddenly feeling distinctly unwell. Something foul seems to have taken hold of me. Has the wind brought it to me, do you think?"

Honoria's thin mouth pursed, though Rose noticed her hands tremble slightly as she adjusted her gloves. "How dreadful. Sadly for you, whatever it is that's come for you has no plan on leaving without getting exactly what she wants."

"As you did with your late husband?" Rose felt reckless and angry. There had been many rumors about Honoria's late husband having suffered a heart attack in his mistress's bed.

For just a moment, what appeared to be genuine hurt flashed across Honoria's face before the mask slipped back into place. "I've no idea what you mean."

"What's one to do when one's husband dies and leaves one penniless? I feel nothing but sympathy, I assure you."

"You'll be sorry if you cross me. I will get what I want." But there was something almost pleading beneath the threat.

"People like you always get just what they deserve," Rose said sweetly.

Honoria scowled but said nothing further, sweeping past Rose into the house.

No sooner had she rid herself of one foe than the next one arrived.

Baron Richard White was soon out of his carriage and standing in front of Rose. Stocky, with a barrel chest and ruddy complexion, he took her hand and pressed his lips to it with what he clearly believed was gallant courtesy.

"Lady Rose, your beauty has not faded since last we met. How fortunate you are that I'm willing to overlook your... spirited nature. Most men would not be so patient with such willfulness in a wife. I have not forgotten our last encounter. Your rudeness is forgiven. However, I'll expect more respect from you going forward. After all, I have a lot to offer you."

Rose's jaw tightened. "Your advances were unwanted. A true gentleman would not have pushed."

He smiled indulgently, as if she were a child expressing a silly fear. "My dear girl, I'm offering you security, protection, a respectable position in Society. In time, you'll come to appreciate the wisdom of this arrangement. Your father and I both want what's best for you, even if you cannot see it yet."

His tone was so patronizingly gentle, so convinced of his own benevolence, that it made Rose's skin crawl more than if he'd simply been crude.

She watched as he lumbered up the steps, feeling tears pricking the backs of her eyes. She would not cry. Not here. It was bad enough that she would be forced to marry this man who thought he was rescuing her. She could not bear anyone's pity.

# CHAPTER NINE

SEBASTIAN, DESPITE HIS exhaustion from the day's manual labor, had not slept well. Regardless, he was up at dawn with the others to eat breakfast before starting work. He'd been assigned to the orchard this morning, tasked with picking ripe apples for Mrs. Carter's party menus. The sun was just coming up when he set to work, carrying several buckets with him to gather the bounties.

As he moved a ladder under the first Codling tree, he thought about what he'd witnessed the day before. He'd been tending to the roses in the late afternoon when he saw finely dressed women and men lounging in the shade of the oak trees on the back lawn. The weather had been warm and a few of them had played a lackluster game of lawn croquet but mostly they lounged about, talking in small groups. Sebastian attempted to keep his head down, but also had strained to hear bits of conversation. Sadly, he'd not been able to hear much at all. He'd caught only a few glimpses of Rose, although he'd heard her laughter several times. And it had nearly stopped his heart.

With his bucket in hand, he climbed the ladder to look for the ripest of the apples for Mrs. Carter's desserts. He plucked them, one by one, and laid each of them into the bucket, careful not to bruise them. It was a quiet morning with only birdsong to keep him company as the sun rose in the eastern sky. No one from the house, other than the servants, would be up and about at this hour. Thus, he nearly fell off his ladder when he heard Rose calling to him from below. He looked down to see her watching him. She lifted her hand to wave.

He hastily climbed down the ladder. "My lady? Is something wrong?"

She shook her head and took a book from the small basket she carried. "I shan't be able to see you later. I'm busy all day with the guests. But I thought you might need a new book."

He glanced down at the book in her hand. Sonnets.

"I worried the novel I gave you might be too hard to read at night when you're tired and thought perhaps poetry might soothe you better after a long day of hard work."

"How thoughtful of you, thank you." Sebastian peered at her closely. Purple smudges under her eyes. She had not slept well either. "Are you well, Lady Rose?"

She tucked a stray tuft of hair behind her ear. "Not really."

"May I be of service?"

"There's nothing to be done. He's here. Baron White, that is. And he's as horrid as I remember. I don't know how I can possibly…marry him."

He knew she referred to all that marriage entailed, including giving her body to him. Sebastian's hands tightened on the ladder rung behind him. The thought of that man touching her—

"My lady, there's something I must tell you. Something that I think will give you hope."

She looked up at him, her face awash in the morning sun. He would count her freckles if he could. Instead, he had to give her a little something to keep her from despair.

"What I'm about to tell you must stay between us."

"Yes, all right."

"Mr. Hale has hired a detective to look into Baron White's past."

Rose staggered backward as if he'd struck her. Her basket tumbled to the ground, the book falling open in the grass. "What?" She pressed a hand to her throat. "A detective? But why—how do you—" She shook her head rapidly. "Why would he do such a thing?"

"He wants to protect you. They all do. Mrs. Carter. Mrs. Blythe. Prudence and Mary. They're all very worried about you."

For a long moment, Rose said nothing. Then she sank into the damp grass, her skirts billowing about her, her face buried in her hands. "Oh, the dears. The absolute dears." When she looked up at him, tears had gathered in her eyes. "A detective. Someone is actually trying to help me."

Sebastian knelt in the grass beside her, fighting the urge to take her in his arms. "Mr. Hale believes if he can find something scandalous or dangerous, then it will save you from having to marry him."

"How do you know this?" Her voice was barely above a whisper.

"He told me."

"But why?" Rose's expression began to shift, wonder giving way to suspicion. "He doesn't know you. You're a gardener. Why would he share something so intimate with you?"

Sebastian's chest tightened. He tried to think of an answer but came up with nothing. A rising panic made it hard to breathe. She was absolutely right. It made no sense that Hale would speak to him in that way.

"Sebastian? What aren't you telling me? Did you know him before you came here?"

He opened his mouth, then closed it. The truth sat on his tongue like poison—that he was no gardener, that his real name was not Doyle, that everything about their meeting had been calculated. That her father had destroyed his family. That he'd come here for revenge, not romance.

"Mr. Hale asked me to look after you, as I mentioned before," he said finally, the words feeling like stones in his mouth. "During that conversation, he said that he'd recently hired a detective."

Her expression had turned to granite right before his eyes. He'd not seen her look this way in any of the times they'd shared together. She'd always looked at him with curiosity and delight. Now, her eyes had hardened into two scuffed emeralds.

"I tell you only to give you hope," he said, feeling suddenly quite desperate. "You mustn't despair, please. The way you've conducted yourself, with such goodness and generosity, has endeared you to the staff. They would do anything for you."

She studied his face as if seeing him for the first time. "There's more to your story, isn't there? Things you're not telling me about your past. The way you can read and the way you speak—they indicate an educated man. Not a man destined to be a gardener."

Sebastian's throat went dry. "I've told you about my mother."

"Yes, you have." She bowed her head, tenting her hands as if to pray. "Still, there's more that you're not telling me. I don't know why you would lie to me, but I know what I can see—that despite whatever secrets you carry, you're a compassionate, warm man who has made me feel less alone."

The words made his fingers tingle. Here she was, praising his character while he deceived her with every breath. If she knew who he really was, what he was really after, would she hate him for it?

"All I want of late is to be here in the gardens with you," she said softly. "It's the only time I feel truly myself. Which makes no sense at all." She lifted her gaze to meet his. "What am I to do now? Trust a detective I've never met? Trust servants who, however dear they may be, have no real power? Trust you, when I'm not even certain who you are?"

The pain in her voice made him want to confess everything. He reached for his handkerchief, his hands trembling slightly. "You must continue as you are, trusting that Hale will find a way out of your marriage to White. Allow the people who love you to look after you."

"And if this detective finds nothing? Or if he finds something on Baron White, but Father simply chooses another terrible man for me to marry?" A tear trickled down her cheek. "What then?"

He pressed his handkerchief gently against her cheek, and she covered his hand with both of hers. The touch sent fire through his veins. "Then we'll find another way," he whispered, though he had no idea what that way might be.

She held his gaze for a long moment, her fingers warm against his knuckles. "We? You speak as if you'll still be here. As if whatever brought you here in the first place won't eventually call you away."

Sebastian felt the ground shifting beneath him. She saw too much, understood too much. Soon she would piece together the truth, and then—God help him.

"I wish I could promise you that," he said. "But you're right to be cautious. You know as well as I that people have motives behind everything they do."

"Indeed. And I would like to know what yours are."

"I cannot tell you more than I already have." He removed his hand from her cheek, though it took all his willpower. "It gives me comfort to have shared these moments with you. At times, I think they may have to sustain me for whatever comes next."

Rose folded his handkerchief into a small square but did not return it to him. "And now I must go before the rest of the household wakes and finds me gone. Prudence will worry if I'm not in my room when she comes for me."

He nodded, rising to his feet and offering his hand to assist her up. For a second or two, she gazed up at him, tears caught in her dark lashes sparkling in the morning light. The urge to tell her everything—his real name, his true purpose, the way she'd somehow become important to him—nearly overwhelmed him.

She took his hand, and the warmth of her soft skin against his calloused palm sent waves of longing through him. "Lady Rose, there has never been a woman more lovely in the history of the world."

She smiled, though sadness lingered in her eyes. "And like the roses, my beauty will fade and I'll be left to wither on a thorny vine."

"Say it isn't so."

"I'm afraid I cannot." She lifted her skirt and turned away, then paused. "Sebastian, I'm not sure why I'm saying this, other than instinct. Please don't disappear without telling me goodbye. Whatever secrets you carry, I've grown…fond of you. I would hate to wake one morning and find you simply gone."

The words were like a dagger to his heart. He watched her walk quickly out of the orchard, dappled light casting dancing patterns over her retreating form, and knew that disappearing without goodbye was exactly what he might have to do.

When she vanished behind the row of hedges, he returned to the ladder with leaden steps. As he climbed the rungs to reach the ripening apples, he wondered if a man could die from the weight of his own deceptions. Nothing was as he'd thought it would be. Most especially the daughter of Lord Wentworth.

HE'D FILLED THREE buckets with apples for Mrs. Carter in less than an hour. Thorncroft had instructed him to deliver them to the kitchen when he'd finished. Thus, he set them into a wheelbarrow and headed out across the gardens toward the manor. When he arrived, one of Mrs. Carter's cooks was just stepping outside, shears in hand, presumably to cut herbs from the beds nearby.

"Good morning," Sebastian said. "Shall I take these inside?"

"Mrs. Carter would be pleased if you could." She scampered away without making eye contact.

He carried two of the buckets in, figuring he'd come back for the third. The kitchen was abuzz with activity, already warm despite the early hour. Feeding a dozen additional people could not be easy. Yet, Mrs. Carter seemed to do it without breaking a sweat.

He placed the apples on the floor near the table, breathing in the delectable aroma of frying bacon, roasted coffee, and cinnamon and cloves warming in a pot of morning porridge.

A crackling fire licked at the iron pot swinging from its sturdy hook in the hearth, and the brick oven radiated heat. When a maid opened it, Sebastian saw loaves of bread turning a delicious golden tan. The long wooden worktable in the center of the room was cluttered with flour-dusted dough waiting to be shaped, a row of eggs in their shells, and a pile of freshly baked scones. A brace of pheasants hung by their feet from a ceiling rafter.

Mrs. Carter stood at the table's end, her sleeves rolled high, wielding a knife as if it were an extension of her arm. Scullery maids darted back and forth, carrying bowls, chopping herbs, and tending the bubbling pots on the range. A young kitchen boy struggled to keep up as he ferried logs from the woodpile to keep the fires blazing.

Sebastian set down the buckets. "I've another one. Shall I bring it in too or store it somewhere else?"

Mrs. Carter glanced up as she wiped her hands on her apron. "Thank you, love. These will do nicely for my tarts and pies. You must've been up with the rooster this morning."

"Whatever you do with them, I know it'll be delicious," Sebastian said politely. "And yes, Mr. Thorncroft asked me to wake early to make sure you have what you needed."

Mrs. Carter blushed, clearly pleased by his compliment and Thorncroft's thoughtfulness. "Amos is such a thoughtful man. You thank him for me if you see him." She paused, her expression growing troubled. "Though I do hope Lady Rose appreciates all our efforts on her behalf. Poor lamb."

Sebastian's pulse quickened. "Is something the matter?"

"Well, I shouldn't speak out of turn," Mrs. Carter said, lowering her voice as she continued chopping. "But I overheard His Lordship speaking with Baron White after dinner last night. Something about moving the ceremony up. Much sooner than planned, from what I gathered."

Sebastian's heart skipped a beat. "How much sooner?"

Mrs. Carter glanced around, then leaned closer. "Within the fortnight, if I heard correctly. The Baron seemed quite insistent about it. Said something about 'settling matters quickly' before returning to his estate." She shook her head sadly. "That poor girl. As if this whole business wasn't rushed enough already."

Sebastian felt the blood drain from his face. A fortnight. That gave Hale's detective barely two weeks to find something damning enough to stop the marriage. It gave Sebastian even less time to decide whether to abandon his mission or press forward, knowing it would destroy Rose's world.

"You've gone pale, love," Mrs. Carter observed, setting down her knife. "Are you feeling poorly?"

"Just—tired, I suppose." Sebastian forced himself to smile. "Mr. Hale asked me to keep an eye on Lady Rose. Apparently Baron White is not to be trusted."

Mrs. Carter's face creased with worry. "Oh, the dear thing. She's been through so much already, losing her mother so young. And now to have her wedding rushed...and to him." She clicked her tongue disapprovingly. "Mark my words, there's something not right about that Baron. The way he looks at the serving girls, and his demands about this and that. A proper gentleman doesn't need to hurry a lady to the altar."

"No," Sebastian agreed quietly. "He doesn't."

Mrs. Carter studied his face with sharp eyes, as if she knew exactly how he felt about Lady Rose.

Heat crept up Sebastian's neck.

Mrs. Carter returned to her work, but a worried crease in her forehead did not lessen.

He went out for the other bucket and placed it next to the others, his mind racing. Two weeks. The detective would have to work quickly. But what if he found nothing? What if Baron White, for all his unpleasantness, had covered his tracks too well?

Still, there was hope in the new constable. Perhaps he was already suspicious of White's and Wentworth's business. And he could count on Hale. The detective may find something damning any day now.

A plump kitchen maid swept past with a tray of fresh butter, while another girl shot Sebastian a curious glance before resuming her work peeling potatoes.

Across the room, one of the footmen entered to fill a silver coffee urn and place a stack of steaming rolls onto a platter.

"Goodness me, it's warm already," Mrs. Carter said, fanning herself with her apron.

"It certainly is." Sebastian reached into his pocket for his handkerchief to wipe the back of his damp neck before remembering that he'd given yet another one to Lady Rose. The memory of her tear-stained face made his chest tighten. Two weeks, and then she'd be trapped forever.

"Is there anything else I can do for you?" he asked, needing to escape before his agitation became too obvious.

Mrs. Carter frowned for a split second, then shook her head. "No, thank you. And take a scone for your trouble. You've grown too thin."

"I doubt that. Not with the food you and the ladies send out for us." Despite his discouraged mood, he would never turn down one of Mrs. Carter's scones. "Thank you. Your scones are a piece of heaven, Mrs. Carter." Sebastian took one from the pile and stuck it in his gardener's belt. A little dirt wouldn't hurt it.

He nodded to the ladies and then hustled toward the door, eager to be alone with his thoughts. He'd only just stepped outside when he heard one of the maids say, "Easy on the eyes, that one."

"Shush now and get back to work," Mrs. Carter said, chuckling.

He didn't stay to hear anything further. His heart felt heavy. Two weeks to save Rose from a fate worse than death. Hale's man had to find something to save Rose. Or the constable?

Strangely enough, that felt more important than his own mission.

# CHAPTER TEN

THAT EVENING, ROSE moved through the entrance of the grand dining room with the practiced grace expected of a hostess, her gloved fingers resting lightly on her father's offered arm as the guests took their places. Prudence had dressed her well. She wore a soft ivory silk gown with delicate gold embroidery along the hem and sleeves. The bodice was modestly cut, adorned with pearl detailing, and a matching gold sash that cinched at the waist. Her dark hair was styled in a classic chignon, accented with a few loose curls framing her face. A simple pair of pearl earrings and a matching necklace exuded understated elegance. If only she had a reason to care what she looked like.

As was tradition, Lord Wentworth took his place at the head of the table, while Rose settled at the opposite end, ready to orchestrate the evening. Footmen, dressed in crisp livery, stood by in silent readiness as the guests arranged themselves.

Rose must be sure to thank Mrs. Blythe for tending to every detail. A crisp white damask tablecloth covered the long surface, set with delicate porcelain plates edged in gold, fine crystal goblets for wine and water, and polished silver cutlery. In the center, a floral arrangement of pale roses and greenery ran the length of the table, interspersed with flickering tapers in ornate candelabras.

Rose could not help but think of Sebastian cutting the roses for her table, his long, capable fingers plucking the thorns from the stems and making sure to pick only the very best blooms.

Gilded sconces cast a warm glow along the deep mahogany-paneled walls, where portraits of Wentworth ancestors looked down with solemn expressions. A massive chandelier of cut crystal hung above the long dining table, its candlelight reflecting in the polished silver and glassware. Heavy velvet drapes, drawn back to reveal the twilight sky, framed the tall windows. An array of silver serving platters were lined up on the sideboard.

She had inked place cards for each guest earlier with her tidy script. With the assistance of Mrs. Blythe, she'd arranged the table with care, ensuring that the evening's delicate maneuvering of potential matches was well supported by seating arrangements, proximity, and conversation.

She'd set Arabella and Philip next to each other, with Lydia, Edmund, and Mr. Whitby and Colonel Barrington taking up the rest of that side of the table. Honoria and Baron White were seated on her father's end of the table, as far from herself as possible. Daphne and Jonathan were in the middle of the side of the table, with Reverend Oakwood. Rose had taken pity on poor Violet and placed her next to her, assuming it would be a relief for Honoria's cousin to have distance between them. The more Rose observed Violet, the more she felt sorry for her. Like Rose, she was being pressured to marry sooner rather than later. At seventeen, Violet seemed so young and vulnerable, which had wakened Rose's maternal instincts.

That said, Violet seemed to be coming out of her shell here in the country. She'd confessed to Rose earlier that she would stay forever if she could. The quiet suited her, she'd said. In addition, like Rose, she enjoyed being outside, reading, or strolling among the flowers. In Rose's opinion, Violet needed a gentle, thoughtful type of man who would spoil her with a life in the country air where she could shine. Tonight, she looked lovely indeed, in a soft lavender gown made from fine muslin, with a delicate silver sash at the waist. Her hair was pinned in a simple twist, accented with a few small pearl hairpins.

Still, she seemed too young for marriage. Rose wished they both could be left alone.

The footmen served with precision, moving soundlessly to refresh wine glasses and replace plates between courses. The first, a white soup with a delicate broth made from almonds, cream, and veal stock, was delicious but somehow tasted bitter in Rose's mouth. Even the freshly baked rolls tasted dry. It was the company, not the meal, Rose decided.

However, the guests seemed to be enjoying the first course more than Rose, as the gentle clink of silver spoons against china mixed with the low hum of conversation.

As the fish course arrived—salmon in a white wine sauce—Rose glanced up to see Honoria staring at her. Probably imagining the day when she would sit where Rose sat now. There was something much like a satisfied cat about the woman.

"Lady Rose," Baron White said from the other end of the table. "I must commend you on the evening's arrangements. It is clear you take great care in your role as hostess."

Rose turned toward him, keeping her expression coolly polite as she placed her hands under the table to hide how they trembled. "Sadly, I've had much practice. Evenings such as this remind me of how much I long for my mother's presence." She would not let her father force her into marriage with an old, disgusting man, for example.

"A skill that will serve you well in your own household." Baron White lifted his wineglass in a silent toast to what he clearly saw as an inevitability. "Speaking of which, I've been discussing with your father the matter of expediting our union. There seems little point in delaying what is already decided."

Rose's fork clattered against her plate. The sound seemed to echo in the sudden silence that fell over their end of the table. "Expediting?"

"Indeed. I see no reason to wait until spring when we could be wed within the fortnight. My estate requires attention, and I'm eager to return with my new bride." His pale eyes gleamed with satisfaction. "Your father has agreed it would be… practical."

Lord Wentworth nodded approvingly from his end of the table. "Baron White makes excellent points. No need for excessive ceremony when the matter is settled."

Rose felt the walls of the dining room closing in around her. Two weeks. The blood rushed from her face so quickly she feared she might faint. "I… that is quite sudden."

"Here, here," Honoria said. She wore a ruby red satin dress that was as loud and gaudy as its owner. The gown had a fitted bodice with intricate black lace detailing, and the sleeves draped elegantly off the shoulder, revealing far too much décolletage. Her dark hair was styled in a series of polished curls, pinned with a garnet-studded comb. "If you wait much longer, you'll be put on the shelf, dear. You really must take care not to become a spinster."

Violet stiffened beside her and then, to Rose's surprise, reached for her hand under the table, giving it a slight squeeze.

"I've been training for it all since I was eight years old," Rose said, with a quick glance at her father. "'Twould be a pity for all my obedience to go to waste."

Lord Wentworth watched her with a bland expression, as if he thought she were harmless. She was. Or perhaps powerless was the better way to describe it.

Baron White chuckled, a sound like grinding stone. "Your obedience will be quite appreciated, my dear. As will your other wifely duties."

The implication in his tone made Rose's stomach lurch. She gripped Violet's hand beneath the table, drawing strength from the girl's quiet support.

To distract herself from her dark thoughts, she glanced around the table to see how her matchmaking was playing out.

Jonathan leaned slightly toward Daphne as they spoke quietly to each other. Dressed in a pale blue muslin gown with delicate lace trim at the sleeves and neckline, she looked exquisite. Her red curls, pinned up with tiny silk flowers, bounced slightly as she laughed at something he'd said.

Across the table, Lydia and Edmund also seemed to be enjoying each other's company. She, too, looked lovely in a sage green gown made of soft, flowing cotton muslin. The sleeves were short, with sheer overlay fabric. Her blond hair was neatly braided and twisted into a bun, with a simple silver comb for decoration.

Arabella was engaged in animated conversation with Mr. Whitby about some philosophical matter, her intelligence clearly impressing the young gentleman.

The second course arrived—a beautifully roasted pheasant, golden and crisp, served alongside honey-glazed carrots and green beans.

Lord Wentworth, ever the composed host, gestured to Colonel Barrington. "You must tell us, Colonel, how fares the regiment? Are the younger officers any better than those of our youth?"

The colonel gave a gruff chuckle, carving neatly into his pheasant. "They are younger, certainly. Whether they are better remains to be seen."

Honoria arched a brow. "And what, Colonel, would you say marks a true officer?"

The colonel considered for a moment. "Discipline. Resolve. A sense of duty that does not waver."

Rose found herself thinking of Sebastian's hands as he'd touched her cheek that morning, the way he'd spoken to her.

Lord Wentworth nodded approvingly at the colonel's words. "Well said."

Rose forced herself to focus on her guests, trying to push away thoughts of her rapidly approaching fate. Two weeks. She'd spent the day reeling over Sebastian's confession about Mr. Hale and the private detective, but now that seemed like her only hope. Would it be enough time?

She shuddered at the thought.

"Are you quite well, Rose?" Violet whispered.

Rose glanced at the girl beside her, touched by her obvious concern. "I'm fine," Rose whispered back. "Just contemplating my future."

"Perhaps we might speak later," Violet said quietly. "After the gentlemen retire for their port."

Rose nodded, grateful for the girl's unexpected support. If she couldn't save herself, at least she might find a way to help Violet avoid a similar fate. Though with only two weeks remaining, Rose wasn't certain she could save anyone at all.

AFTER SUPPER, THE men went to the parlor to enjoy port and cigars, leaving the women to convene in the drawing room.

Rose poured tea with practiced grace, her hands steady only because she willed them to be. She could feel Honoria's gaze trailing her like a wasp circling a picnic. A fragrant arrangement of roses adorned the marble-topped table, their scent delicate, nostalgic. Sebastian again.

Honoria had installed herself at the center of the room, sitting with the poise of a woman who had learned to command attention through sheer force of will. Beside her, Violet shrank into the upholstery, the confidence she'd shown earlier snuffed out. She kept her eyes lowered, hands clasped in her lap, silent since their arrival.

Across the room, Arabella Kingsley lounged in her armchair like a general studying the terrain. Her sharp gaze flicked between Honoria and Rose, waiting. Lydia sat upright, chin slightly lifted, her expression unreadable—but the light tap of her fingers against the teacup betrayed her temper. Even Daphne, usually all brightness and chatter, was unusually quiet, her wide blue eyes flitting from Rose to Honoria with concern.

Honoria broke the silence with a thoughtful sigh and set down her cup. "The country is so peaceful compared to London,

don't you think? Though I confess, I find myself grateful for the quiet these days. There's something to be said for stability after years of uncertainty."

Arabella's brows arched. "Are you planning to stay on as Rose's guest indefinitely?"

Honoria's smile was warm, almost maternal. "I hope to make myself useful wherever I'm needed. Lord Wentworth has been so generous, and I know how difficult it can be for a young woman without her mother's guidance." Her eyes settled on Rose with what appeared to be genuine concern. "Especially during such an important time in her life."

"Important time?" Daphne asked.

"Why, her engagement, of course. Baron White is a wonderful match for her." Honoria's voice carried the tone of someone sharing delightful news. "A connection that could provide such security for Rose's future."

Arabella's voice was cool, probing. "Why concern yourself with Rose's marriage prospects? If you and Lord Wentworth intend to marry, surely her affairs are her own."

Honoria's expression flickered—just for a moment—with a hint of something harder just beneath the surface. "I've learned that in matters of family, we're all connected. A father's peace of mind affects the entire household." She smoothed her skirts, regaining her composure. "I've seen what happens when young women reject suitable matches out of romantic notions. The consequences can be devastating."

"What consequences?" Rose asked quietly.

Honoria leaned forward slightly, her voice dropping to a confidential tone. "I knew a girl once—beautiful, intelligent, much like yourself. Her family found her an excellent match, but she refused. She became increasingly agitated, prone to episodes. Her family grew concerned about her nerves." She paused, letting the words settle. "Eventually, she required care. Professional care. It broke her father's heart, but what choice did he have?"

The room had gone very still.

"Are you suggesting—" Lydia began.

"I'm suggesting nothing," Honoria said gently. "I'm simply sharing what I've witnessed. Sometimes the kindest thing a parent can do is intervene before a situation becomes irreversible." Her gaze found Rose again. "Especially when a young woman shows signs of distress. Refusing food, appearing overwrought, making wild accusations about perfectly respectable gentlemen."

"Wild accusations?" Arabella repeated.

"Oh, I don't mean to suggest Rose has done anything of the sort," Honoria said quickly. "But I can see the strain she's under. The way she startles at shadows, the pallor, the trembling hands." She gestured delicately toward Rose. "These are concerning symptoms. Any loving father would take notice."

Rose's jaw clenched. "There's nothing wrong with my nerves."

"Of course not, dear." Honoria's voice was soothing, the tone one might use with an invalid. "But others might not see it that way. Especially if you were to refuse a generous offer from Baron White without reasonable cause. Society has such rigid expectations for young ladies, and when those expectations aren't met..." She spread her hands helplessly. "Well, people draw their own conclusions."

Lydia set down her teacup with more force than necessary. "You're threatening her."

Honoria's eyes widened in apparent shock. "Threatening? My dear Lady Norbury, I would never. I'm simply concerned for Rose's welfare. Having been a young woman without prospects myself, I understand how frightening the world can seem." Her voice caught slightly. "How desperate one becomes for security, for protection. Baron White offers both."

"And if she refuses him?" Arabella pressed.

"Then I hope she has a very good reason," Honoria said, her warmth cooling by degrees. "Because refusing an honorable proposal without cause raises questions about a woman's judgment. Her stability." She glanced around the room. "I know you ladies mean well, but you live in a different world than most of us. You have your own estates, your own incomes. You can afford to be idealistic."

The barb hit its mark. Rose saw Daphne flush, knowing her precarious financial situation.

"That may be true," Arabella said carefully, "but it doesn't give anyone the right to coerce a woman into marriage."

"Coerce?" Honoria laughed softly. "What a dramatic word. I prefer 'guide.' After all, who among us hasn't needed guidance at some point? I certainly did." Her expression grew distant for a moment. "I was young once, full of dreams and romantic fantasies. I thought I could choose my own path." She refocused on Rose, her smile returning. "I learned better. We all do, eventually."

"Some of us don't need that education," Lydia said sharply.

Honoria tilted her head, studying Lydia with newfound interest. "Indeed? With your circumstances, I would think you'd see the wisdom in my counsel."

The implication hung in the air. Lydia had no dowry. Thus, she and Rose were in similar predicaments. No one wanted them.

Lydia's face went rigid, and she clasped her hands so tightly in her lap that her knuckles whitened.

"That's enough," Rose said, standing abruptly. Not shaking. Not weeping. Her expression was calm. She would not let this horrid woman see her angst. "You've made your position clear, Mrs. Blackwell. And you've exhausted your welcome."

Honoria rose gracefully, unruffled. "I understand you're upset, dear. Strong emotions are natural when facing such important decisions." She snapped her fingers at Violet, then gestured for her to rise to her feet. "But I hope you'll consider what I've said. I advise with your future in mind. Someday, you'll see that clearly."

She helped Violet to her feet, her grip firm but appearing gentle. "Come, darling. We've imposed long enough."

Violet didn't speak, but she turned at the doorway, her eyes meeting Rose's with a look so full of sorrow and sympathy that it pierced straight through her. In that glance, Rose saw her own future reflected—another woman trapped by circumstance, dependent on male protection, forced to smile while her gilded cage grew smaller.

The moment the door shut behind them, the ladies erupted.

Daphne let out a breath she'd clearly been holding. "That was… vile. She is vile. I'm sorry, sweet Rose."

Lydia shook her head, voice tight. "How could anyone be born that mean?"

"Maybe she wasn't," Daphne murmured. "Maybe this world made her that way."

"I don't know about either of you, but I'm suddenly in need of something stronger than tea." Arabella stalked to the drinks cart and poured herself a generous measure of sherry. "Anyone else?"

Daphne and Lydia nodded, rising to pour their own. Arabella poured a fourth glass and returned to press it into Rose's hands.

Rose hadn't moved. She was afraid if she did, she might shatter.

Arabella sat beside her, voice gentling. "We'll figure a way out of this. I meant what I said—I'll take you in, if it comes to that."

Rose looked up, her voice a thread. "You'd really do that? Even knowing the scandal could destroy you?"

"Let me worry about my reputation," Arabella replied, though the subdued edge in her tone betrayed the weight of it. "What matters now is keeping you safe. And sane."

"We will all help," Lydia added firmly. "Arabella and I have the means, and we'll use them."

"I'll do what I can too," Daphne said. "Even if it's just standing beside you."

Rose's hands trembled around the glass. "That means more than you know. I've always wanted a family of my own. To love a good man and have children together. I used to think that might fill the space left by Mummy. But if I marry him, all those dreams are merely dreams. Never to come true. It's either marry Baron White, or they'll have me put away."

She trailed off. The unspoken words were louder than anything she could have said.

Arabella's expression darkened. "Proving you unfit wouldn't be easy, but if your father's determined, it's not impossible."

"I have to wonder—why Baron White?" Rose asked, thinking out loud. "There are other wealthy men."

Arabella hesitated. "Have you ever wondered why your Season went so poorly?"

Rose's throat tightened. "Father told me it was because I was awkward. Too bookish and quiet. He mentioned my lack of conversational skills."

"And you believed him?"

"What else was I to think? I was ignored at every ball. I sat against the wall like a forgotten chair. Even the fortune hunters kept their distance."

Arabella leaned forward, elbows on her knees. "There's a reason for that. And it has nothing to do with your character or beauty. Your father is not the man Society pretends he is."

Daphne frowned. "What do you mean?"

Arabella lowered her voice. "Most of his wealth doesn't come from his lands. It never has."

Rose stilled. "What are you saying?"

"I had my suspicions," Arabella said. "So I asked around—carefully. Men talk, especially when they've had too much to drink. Or when they're in my bed." Her tone was dry, but her eyes were sharp. "And I listened."

"And?" Rose's voice was barely above a whisper.

Arabella's jaw tightened. "He's a smuggler, Rose. One of the most powerful in the region. French brandy, mostly."

Daphne gasped.

Rose said nothing. She couldn't move. Couldn't breathe.

Deep down, some part of her had known. The locked doors. The uninvited visitors. The money that flowed far too easily.

Arabella's gaze softened. "I couldn't understand why your Season was such a failure. You're a viscount's daughter. You should've had suitors lined up. But from what I heard, the rumors started before your first debut. Just whispers—but enough to keep decent families away."

Rose exhaled all at once, her body sagging under the weight of it. "So it was him," she said hollowly. "He poisoned the well and then blamed me for it."

"You poor thing," Daphne whispered. "You deserve so much better."

"The worst part was believing it," Rose said. "That there was something wrong with me."

"But, again, why White?" Lydia asked, beginning to pace near the unlit hearth. "Of all the men—"

"It's obvious," Arabella said grimly. "White isn't just his friend. He's his business partner. The marriage is a safeguard. It ties White to your father permanently."

Rose's stomach turned. "So I'm insurance that the partnership will remain. Father must not trust White fully. He wants to make sure they're connected in more ways than one."

"Exactly."

Rose took a long sip of sherry, trying to still the shaking in her hands. "All those nights I sat alone, thinking no one wanted me. And all along it was him. It was always him."

"I should like to kill them both," Daphne muttered, cheeks flushed with fury. "I've never had a violent thought until today."

"I was a fool not to see it sooner," Rose said. "I've been so naïve. So accepting."

Suddenly, a sharp pain lanced through the side of her head— then a voice, soft and urgent, echoed in her mind.

*I know what you've done.*

She stiffened, breath catching.

The room tilted. Shadows flickered. Candlelight danced along the walls like specters.

*I know what you've done.*

Arabella touched her arm. "Rose?"

She blinked rapidly, trying to surface. "I'm… I'm fine."

"Rose, you've gone pale," Daphne said, alarmed.

But she wasn't fine. Not even close. Because she recognized the voice now.

Her mother's voice.

*Mummy.*

And if her mother was trying to tell her something from beyond the grave… then the truth about her father didn't end with smuggling.

It went much, much deeper.

# CHAPTER ELEVEN

SEBASTIAN ROSE AT dawn that morning, wanting to get some of his tasks done early so that he could do as Hale asked and keep an eye on Rose during the day. According to Hale, the gentlemen houseguests were leaving after breakfast for a shooting party, so he did not expect Rose to confront any trouble later that day. But White could cause trouble before they left.

After a quick meal of a biscuit he'd stuck in his pocket from dinner the night before and a cupful of cold water from the well, he headed out to work. The rest of the gardeners were only just stirring, dressing, and grousing, but he paid them no mind. His mission today was to keep watch over Rose.

Dew had dampened the tips of his boots by the time he reached the rose garden. He turned a corner but stopped. Voices were coming from behind the trellis. A soft, feminine voice that could only be Rose's, followed by a gruff, masculine one.

He leapt to action, running around the row of manicured shrubs and into the rose garden. There, trapped in front of the swing, was Rose. A barrel-chested man in a fine coat stood before her, his back to Sebastian. Thick black hair. Rotund.

White.

"Baron White, please, just leave me alone. Please. I've just come to read."

Why was he here and not with the other men?

"We'll be man and wife soon enough. Give me a little kiss

before I head out to the shooting party." White pressed ever closer to Rose.

She pushed at him with her hands, but her small frame was no use against the brute. "Leave me alone."

"But I've gone to so much trouble, getting up before daybreak to follow you out here. Away from prying eyes." His voice carried the rough edges of a man used to getting his way through intimidation rather than charm.

"I said no."

His laugh was coarse, dismissive. "You'll learn to mind your tongue once we're wed, girl. I have no patience for disobedience."

Sebastian stepped forward, his heart hammering. "Sir, you need to step away from the lady."

White barely glanced over his shoulder. "Bugger off, boy. This is none of your concern."

"Lady Rose appears distressed," Sebastian said, trying to keep his voice steady. "Perhaps you should—"

"Perhaps I should what?" White wheeled around fully now, his broad face flushed with annoyance. "Take orders from some grubby gardener? I don't think so." He looked Sebastian up and down with obvious contempt. "You forget your place."

Sebastian's jaw clenched. Behind White, he could see Rose gripping the swing's rope, her knuckles white. He made eye contact, and tilted his head toward the house. She got the hint and tore out of the garden without a backward glance. "My place is to ensure the safety of Lady Rose."

"Your place is to trim hedges and keep your mouth shut." White took a step toward him, his barrel chest leading. "Unless you'd like to find yourself without employment. Or worse."

The casual threat sent a spike of anger through Sebastian's chest. He'd dealt with bullies before—men who thought their position gave them the right to abuse others. "I'm humbly asking you to leave Lady Rose alone."

"Are you now?" White's smile was more a grimace, as if he

had need of a chamber pot. "Well, what you'd like matters about as much as what she'd prefer. Which is to say, not at all."

That did it. Sebastian moved forward, but White was ready for him—the older man might be soft around the middle, but he was clearly strong. But he was not expecting Sebastian's speed. Years of physical labor had made Sebastian quick and wiry, and he managed to grab White by the lapels and shove him backward against the trellis.

"I said leave her alone," Sebastian growled.

White's eyes flashed with genuine anger now. "You stupid boy. Do you have any idea who you're laying hands on?" He tried to push Sebastian off, but couldn't get the leverage. "I'll have you flogged. I'll have you transported."

Sebastian's grip tightened. The rage that had been building since he'd heard Rose's frightened voice was making his vision blur around the edges. Almost without thinking, his hand went to his tool belt, fingers closing around his gardening shears.

"Let go of me!" White said.

"Not until you give me your word you'll stay away from her."

"My word?" White laughed harshly. "You think I owe you anything, you worthless—"

The shears were in Sebastian's hand now, the metal warm from his palm. He held them up where White could see them, and the older man's words died in his throat.

"You are mad," White breathed.

Sebastian's heart was pounding so hard he could barely think straight. What was he doing? This was insanity. He would pay for this, one way or another. However, the image of Rose cowering, of this brute putting his hands on her, spurred him forward. "You keep your hands off her," he said through gritted teeth.

White's gaze darted between Sebastian's face and the shears. For a moment, Sebastian thought he might call his bluff—and then what? What would he do then?

"You're out of your bloody mind," White said, but there was

something different in his voice now. Uncertainty.

"Maybe I am." Sebastian surprised himself with how steady he sounded. "Maybe that's what happens when you watch monsters like you prey on innocent women."

"You don't know what you're getting into, boy." White's voice dropped lower. "This isn't some tavern brawl. There are people involved here who'd gut you for looking at them sideways."

Something in his tone made Sebastian pause. Not fear, exactly, but wariness. As if White wasn't just talking about his own connections.

"What people?" Sebastian asked.

White's eyes narrowed. "What's it to you?"

Sebastian's mind raced. He was in too deep now to back down, but he was clearly missing something important. White's fear seemed focused on something beyond just Sebastian's threats. "Maybe it matters more than you think."

"Does it?" White studied his face more carefully. "Who sent you here?"

The question caught Sebastian off guard. "What?"

"Don't play stupid with me. Nobody just happens to end up working at Wentworth's estate." White's voice grew more suspicious. "Especially not someone who knows enough to ask about my business associates."

Sebastian's pulse quickened. He was walking a tightrope now, and one wrong word would send him tumbling. But White's assumption might be his only chance. "What makes you think someone sent me?"

"Because that's how this game works, you fool." White's fear was giving way to calculation. "The question is whether you're working for Talbot or someone else entirely."

Talbot. Sebastian filed the name away, trying not to let his relief show. "And what if I am?"

"Then you're a long way from home," White said grimly. "And Wentworth's going to want to know why Talbot's sniffing around his territory."

Sebastian forced himself to hold White's stare. "Maybe Wentworth should be more worried about why his territory is worth sniffing around."

It was a guess, but it seemed to land. White's face darkened. "We had an agreement."

"Agreements change." Sebastian was making it up as he went along, praying his ignorance wouldn't show. "Especially when one party starts getting ambitious."

"I don't know what Talbot's told you, but we've stuck to our side of things."

"Have you?" Sebastian tightened his grip on the shears, using White's assumption to buy himself time to think. "Because from where I'm standing, it looks like you're expanding your operations. Taking on new responsibilities."

White's gaze flicked toward the house, and Sebastian realized he was thinking about Rose. About the marriage arrangement.

"That's business," White said carefully. "Personal business. Nothing to do with our other arrangements."

"Everything's connected," Sebastian said, hoping he sounded more confident than he felt. "You know that."

For a long moment, they stared at each other. Sebastian could feel sweat gathering between his shoulder blades despite the cool morning air. If White called his bluff now, he was doomed.

"What does Talbot want?" White asked finally.

Sebastian's mind raced. What would someone like Talbot want? Territory? Money? Revenge? "What do you think he wants?"

"Don't play games with me."

"I'm not playing anything." Sebastian let some genuine anger creep into his voice. "I'm here to make sure certain lines don't get crossed. And what I just witnessed." He gestured toward where Rose had been standing. "That was crossing a line."

White's expression shifted, confusion mixing with wariness. "What's the girl got to do with Talbot?"

Sebastian realized he'd made a mistake. He was supposed to be here about the smuggling business, not protecting Rose. Think. Think. "She's connected to this estate. This estate is connected to your operations. Everything's connected, like I said."

It was thin, but White seemed to accept it. "So what now?"

"Now you keep your hands off her. And you tell Wentworth that his guest workers are watching." Sebastian stepped back, lowering the shears but not putting them away. "Any problems with that arrangement?"

White straightened his coat, his face a mask of barely controlled fury. "You tell Talbot he's playing a dangerous game. Wentworth's not going to stand for this interference."

"Then maybe Wentworth should have thought of that before he started expanding his business into territories that don't belong to him."

White's jaw worked silently for a moment. Finally, he gave a curt nod. "We'll see how long your employer's protection lasts, boy."

He turned and stalked away, moving with the stiff dignity of a man who'd been humiliated but wasn't ready to admit it.

Sebastian watched him go, his hands shaking now that the confrontation was over. What the hell had he just done? He'd threatened a baron, impersonated some criminal named Talbot, and somehow convinced a smuggler that he was a spy.

The shears felt impossibly heavy in his hands. He'd been ready to use them. The realization made his stomach churn.

But Rose was safe. For now.

He sank onto the swing, trying to process what had just happened. He was in far deeper than he'd ever intended, and he had the sinking feeling that this was only the beginning.

SEBASTIAN DIDN'T SEE Rose again until just after noon. The men had gone off to their shooting party by then, leaving the women to do as they pleased for the afternoon. However, when he casually walked by the patio where the women had gathered to paint, he didn't see Rose among them.

He figured she was probably upstairs in her room, recovering from the trauma of the morning. The memory made his chest tight. He couldn't shake a feeling of dread. Had he made everything worse with his lies and threats? White was no fool.

Mrs. Carter had asked him to pick some of the dessert apples for her cheese platters, so he went out with his bucket to the orchard, his mind churning with everything he'd learned. His instincts to protect Rose seemed to be overriding everything else lately, including his resolve to prove her father a murderer. He couldn't understand what was happening to him, only that she was never far from his thoughts—and that had definitely not been in his plan.

He conjured images of his siblings, hoping they would remind him of what he was truly doing there. His duty was to them. He mustn't forget it.

When he reached the orchard, he spotted Rose sitting with her back against the trunk of one of the larger trees. She had her knees pulled up and her face in her hands, her shoulders shaking with quiet sobs.

He approached cautiously, not wanting to startle her. When he was a few feet away, she lifted her tear-stained face to look at him. "Hello, Sebastian." She wiped her eyes with a handkerchief—his handkerchief, he realized with a jolt, not her own delicate lace variety.

"Lady Rose." He knelt beside her, keeping a careful distance. "Are you all right?" The sight of her red-rimmed eyes made something violent twist in his chest. White deserved worse than threats.

"I am fine." Her voice sounded hoarse from crying. She patted the grass beside her. "Will you sit with me?"

He glanced around to see if anyone was about. Thorncroft and his staff often took their midday rest during the heat, dozing under trees with water and fruit. Still, he sat several feet away, far enough to explain their presence as innocent concern if they were discovered.

"I wasn't sure you'd still be here," she said quietly. "I was terrified they'd run you off or called the authorities. The thought of never seeing you again was too much to bear." Fresh tears spilled down her cheeks.

"I am still here. I made sure of that."

"What did you do? I saw you with the garden shears, and then I—" She flushed. "I hid behind a bush. I thought you might hurt him, and if the constable came…" She shuddered. "I ran before I could see too much. In case they questioned me later."

Sebastian's stomach knotted. She'd been protecting him even while terrified. "I found a way to handle it."

"I would like to hear about it, but first I need to tell you something." Rose was quiet for a long moment, her fingers clenched in her lap. "Last night, my friend Arabella gave me information." Her voice caught. "About my father."

"What about him?"

"She says he's a smuggler." The words came out in a rush, as if she couldn't bear to hold them any longer. "That Baron White is his partner. That my failed Season, all those empty dance cards—it wasn't because I was awkward or shy. It was because of the rumors about my father's true business."

Sebastian's heart began to pound.

"You don't look surprised," she said, studying his face, her eyes widening in obvious alarm. "Sebastian, you don't look surprised at all."

He closed his eyes briefly. "No. I'm not."

"You knew?" Her voice rose. "How could you possibly— you've only been here a few weeks, and I've lived here my entire life and never suspected?"

"I couldn't sleep one night. I went to check on my horse and saw a delivery wagon. French brandy, from the look of the crates. There was a man supervising. I didn't realize until later that it was White."

Rose stared at him, her face cycling through hurt, confusion, and something that might have been betrayal. "You've known this whole time that my father is a criminal, and you said nothing?"

"I didn't know how to tell you. I didn't know if you were involved."

"If I was involved?" She laughed bitterly. "How could I be involved? Father keeps everything important from me."

"That's not what I meant."

"Then what did you mean?" Her eyes were bright with unshed tears. "Because it seems like everyone knows the truth about my life except me."

Sebastian felt like he was drowning. Every word he spoke seemed to make things worse, and the worst part was that he was still lying to her. About why he was really here. About who he was. About what he intended to do.

"I'm sorry," he said helplessly. "You're right. I should have told you."

"Why didn't you?"

*Because I came here to prove your father framed my father, and I didn't want you to suspect my motives. Because I'm using your trust to get closer to the truth. Because I'm exactly the kind of liar you're talking about.*

"I was trying to protect you," he said instead.

"From what? The truth?" She wiped her eyes roughly. "How is keeping me ignorant protecting me?"

He had no good answer for that.

Rose was quiet for a long moment, pulling up blades of grass and letting them fall. "I feel like such a fool. My whole life feels like a performance where everyone knew their lines except me."

"You're not a fool—"

"Aren't I? My father blamed me for my failed Season. Said I

was too strange. Not pretty enough." Her voice cracked. "And I believed him. I spent two years thinking there was something fundamentally wrong with me."

Sebastian's hands clenched into fists. "There's nothing wrong with you. Your father's the one who—" He stopped himself before he said too much.

"Who what?"

"Who lied to you. Who let you blame yourself for his choices."

Rose nodded slowly. "Now I understand why he wants me to marry White. It's not about my future or my security. It's about their business partnership."

"I fear so," Sebastian agreed quietly.

"Tell me about this morning," she said. "What did you do to White?"

Sebastian rubbed the back of his neck. "I convinced him I was working for one of his competitors. Someone named Talbot—he mentioned the name himself, so I just went with it. I had to think quickly."

"You pretended to be a spy?"

"I made the whole thing up as I went along. But it worked because he's obviously guilty of something. When someone's paranoid about their enemies, they're easier to manipulate."

Rose stared at him for a long moment. "That was incredibly clever. And dangerous."

"I wasn't going to let him hurt you."

"Who are you really, Sebastian?" The question was soft, but it hit him like a blow to the chin. "Because a simple gardener doesn't think like that. Doesn't act like that."

His throat felt tight. "I am someone who believes in protecting people who can't protect themselves."

"That's not an answer."

"It's the only answer I can give you right now."

"Why?" Her green eyes searched his face. "What are you hiding?"

*Everything.* "It is complicated."

"More complicated than discovering your father is a criminal who's been lying to you your entire life?"

Sebastian winced. "Lady Rose, I promise you, someday I'll explain everything. But right now I can't."

"Right now you need me to trust you even though you won't trust me." Her voice was flat, resigned.

"It's not about trust."

"Then what is it about?"

He wanted to tell her. The words were right there, pressing against his teeth. *I'm here because I think your father ruined our family. Because I need to prove it. Because everything I've done, every kindness I've shown you, has been in service of that goal.*

But looking at her now—broken and confused and desperately trying to piece together the truth of her own life—he couldn't do it. Not yet.

"I'm sorry," he said. "I know that's not enough, but it's the best I can do right now."

"No, it is not enough." She was quiet for a moment, then sighed. "But you did risk yourself for me today. That has to count for something."

They sat in silence, the weight of everything unsaid a barrier between them.

"There's something else," Rose said finally. "Something that happened last night, after Arabella told me about Father."

"What?"

"I heard a voice in my head. My mother's voice." She spoke carefully, as if testing the words. "She said, 'I know what you've done.' But it felt like a memory. Something I'd heard before."

Sebastian's heart stopped. "When? When do you think you heard it?"

"I don't know. But she sounded frightened when she said it." Rose's voice dropped to a whisper. "What if she discovered the truth about his business and confronted her? What if he was the one who...hurt her. It's too awful to think about. Yet, I must consider it."

*What if she saw him kill her?* Sebastian thought, his pulse hammering. "Do you remember anything else? From around that time?"

"I have nightmares sometimes." Rose played with the ribbons of her bonnet, staring just beyond him. "I'm standing in a doorway, watching my mother by a window. But when she turns around, her face is destroyed. Blood everywhere. And she tells me to run, but her voice is wrong. Like something evil is speaking through her."

The description sent ice through Sebastian's veins. "How long have you had these dreams?"

"Always. Since I was small." She looked at him with haunted eyes. "You think it means something, don't you? You think I might have seen something?"

"I don't know," Sebastian said carefully. "But trauma can make children forget things. Protect themselves by burying memories that are too painful."

"Or maybe I'm just imagining things. Maybe my mind is creating connections that aren't there."

"Maybe." But Sebastian didn't think so. Not with the fear in her voice, the precision of those details.

Rose was quiet for a long moment before she said, "I'm scared, Sebastian. Not just of White, but of my father. What if he thinks I know something?" She shuddered. "He and Mrs. Blackwell have said they will have me committed if I don't marry White. What if he thinks I remember and decides to commit me or worse?"

Sebastian wanted to pull her into his arms, to promise her that he'd keep her safe, that he'd find the truth and make her father pay for everything he'd done. But he couldn't do any of those things without revealing why he was really there.

"I won't let anything happen to you," he said.

"How can you promise that when you won't even tell me who you are?"

The unanswerable question.

Rose stood up, brushing grass from her skirts. "I should go. Prudence will be looking for me."

Sebastian rose as well, fighting the urge to reach for her. "Lady Rose, wait a moment."

"I need time to think." She backed away, as if she were suddenly frightened of him. "About everything. About what I can trust and what I can't. Of who I can trust and who I can't."

His vision blurred and he felt as if he might crumble right before her. He knew he deserved what she said.

"Please be careful," he said. "Stay with your maid or the other women. Don't go anywhere alone."

"I will." She paused at the edge of the orchard. "Do be careful, Sebastian. These are dangerous men and you've made yourself a target."

Sebastian watched her walk away, her shoulders straight despite everything she'd learned. She was stronger than she knew, braver than she gave herself credit for.

But she was also right not to trust him completely. Because the truth was, he was still lying to her about the most important thing of all.

# CHAPTER TWELVE

AFTER SHE RETURNED to the manor, Rose suggested to the ladies that they take a walk through the meadows and down to the creek where a deep pool of water awaited. Rose knew the property well and had always found solace in the secluded spot. The ladies had been delighted at the prospect of an afternoon adventure away from the stifling atmosphere of the house. Fortunately, Honoria had gone with the men to observe the shooting party. Violet, on the other hand, had eagerly joined Rose and the others for an outing away from her cousin's watchful eye.

The five of them set out in the mid-afternoon, with the sun hanging warm and golden over the rolling hills. They walked arm in arm out of the manicured gardens and onto the wilder paths of the estate, their skirts brushing against the tall grasses. Foxglove, buttercups, and heather dotted the hillsides in bursts of color. The wind carried the scent of fresh hay from a farm in the valley below, mingling with the distant bleating of sheep. Cicadas provided a drowsy summer chorus.

If only she could enjoy it all. Instead, her stomach remained knotted with worry, her thoughts scattered like leaves in a storm.

"Such a glorious day," Daphne said, sighing with pleasure as she knelt to pluck a buttercup. "Did you know that if you hold this under your chin, it will tell you if you fancy butter?"

"What a silly notion," Arabella laughed. "Though I suppose

it's as reliable as any other test of affection."

"Who among us doesn't fancy butter?" Violet asked, adjusting her bonnet ribbon.

"You're all terribly practical and no fun at all," Daphne said, grinning.

Rose forced herself to smile, even though their gentle teasing couldn't distract her from the morning's revelations.

Lydia linked her arm with Rose's. "Would you care to share what's troubling you? We've proven ourselves trustworthy confidantes, have we not?"

"Did something happen?" Arabella asked.

Rose's throat tightened with emotion. "You've all been such dear friends. Yes, something happened this morning. With Baron White."

"Dear me," Daphne said. "Do tell us everything."

Rose proceeded to recount the entire incident in the rose garden, sparing no detail of White's unwelcome advances or Sebastian's dramatic intervention. She also told them about the use of the garden shears. "If Sebastian hadn't appeared when he did, I don't know what would have happened." She shuddered at the thought.

"This Sebastian, he's one of the gardeners?" Arabella asked.

"The tall, handsome one with the serious expression," Violet said.

"Ah yes, I've noticed him." Arabella's eyes glinted with interest. "He's quite delicious."

"I agree. And he seems almost noble," Lydia said. "The way he walks, the set of his shoulders."

"He was educated as a youth," Rose said. "He told me his mother had him out of wedlock and fell from grace, but she made sure he was educated."

"How mysterious he is," Arabella said. "I do enjoy a mystery. Particularly one that comes with such appealing packaging."

"Arabella!" Daphne said, her cheeks flushing scarlet.

"What? I'm a widow. I'm allowed to appreciate a fine-looking man." Arabella lifted her face to the sun, letting her bonnet fall back. "Life's too short for false modesty."

"You'll freckle," Daphne said.

"Let me freckle. I'll powder over them if needed."

"Can we return to the matter at hand?" Lydia asked. "This Sebastian actually threatened Baron White with gardening shears?"

Rose nodded, unable to suppress a small smile. "He was magnificent. Completely fearless."

She explained how Sebastian had convinced White he was a spy for a rival operation.

"How remarkably clever," Arabella said.

"Yes, but it raises questions," Lydia said. "What sort of gardener thinks so quickly on his feet? Who speaks like a gentleman but works with his hands?"

"Perhaps he really is a spy," Daphne suggested breathlessly. "For this Talbot person."

Rose felt her stomach drop. "I hadn't considered that possibility." Why hadn't she?

"The simplest explanation is often the correct one," Lydia said.

"But what do you think?" Arabella asked Rose directly.

"I honestly don't know what to think anymore," Rose said. "Everything I believed about my life has been turned upside down. I feel like such a fool."

"You must be cautious, Rose," Lydia said. "This man's true motives are unclear."

"If you knew him as I do, you wouldn't say that," Rose said, thinking of their quiet conversations in the garden.

"How well do you know him?" Arabella asked with keen interest.

Rose felt heat rise in her cheeks. "I've spent time with him in the rose garden. He loves books and has no access to them, so I've shared some of mine."

"How generous of you," Arabella said with a knowing smile.

"It was merely kindness," Rose said.

"Of course it was," Daphne said soothingly, though her expression remained worried. "But Rose, with everything else happening, please do be careful."

"I know it sounds foolish, but I'm drawn to him in a way I've never experienced before," Rose said. "It frightens me how much I care about him."

"Attraction can cloud judgment," Arabella said, though not unkindly. "Especially when one has little experience with it."

"We're almost there," Rose said, eager to change the subject as they approached a thicket of trees. "The pool is just beyond those willows."

As they drew closer, the sound of voices and splashing water reached their ears.

"What's that?" Violet whispered.

"It seems we're not the only ones who had this idea," Arabella said. "Shall we turn back?"

"Absolutely not," Daphne said. "We must see who it is."

"Daphne! How wonderfully wicked of you." Arabella laughed. "I heartily approve."

"What if they're dangerous?" Lydia asked.

"Then it's fortunate I came prepared," Arabella said, patting her reticule meaningfully.

"You carry a weapon?" Daphne asked.

"A small pistol. A woman must protect herself."

Rose felt a chill. The casual mention of weapons reminded her uncomfortably of Honoria, who Violet had mentioned also carried a pistol.

They approached the clearing cautiously, the sound of male laughter and splashing growing louder. When the trees parted to reveal the sun-dappled pool, Rose's breath caught in her throat.

Six men lounged in the clear water, their discarded clothes scattered along the bank. For a moment, all five women froze in shocked silence.

Rose's gaze found Sebastian immediately. He stood in the

shallows, water streaming from his dark hair, droplets catching the afternoon light as they traced paths down his chest and shoulders. She should look away—propriety demanded it—but she found herself unable to move.

It was then that she saw his back.

A network of scars crisscrossed the bronze skin from shoulder to waist. Some were thin silver lines, faded with time. Others were thick, raised welts that spoke of deliberate cruelty. One particularly vicious mark ran diagonally across his shoulder blade, the kind left by a whip wielded with practiced brutality.

Rose pressed her hand to her mouth, bile rising in her throat. Who could have done such a thing? And when? Most of the scars looked old, as if inflicted when he was much younger. A boy, perhaps, unable to defend himself.

She should turn away, should respect his privacy, but the sight of those marks filled her with such fierce, protective anger that she couldn't move. Someone had hurt him. Repeatedly. Savagely.

Sebastian turned and their eyes met across the water. His expression shifted from surprise to something like mortification as he realized what she must be seeing. He didn't move to cover himself or dive deeper into the water. He simply stood there, exposed and vulnerable, watching her with wary resignation.

Time seemed to slow. She wanted to run to him, to somehow shield him from the memory of whatever had left those marks. Instead, she could only stand frozen, her heart breaking for the pain he must have endured.

One of the younger gardeners spotted them and let out a yelp of alarm. "Lord preserve us—ladies!"

Chaos erupted as the men scrambled for their clothes, dove underwater or rushed toward the bank. Sebastian remained motionless, his gaze still locked with Rose's, as if he were testing her reaction to his scarred body.

"Rose, we must go," Lydia said urgently, tugging at her arm.

Rose tore her gaze away, her heart hammering. "Yes. Of

course."

They hurried back through the trees, the men's panicked voices following them.

"Sweet Mary, if his lordship hears about this."

"We'll be out on our ears before supper."

"Never thought we'd be entertaining the quality today."

Only when the voices faded did any of the women dare speak.

"Well," Daphne said, her face crimson. "That was... educational."

Arabella laughed delightedly. "Educational indeed. Did you ladies enjoy your anatomy lesson?"

"I've never seen..." Daphne trailed off, fanning herself with her hand.

"A man without his clothes?" Arabella supplied helpfully. "They're quite different creatures when undressed, aren't they?"

Violet made a small, strangled sound and pulled her bonnet lower over her face. "If my cousin discovers what we've witnessed, she'll be terribly angry I went with you. She thinks you're all bad influences on me. Not that she truly cares about me, but you know how she is."

"She won't find out," Arabella said. "Those poor men are far more concerned about their reputations than we need be about ours. They were the ones behaving improperly."

"I rather suspect they'll pretend this never happened," Lydia said, nodding.

"The scars." The words burst out of Rose. "Did you see Sebastian's back?"

The mood sobered instantly.

"Yes," Arabella said. "Difficult to miss."

"What could cause such marks?" Rose asked, though she suspected she already knew.

"A whip," Violet said, her voice barely audible. "Or a riding crop."

"Violet," Arabella asked, "how do you know such things?"

"My father," Violet whispered. "He has a terrible temper. My brother Robert bears the worst of it." She touched her ribs gingerly. "I know what such marks look like."

The revelation made Rose's stomach drop.

Arabella stopped walking entirely, her face darkening with fury. "Your father beats you?"

"Not physically, although words can hurt," Violet said quickly. "But Robert. My brother. He has been beaten more times than I can count. One time Father broke his arm." She shuddered. "It is why I want to marry, to escape my father."

"Oh, Violet," Rose said, taking the younger woman's hands. "I had no idea."

"There are too many bad men in this world," Violet said. "But there's not much we can do about it."

They walked in heavy silence. Rose's mind kept returning to Sebastian's scars, to the resignation in his eyes when he'd seen her looking. How many others carried such hidden wounds? How many suffered in silence behind closed doors?

As they crested a small hill, Rose's mother's voice suddenly echoed in her mind, clear as if she were standing beside her.

*You and your partner could hang for this. And then what happens to Rose?*

Rose stumbled, her breath catching. The voice was so vivid, so real, that she looked around expecting to see her mother standing there.

"Rose?" Daphne caught her arm. "Are you quite all right?"

"I..." Rose pressed her hand to her temple. "I'm fine. Just overheated, I think."

But she wasn't fine. The voice had been different this time—not just a fragment, but a complete sentence. And it suggested her mother had known about the smuggling, had confronted her father about it.

*And then what happens to Rose?*

Her mother had been afraid. Not just of the legal consequences, but of what would happen to her daughter if her father were caught. Her earlier suspicions were growing too strong to ignore.

"Let's return to the house," Rose said shakily. "I could use something cool to drink."

The ladies agreed, but Rose could feel their concerned gazes upon her. She was falling apart, piece by piece, and she wasn't sure how much longer she could hold herself together.

As they walked back toward the manor, Rose found herself thinking about her father and his secrets. How many more was he hiding? Could it be a murder? That of his own wife? Was it possible?

THAT EVENING, ROSE stood in front of the mirror while Prudence helped her dress. They'd chosen a dark blue silk, with delicate silver embroidery along the neckline. Prudence had fixed her hair in an elegant updo, with tendrils framing her face. At any other time, Rose might have admired the soft sheen of the fabric that draped to the floor with a slight train. But tonight, her reflection looked like a stranger. Pale, hollow-eyed, fragile.

"My lady, is something amiss? You've barely said a word," Prudence said, adjusting the drape of Rose's sleeves.

Rose stared at herself in the mirror, seeing echoes of her mother in the shape of her eyes, the curve of her mouth. How many times had her mother stood in this very spot, preparing for an evening she dreaded? How many nights had she smiled and played her role while fear gnawed at her heart?

"I've been having those dreams again. The ones where my mother's trying to tell me something." Rose turned from the mirror to face her maid directly. "And lately, I've been hearing her voice when I'm awake. Clear as if she were standing beside me."

Prudence's face went carefully blank, the expression she wore when trying to hide something. "Dreams can feel very real when we're grieving or troubled."

"This isn't grief, Prudence. This is memory." Rose studied her maid's face. "What do you remember from the night she was killed?"

"My lady, I don't think—"

"Please." Rose caught Prudence's hands. "I need to know. I feel like I'm going mad, hearing fragments of conversations, seeing pieces of things I can't quite grasp. Help me understand."

Prudence closed her eyes briefly, as if steeling herself. When she opened them, her expression was resigned. "What would you like to know?"

"Tell me about Lizzie."

Prudence sank into the chair beside Rose's dressing table, suddenly looking much older than her years.

"Lizzie was your mother's lady's maid. Had been since Lady Eleanor was first married. They were..." Prudence paused, choosing her words carefully. "They were more like sisters than mistress and servant. Your mother trusted her completely."

"And she died just days after my mother."

"A riding accident, they said. Her horse spooked and threw her." Prudence's voice was bitter. "But Lizzie was the finest rider among all the staff. She could handle any horse in the stable."

Rose felt a chill run down her spine. "You don't think it was an accident."

"None of us did. Mrs. Carter, Mrs. Blythe, and I—we all knew something was wrong. But when we tried to speak to the constable..." Prudence shook her head. "He wouldn't hear a word against his lordship."

"His lordship?" Rose's voice came out as a whisper.

Prudence looked stricken, as if she'd said too much. "Lady Rose, perhaps we shouldn't speak of this."

"Tell me." Rose's voice was stronger now, edged with determination. "Tell me what you suspected."

For a long moment, Prudence said nothing. Then, as if a dam

had burst, the words came tumbling out.

"The night your mother died, the three of us sat with Lizzie in the kitchen afterward. She was beside herself with grief, couldn't stop weeping. And then she said something terrible." Prudence's voice dropped to barely above a whisper. "She said that earlier that evening, Lady Eleanor had pulled her aside and told her, 'If anything should happen to me, tell the constable to look closely at my husband.' And Lady Rose, we know there were other times when he was aggressive with her. Lizzie used to tend to her bruises."

Rose hugged her middle, stumbling backward. Her legs gave out as she sank onto the edge of her bed. The room seemed to tilt around her, black dots dancing before her eyes.

"No. No, that can't be right."

But even as she said it, fragments of memory began surfacing. Her mother's voice, urgent and frightened: *You and your partner could hang for this. And then what happens to Rose?* Another voice, deeper, male, angry in response.

"Lady Rose?" Prudence was beside her in an instant, steadying her with gentle hands. "Should I fetch some water?"

Rose couldn't speak. Her throat felt closed, her chest tight. Her mother had known. Had suspected her own husband might hurt her. Had tried to protect herself, to leave some trail for justice to follow.

And then Lizzie, who had carried that message, had died just days later.

"The constable," Rose managed to say. "Did you tell him what Lizzie said?"

Prudence's face darkened. "We tried. But he was already bought and paid for, wasn't he? Wouldn't even speak to us properly. Said the word of servants wasn't worth the breath it took to speak it."

"So Lizzie died for nothing." Rose's voice was hollow.

"Not for nothing. She tried to honor your mother's wishes. We all did, in our way." Prudence knelt beside the bed, taking

Rose's cold hands in her warm ones. "But we were powerless, my lady. Just servants in a house where terrible things happened and no one with authority cared to see justice done."

Rose closed her eyes, trying to make sense of it all. Her father—the man who had raised her, who had scolded her for her failed Season, who was now trying to force her into marriage—had he really killed her mother? And then murdered an innocent young woman to cover his tracks?

"There's something else," Prudence said hesitantly. "I probably shouldn't tell you, but… I think Mary knows more than she's ever said."

"Mary?" Rose's eyes snapped open. "Our Mary?"

"She was just a scullery maid then, barely thirteen. Quiet little thing, always in the shadows." Prudence worried at her lower lip. "But the morning after it happened, I found her in the pantry, shaking like a leaf. When I asked what was wrong, she just kept saying 'I didn't see nothing, I didn't hear nothing' over and over. But the way she said it made me think differently."

"Like someone had told her to say it."

"Exactly." Prudence's voice was grim. "I've always wondered what she might have witnessed. But she's never breathed a word, not in all these years."

Rose felt something cold and hard settle in her chest. Fear, yes, but also anger. How many people had suffered for her father's secrets? How many had been silenced or killed to protect his crimes?

"Lady Rose," Prudence said urgently, "you must promise me you won't do anything rash. If what we suspect is true, then you're in terrible danger. Especially now, asking questions. You're bound to anger him."

"I have to know the truth. I can't live like this anymore, hearing fragments, seeing pieces. I feel like I'm drowning in lies."

"Then we must be very, very careful about how we proceed." Prudence stood, smoothing her skirts with shaking hands. "Perhaps we could speak to Mary together, when his lordship is away from the house. And we must tell no one else of our suspicions."

Rose nodded, though her mind was already racing ahead. Tonight at dinner, she would have to sit across from her father and smile. She would have to pretend she didn't suspect him of murdering her mother and an innocent young woman. She would have to act as if her world hadn't just crumbled to pieces.

"How do I face him?" she asked, her voice breaking. "How do I sit at that table and pretend everything is normal?"

"I don't know," Prudence said. "But I do know that you're strong and smart. Somehow, you will triumph. I just know you will."

Rose looked at herself in the mirror again. The frightened girl was still there, but something else was emerging too. Something harder, more determined. Her mother had tried to leave a trail, tried to ensure the truth would come out.

Rose would honor that. Whatever the cost.

"Please help me with my jewelry," she said, her voice steadier now. "If I'm going to perform tonight, I might as well look the part."

But as Prudence fastened her necklace, Rose caught sight of her own eyes in the mirror. They looked different now—older, sadder, but also resolute.

Tonight, she would begin asking the right questions. And this time, she wouldn't stop until she had answers.

# CHAPTER THIRTEEN

SEBASTIAN SPENT THE evening in his own private hell, unable to shake the image of Rose's face when she'd seen his scars. The shock in her eyes, the way her hand had flown to her mouth, played over and over in his mind like a cruel refrain.

He'd eaten supper with the others but barely tasted the food. While the rest of the men had moved on to joking about their unexpected encounter with the ladies, Sebastian felt as though his skin had been stripped away, leaving every nerve exposed.

"Reckon Lady Rose got quite an eyeful," one of the younger gardeners was saying with a nervous laugh. "Think she'll tell his lordship?"

"Nah," Thorncroft replied. "Mrs. Blythe says the ladies won't make trouble for us. We weren't doing nothing wrong, just cooling off after a hot day's work."

Sebastian pushed back from the table. He couldn't bear to listen to them discuss Rose, couldn't stand the thought that she might be upstairs right now, disgusted by what she'd seen. The scars told a story he'd never wanted to share—of helplessness, of being at another man's mercy, of pain that had marked him inside and out.

"Where you off to, Sebastian?" Thorncroft called.

"Getting some air," Sebastian muttered, and fled before anyone could follow.

The stables were quiet at this hour, save for the occasional creak of wood and the soft shifting of hooves against straw. Sebastian made his way to Tempest's stall, desperate for the comfort of his oldest friend.

The stallion nickered softly in greeting, and Sebastian felt some of the tension leave his shoulders. "Hello, old boy." He spoke softly, running his hand down Tempest's sleek neck. "I've had better days. How about you?"

He pulled a sugar cube from his pocket, offering it on his palm. Tempest's warm breath tickled his hand as the horse accepted the treat, and for a moment, Sebastian could almost pretend he was back in Brighton with his brother, that none of this nightmare was real.

"She saw them. All of them. Every mark he left on me." His throat tightened. "You should have seen her face. The horror in her eyes. How can I expect her to look at me the same way now?"

Tempest nudged his shoulder gently, as if sensing his distress.

"I keep forgetting why I came here," Sebastian continued, the words tumbling out like a confession. He continued to speak, only silently, unsure of who might be about to hear him. *When I'm with her, everything else fades away. James and Sophia, justice for Papa—it all becomes secondary to the way she smiles, the sound of her laugh.* He pressed his forehead against Tempest's neck. *What kind of man does that make me? What kind of son?*

"Sebastian, there you are."

Sebastian spun around, his heart hammering. Tobias Hale stood in the stable doorway, his expression unreadable in the dim light.

"Christ, Hale. You nearly gave me heart failure."

"Apologies. I've been looking for you." Hale stepped closer, and Sebastian noticed he carried a folded paper in his hand. "Heard you'd slipped away from the others."

"Needed some quiet," Sebastian said, embarrassed to be caught talking to his horse like a madman. "What's that you have there?"

Hale's expression grew grim. "Information. About Baron

White." He glanced toward the stable doors, then lowered his voice. "I've had a man making inquiries in London. Discreetly."

"And?"

"It's worse than we suspected." Hale unfolded the paper, though he didn't look at it. "The devil has a history. A long, ugly history that's been covered up with money and influence."

Sebastian's jaw clenched so hard his teeth ground together. "What kind of history?"

"The kind that involves young women. Servants, mostly. Girls with no power, no protection." Hale's voice was tight with controlled anger. "My contact found records—payments to families, sudden departures, accidents that weren't accidents."

"How many?" Sebastian asked, though he wasn't sure he wanted to know.

"At least six that we can verify. Probably more." Hale met his eyes. "One girl was barely sixteen. Worked at his London house. Got herself with child—his child, most likely—and tried to tell someone about it. A week later, she was found drowned in the Thames. They said it was a suicide but who knows?"

The rage that hit Sebastian was so sudden and fierce it nearly knocked him backward. His hands clenched into fists, and for a moment he saw white at the edges of his vision.

"Easy," Hale said quietly. "I know. I felt the same way when I read it."

"We can't let him have her," Sebastian said through gritted teeth. "I don't care what it costs. Rose will not become another name on that list." He paused, thinking about how to tell Hale about his morning encounter with White. "I had an incident with White this morning. In the rose garden."

Hale's eyebrows shot up. "What kind of incident?"

Sebastian told him everything—White's assault on Rose, the garden shears, the desperate bluff about being Talbot's spy. With each detail, Hale's expression grew darker.

"Heaven forbid, Sebastian. You could have been killed."

"He had his hands on her," Sebastian said simply. "I would

have done worse if necessary."

Hale was quiet for a long moment. "You know this changes things. White will be watching you now, looking for any excuse to have you removed."

"Let him watch. I meant what I told him. As long as I'm here and safe, so is he. But if anything happens to me…"

"Then what? You're bluffing with cards you don't have."

Sebastian's smile was sharp and cold. "Am I? White doesn't know that. His guilty conscience is doing half the work for me."

"Still, we're working on borrowed time now." Hale folded the paper and tucked it back into his coat. "Which is why I have a proposal. You may not like it."

"I'm listening."

"The masquerade ball is in three days. I want you to attend."

Sebastian stared at him. "As what? A guest?"

"Exactly. I have a contact—Mr. Nathaniel Clarke, son of a wealthy merchant. His family was ruined by White's business practices, so he's more than happy to lend us his invitation. You'll wear his name and a mask that covers your entire face."

"And do what? Dance the night away while Rose is trapped with that monster?"

"Gather information. These men become loose-tongued when they're drinking and think they're among friends. You might overhear something useful." Hale paused meaningfully. "You'll be able to keep an eye on Rose. Make sure White doesn't corner her again."

Sebastian's pulse quickened at the thought. To be near her, to speak with her without the barrier of their supposed class difference, even for one night, was a dream too good to be true.

"It's dangerous," he said, more to himself than to Hale. "If I'm discovered."

"You won't be. Not if you're careful. The key is to leave before the unmasking at midnight. Like Cinderella, only hopefully without losing a shoe."

Despite everything, a smile tugged at his lips. "And if this works? If we find what we need to bring them down?"

"Then Rose will be free." Hale's expression softened slightly. "She'll lose everything else—her home, her position, her dowry. She'll be ruined by association when the truth comes out. But she'll be alive, and she'll be free to choose her own path."

The weight of that settled over Sebastian like a shroud. Even if they succeeded, even if they saved her from White and brought her father to justice, Rose would suffer for it. She would lose everything she'd ever known.

"She'll hate me," Sebastian said quietly. "When she learns what I've done, who I really am, why I came here—she'll never forgive me."

"Maybe. Or maybe she'll understand that you saved her life." Hale studied him carefully. "You must do what is right and hope for the best outcome for all of us."

"I didn't expect to feel conflicted. But Lady Rose? She's innocent in all of this. I'm about to wreck her life."

"Lizzie came to me the night Lady Wentworth died. Terrified, sobbing. Said Lady Wentworth told her to go to the constable if anything happened, to tell them to look closely at Lord Wentworth." Hale's voice cracked slightly. "Two days later, she was dead. I should have protected her. Should have gotten her away from here the moment she told me what Lady Wentworth had said." Hale's eyes were bright with unshed tears. "Instead, I let her stay, thinking we were safe, thinking Wentworth wouldn't dare hurt a servant. I was wrong."

Sebastian felt his own throat tighten. "I'm sorry."

"It's why I'm helping you. Not just for justice, though that matters. But because I couldn't save Lizzie, and I'll be damned if I'll let another innocent woman die on my watch."

They stood in silence for a moment, united in their grief and their determination.

"The ball, then," Sebastian said finally. "I'll do it."

"Good. I'll have the costume and invitation delivered to my cottage tomorrow. You'll dress there." Hale turned to go, then paused. "Faith, Lord Ashford. Have faith."

After Hale left, Sebastian remained in the stable with Tempest, thinking about how brave he would have to be to go to that ball disguised as another man. He'd not wanted to play a part in a play but it seemed that was all he did of late. Pretend to be someone he was not. And at what cost? To Lady Rose? To himself? To Hale? To all of those hurt by Wentworth? Would this risky decision be the one to bring redemption or would he hang as his father had?

He'd said he would die trying to clear their family name if it came to that. However, the fervor with which he'd planned his revenge was starting to fade. In its place? Lady Rose's well-being. How could he possibly reconcile the two when they were in opposing directions?

THE NEXT MORNING, Sebastian was up and headed to the rose garden as the sun was rising. He had no idea if Rose would come visit him, but he wanted to be there if she managed to get away.

To his surprise, she was already there, sitting on her swing, so pretty that it took his breath away. She jumped to her feet the moment she saw him. He rushed to her, as if his feet had wills of their own. The leap in his heart scared him more than almost anything had in his life.

*Seeing your father hanged. Don't forget that fright.*

He managed to keep himself from touching her, but it took every ounce of will he had. Instead, he scrutinized her face for clues to her emotional state. Who knew what she'd had to endure since last he saw her? Dark circles shadowed her eyes, and her fingers worried the fabric of her skirt.

"Who did that to you?" Rose blurted out, without preamble.

His throat tightened. The lie he'd practiced felt like ash in his mouth. "The family I lived with after my mother's death was cruel. Any small infraction was punished." He forced himself to meet her eyes. "With glee."

"How could anyone hurt a child like that?" Her voice broke, and she reached toward him before catching herself, her hand hovering in the space between them.

The almost-touch sent heat racing through him. He clenched his fists to keep from closing that distance. "May I ask you something?"

"Anything."

"Has your father ever laid a hand on you?" The words came out rougher than he intended.

Her eyes widened. "No. His cruelty comes in words only." She sank onto the swing, her knuckles white as she gripped the ropes. "Though I don't think—I don't think it was the same for my mother."

Sebastian's pulse quickened. "What do you mean?"

"I heard her voice again last night." Rose's voice dropped to barely above a whisper. "She said, 'You and your partner could hang for this, and then what happens to Rose'?"

"Do you have any idea what it means?"

She bit her lower lip, a habit he'd noticed when she was thinking hard. "I think… I think it's from the night she died. As if I heard her and Father arguing." Her breath came faster. "But it's like trying to hold water. The memory slips away. Do I sound mad?"

"Not at all." He wanted to take her hands, to offer comfort, but didn't dare. "I know someone who witnessed violence as a child of eight. She can't remember it, though her brother does. Sometimes we bury what's too painful to bear."

"I was eight when Mother died." Rose's voice grew smaller. "The same age as the girl you speak of."

"Do you remember anything else from that night?"

She nodded slowly. "My governess let me peek into the ballroom to see Mother in her gown. She looked like a fairy tale princess." Her shoulders began to shake. "But after that… nothing. Not when they told me she was gone, not the funeral, not even the weeks after. I loved her so much, Sebastian. I was lost without her. I still am."

The raw pain in her voice made his chest ache. His hand moved toward her before he could stop it, hovering near her side. "So it's possible you saw something that night. Something your mind couldn't handle."

"That's what I keep thinking." She pressed her palms to her eyes. "What if I overheard them fighting about his business? What if she found out what he really was and he lost his temper?"

Sebastian's stomach clenched. He was walking a knife's edge between truth and deception. "What are you saying?"

Rose lifted her head, tears clinging to her lashes. "A week ago, I would have sworn Father could never do such a thing, but now?" She drew a shuddering breath. "Prudence told me about Mother's lady's maid, Lizzie. How she died in that riding accident."

"Hale's fiancée. He told me he believes Hargrave spooked the horse. Mrs. Blythe and Mrs. Carter think the same thing."

"How do you know that?"

"I overheard them talking one afternoon."

"He had her killed to keep Prudence quiet about what she knew." Rose's voice grew stronger, anger threading through the pain. "And Prudence said Mother had told Lizzie that if anything happened to her, to tell the constable to look at her husband."

"Hale told me the same thing."

"Father was paying off the constable." Rose's eyes flashed. "He refused to hear anything from the servants about what they knew about my mother's death. And then Lizzie died too." She leaned forward, studying his face intently. "Prudence told me something else. She thinks Mary knows more than she's confessing."

His heart hammered against his ribs. How much could he reveal without destroying everything? "Prudence and Finch have mentioned similar things to me." He told her about their interaction at the pub, when he'd asked for information about

Lady Wentworth. "Mary was definitely not telling us everything she knew. Prudence pressed but she wouldn't say anything."

"Prudence wants me to ask Mary directly." Rose's jaw set with determination. "I see how the servants flinch when Father raises his voice, how they look over their shoulders when Hargrave's near. I've not been completely blind to the truth." She stood abruptly, pacing to the garden's edge. "They're not just servants to me, Sebastian. They're the only family I've had since Mother died."

"I know." He rose, taking a step toward her.

"No, forgive me." She whirled back, her hand pressed to her throat and stared at him for a long moment, a raw vulnerability flickering in her eyes. "What should I do, Sebastian? How do I face all of this?"

"Talk to Mary. Today, if you can manage it."

"It's going to hurt, isn't it? Whatever she tells me."

He nodded, grimacing. "I wish I could spare you this pain."

Rose stepped closer, close enough that he could see the gold flecks in her green eyes. "There is one thing you could do."

His breath caught. "What?"

"Tell me who you really are."

He hung his head, hands trembling with the urge to confess everything—his real name, his quest for justice, how desperately he was falling for her despite every reason he shouldn't. Instead, he forced out, "I cannot. Not yet."

Something shuttered in her expression. "Then you wouldn't really do anything to help me, would you?" Her voice turned cool, distant. "I understand, of course. Your secret must be quite powerful if you can't trust me with it. Even after everything we've shared."

She moved toward the garden path, her spine straight as a queen's. Sebastian's throat worked, the truth clawing at him. *Tell her. Tell her now.*

But James's face flashed in his mind, then Sophia's. The weight of justice for his family pressed down on him.

"Rose—"

She paused without turning. For a heartbeat, he thought she might come back to him. Then she continued walking, disappearing around the corner of the manor house.

Sebastian stood alone among the roses, his hands clenched so tight his nails bit into his palms. He was losing her with every lie, every half-truth. And when she finally learned who he really was—when she discovered he was the son of the man her father had destroyed—he would lose her forever.

But he had to keep going. For James. For Sophia. For justice.

Even if it destroyed the only chance at love he'd ever known.

# CHAPTER FOURTEEN

ROSE WENT DIRECTLY into the house and downstairs to the servants' quarters to ask for Mary's whereabouts. One of the scullery maids told her Mary was in the linen room. Rose paused outside the door, her hand on the brass handle, knowing that once she asked these questions, there would be no taking them back.

Mary stood at the worktable, folding linens with precise, mechanical movements. But Rose saw the tension in her shoulders and the way her fingers clenched just a little too tightly around the fabric when she saw that it was Rose.

"My lady." She dipped into a stiff curtsy, eyes flickering downward.

"I'm sorry to interrupt your work." Rose took a step closer, studying Mary's face. "But I need to ask you something about my mother."

Mary's hands stilled for just a moment before resuming their folding. "Of course, my lady."

Rose drew a breath, thinking of Baron White's cold eyes across the dinner table last night, the way he'd looked at her like she was already his. If she was going to escape that fate, she needed the truth. All of it.

"The night she died. You were here, were you not?"

The linen slipped from Mary's hands entirely. She bent quickly to retrieve it, but Rose caught the sharp intake of breath, the way Mary's lips moved in what looked like a silent prayer.

"I—yes, my lady. But I didn't see anything."

Rose could remember when Mary had first come to work for them. A thin, frightened girl with hollow cheeks who used to shrink into corners. Even now, grown into a capable woman, that old fear clung to her like smoke.

"What do you remember about that night?" Rose asked gently.

Mary's knuckles went white around the fabric. "The constable came. We were told to stay away from the east wing." She spoke too quickly, words tumbling together. "That's all."

"Mary." Rose stepped closer. "Please. I think you saw something that night."

"I didn't." But Mary couldn't meet her eyes.

Rose felt her chest tighten. She touched the small locket at her throat. It was her mother's locket. Her father had given it to her when she turned sixteen. Back when she still had hope of a happy life.

"I don't believe that," Rose said.

Mary's hands began to shake. The linen trembled in her grip.

"I can't." The words came out strangled.

"Why not?"

For a long moment, Mary said nothing. When she finally spoke, her voice was barely a whisper. "Because I need this position, my lady. I have my sister to think of."

Rose frowned. "Your sister?"

"Annie. She's eleven, born with a twisted foot. Can't work, can't care for herself." Mary's voice cracked. "If I lose my wages, if Lord Wentworth dismisses me, we'll starve. And he would dismiss me, my lady. He'd make sure I never found work anywhere. Or worse."

The desperation in Mary's voice made Rose's throat ache. But she thought of Baron White again, of the marriage contract her father was so eager to sign, and pressed on.

"Mary, if you know something about my mother's death, you

must tell me."

"Don't." Mary backed toward the wall, shaking her head violently. "Don't ask me this. You don't know what kind of men you're dealing with."

Ice ran down Rose's spine. "You mean my father?"

Mary's lips parted, but no sound came. Then, so quietly Rose almost missed it: "And Hargrave."

The room went cold. Rose gripped the edge of the worktable, her knees suddenly weak. Now she was getting somewhere. Get her to talk about Hargrave, a voice whispered in her ear. "What did he do?"

Mary pressed herself against the wall, eyes wide with terror. "I saw what happened to Lizzie. She said too much, and they took care of her." Her voice broke. "Please, my lady. Let this be. What good does dragging it up do now?"

Rose stared at her, pieces clicking into place with horrible clarity. Lizzie had known the truth and they killed her because of it. All so obvious now. How could she not have put this together before? Because she had blinders on, that's why. She hadn't been brave enough to see the truth, even though it had been right in front of her this entire time.

"If what I suspect is true," Rose said carefully, "if my father and Hargrave were involved in my mother's death, then exposing them would protect you. And me."

Mary let out a bitter laugh. "You think the law cares about protecting servant girls? About protecting you?" She shook her head. "Rich men make the rules, my lady. The rest of us just try to survive them."

The words settled into Rose's chest like stones. Even if she proved her father's guilt, even if she escaped Baron White's bed, what justice would there really be? Men like her father always found a way to land on their feet.

But the alternative was accepting Baron White's hands on her body for the rest of her life. Living with the knowledge that her father had killed the person she'd loved most in the world.

"My mother wouldn't have wanted me to just survive," Rose said, more to herself than to Mary. "She would have wanted me to fight."

Mary's face crumpled. For a moment, she looked like that frightened thirteen-year-old again. "I wish I could help you, my lady. I truly do. But Annie is my family." She clutched the linens to her chest like armor. "I'm all she has."

Without another word, she grabbed the remaining linens and fled, leaving Rose alone with the weight of what she now knew and the terrible choice ahead of her.

*Rich men make the rules. We just survive them.*

But survival, Rose was beginning to understand, came in many forms. And she was no longer sure she could live with the safest one.

ROSE KNOCKED ONCE on her father's study door and waited.

"Who is it?" came the clipped reply.

She opened the heavy door and stepped inside without waiting for permission. The familiar scents of leather, pipe smoke, and brandy clung to the room. Lord Wentworth sat behind his imposing mahogany desk, swirling amber liquid in a crystal glass, eyes flicking to hers with visible irritation.

"What is it now, Rose? I'm expecting company."

"I need a moment of your time." She kept her voice steady.

He gestured to the chair opposite his desk. "Sit, then."

"I'd rather stand."

His brow lifted. "Suit yourself."

She drew a slow breath. "I've been thinking about Mummy."

Fear flickered in his eyes—quick, controlled. But she caught it.

He leaned back. "What good does that do you?"

"It might do me quite a lot. If I finally learn the truth of what happened to her."

He sighed like a man forced to explain arithmetic to a stubborn child. "What truth is left to uncover? Lord Ashford killed her. He was tried, convicted, and hanged. A tragedy, yes, but not a mystery."

"A tragedy," she repeated. "Is that the same as a murder?"

He studied her. "Sometimes they're one and the same."

"I've been wondering about the candlestick. Why someone as intelligent as Lord Ashford would leave the murder weapon in plain sight."

He scoffed. "Ashford was intelligent, yes, but passion makes fools of clever men. He loved your mother. Or thought he did. He couldn't have her, and in the end, he snapped. That's all there is to it."

"From what I've heard, they were simply friendly acquaintances."

"Oh, Rose," he said with a tired shake of his head. "Your mother was warm. Charming. Men misinterpreted her kindness all the time. Ashford believed her affection meant something. He became obsessive. Delusional."

She took a step closer. "You told me once they were friends."

"They were. But even friendships can turn sour when one party wants more. She chose me, and he never recovered from the loss."

"You're saying he killed her because he couldn't have her?"

"A lovers' quarrel gone too far. That's the theory the Crown accepted, and frankly, so should you."

"I remember her crying that night," Rose said. "I remember raised voices. Yours."

He waved that off. "She was an emotional woman. You know that. Like you."

"No. Don't compare us in that tone. She wasn't unwell. She wasn't hysterical. She was afraid. Of you."

His fingers stilled on the brandy glass. "You were a child. You remember fragments. Not the truth."

"I remember her love. Her steadiness. Her warmth. The way

her hands trembled when you walked into a room."

His gaze cooled. "Careful, Rose."

She pressed forward. "You want me to believe Lord Ashford was the villain. But what if he wasn't? What if you chose him because he was easy to blame?"

His voice lowered. "That's a dangerous thing to suggest."

"Dangerous for me, you mean?"

He stood slowly, stepped around the desk. Close enough for her to smell the brandy on his breath. Smuggled, no doubt.

"You're imagining things. Like your mother. She said terrible things when she was upset. Accused me of all sorts of betrayals. She wasn't well. I should have had her treated. I won't make that mistake with you."

Her stomach turned. "She didn't need treatment. She needed safety. What was it she found out, Father? What did she threaten to expose?"

His jaw flexed. "You don't know what you're talking about."

"Don't I?" She leaned in, lowering her voice to a thread. "Why do you really want me to marry Baron White? What does he know?"

His silence was answer enough.

"I know who he is to you," Rose continued. "He's not a suitor. He's leverage. You want to bind him to you—legally, socially—because he knows too much."

Wentworth smiled. It was tight, cold. "And where did you come by these fairytales?"

"I know about the smuggling. And I know my marriage to him has nothing to do with my future and everything to do with yours."

The mask slipped for a breath, his jaw twitching before he forced it still. "Do you think your little theories make you clever? You live in luxury because of me. Because I've made the difficult choices."

She met his eyes. "And did you make a difficult choice the night Mummy died?"

He moved in close, his voice a blade. "You will shut your mouth. Or you won't open it again."

Her breath hitched, but she held her ground. "I am not afraid of you." All lies. She was terrified.

"You should be." He straightened, tone now cold and smooth. "The only thing that matters is power. I have it. And you, Rose, will do as you're told. You'll marry Baron White."

"I won't."

"You will. Unless you'd prefer to be sent for an extended rest, like your mother should have been. Or perhaps a longer sleep—one that reunites you with her entirely."

The room spun, but she forced herself to remain still.

"I'll run," she said. "I'll disappear before I let you do this to me."

"There's nowhere you can run that I won't find you." He smiled, small, cruel. "The wedding will take place the day after the masquerade ball."

The floor felt unsteady beneath her feet. She glanced down instinctively, and something caught her eye.

Just beside his polished boots, a floorboard warped slightly along the edge. Loose. Moveable. A hiding place? How had she not noticed it before? The rug was not where it usually was. Someone had moved it back a few inches. Not enough to notice.

Why? And who?

When her eyes lifted again, Wentworth was watching her. He had seen her see it.

Her heart thundered in her chest. She had to get out—before his rage boiled over. Before he did what she now believed he was capable of.

She lifted her chin. "I will not be your pawn. I'd rather die than marry him."

"Is that right?"

"It is. So do what you must, Father. And I will do the same."

She turned and fled. His voice followed her out, soft and venomous:

"I certainly shall, dear daughter. You can count on it."

She ran all the way to her room, locking the door behind her with shaking hands. No footsteps followed. Only silence.

She collapsed to the floor, drawing her knees to her chest, and let the tears come.

She wept for her mother. For the life they never got to share. She wept for herself, for the part of her that had still hoped to be wrong.

But she wasn't.

Her father was a smuggler. A liar.

And he might very well be a killer.

If she defied him, he wouldn't hesitate to make her disappear too. But she must do it anyway.

# CHAPTER FIFTEEN

HALE HAD ASKED Sebastian to meet him in his private quarters to dress for the ball. Sebastian's stomach churned as he approached the small stone cottage near the edge of the orchard. The modest dwelling sat tucked away from Wentworth Manor's grandeur, close enough for the steward to be summoned yet hidden from prying eyes. Ivy curled up the weathered stone walls, and the thatched roof had darkened with age.

He knocked once and waited. Soon, Hale opened the door, glancing left and right before ushering him inside.

"All is well?" Hale asked, closing the door firmly behind them.

"As well as can be expected. The carriages are arriving. I should not tarry long."

The cottage was practical and orderly, much like Hale himself. A large wooden desk dominated one wall, covered in neat stacks of ledgers and estate maps. A single bookshelf held volumes on land management alongside a few worn novels. The windows stood open, letting in the warm summer evening air.

Hale gestured toward the bed, where fine clothing lay waiting. Sebastian approached slowly, his breath catching as he touched the dark green velvet coat. The fabric was softer than anything he'd worn in years.

"I have not dressed as a gentleman. Ever."

"Tonight you reclaim what was stolen from you." Hale

moved to his desk and withdrew a wooden box. "This was not easy to commission on short notice, but I know a woodworker who asks no questions."

He lifted out a mask unlike any Sebastian had seen. It was carved from dark-stained wood, heavier than expected, with intricate details of leaves and vines that seemed to emerge from the wood itself. The face bore the squared jawline of a Venetian Bauta, but the organic patterns gave it an otherworldly quality.

"The Green Man," Sebastian said, recognizing the ancient symbol.

"Precisely. He exists between worlds—neither fully civilized nor entirely wild." Hale held the mask carefully. "Rather fitting, would you not say?"

"Perhaps too much so?" Sebastian took it, running his thumb along the smooth curves. The eye holes were narrow but functional, and the extended mouthpiece would not only conceal his features but alter his voice as well.

"I have prepared a bath." Hale gestured toward a tub behind a screen. "Take your time. Call when you are ready."

Alone, Sebastian stripped away his work-worn clothes and slipped into the tub. The warm water felt like absolution. He scrubbed away the grime of servitude, watching the dirt swirl away with something that might have been his old self.

When he emerged, he felt lighter somehow. Cleaner in more ways than one.

He began with the undergarments, then the black wool trousers that fit as though tailored for him. The white linen shirt was crisp against his skin. A charcoal brocade waistcoat came next, cut to flatter his lean frame.

Then the coat. The forest-green velvet seemed to transform him with its weight and richness. Dark embroidery traced the lapels like ivy on stone. He tied the emerald silk cravat, remembering his father doing the same. Finally, the black leather gloves that would hide the calluses that marked him as a working man.

"Hale," he called out. "I am ready."

The steward returned, and his expression shifted almost imperceptibly. "Lord Ashford, welcome back."

Lord Ashford. The man he was meant to be. Had he found him once again? He moved to the small looking glass and stared at his reflection. The man looking back was someone he'd not seen as an adult—straight-shouldered, well-dressed, every inch a gentleman. Yet the eyes held knowledge the old Sebastian had never possessed.

"I had forgotten what it feels like to be dressed in finery," he said, his voice rough with emotion. He adjusted his cravat with fingers that trembled slightly. "These years… they have changed me. Made me into a man filled with rage and thirst for revenge. I can almost remember who I used to be when I see myself now."

"Like it or not, our hardships define who we are." Hale handed him the mask. "You understand suffering. Loss. That will make you a better man than you would have been. More compassionate. Generous even."

Sebastian took the mask, weighing it in his hands. "And if I am discovered?"

"Then we shall face whatever comes. But tonight, you are Nathaniel Clarke—a merchant with money enough to attend but not so prominent that anyone will scrutinize you closely. The real Clarke rarely appears at such events, and the mask will ensure no one looks too closely."

Sebastian positioned the mask carefully, tying it securely. The transformation was complete. He was neither Sebastian the gardener nor entirely Lord Ashford, but something new. Something dangerous.

In the glass, the Green Man stared back at him. Despite the seriousness of the occasion, Sebastian smiled.

"Shall we proceed?" Sebastian asked. Even through the mask, his voice carried a note of authority he'd thought lost forever.

Hale nodded. "It goes without saying that you must be careful. But I'll be keeping watch too."

Sebastian held out his hand and the men shook. "Thank you, Hale. Pray that all goes well."

IN HIS BORROWED finery, Sebastian stood in shadow watching carriages arrive at Wentworth Manor's sweeping drive, steeling himself for what lay ahead. Though he'd learned to dance as a child, years had passed since he'd attempted such grace. He hoped his feet would remember what they'd once known. Tonight, he must not merely blend in. No, that would not be enough. He must convince the very people who had cast him out that he belonged among them.

From within the grand house, candlelight spilled through tall windows, accompanied by the soft strains of a string quartet.

Sebastian stepped from the shadows and fell in behind a newly arrived couple, checking his mask one final time as they climbed the marble steps.

A footman ushered him through the grand entrance hall, a cavernous space lined with white marble columns, the air thick with the scent of polished wood and elaborate floral arrangements. Flowers from the very gardens he tended. The irony was not lost on him.

Guests gathered in the foyer, removing cloaks and murmuring behind their masks. Sebastian forced his stride to remain confident despite the dampness of his palms beneath his leather gloves. When the doors to the receiving hall opened, he found himself face to face with Lord Wentworth and Lady Rose.

His pulse held steady as he approached.

Lord Wentworth, resplendent in a black coat and gold-trimmed waistcoat, greeted guests with cool politeness. His gilded stag mask suited him perfectly. He would naturally choose the symbol of a creature that ruled the forest through size and antler.

And then there was Rose.

She stood beside her father like a figure from a dream, her gown of gold and silver catching every flicker of candlelight. A delicate crescent moon mask covered the upper portion of her face, adorned with tiny pearls and starbursts that gave her an otherworldly quality. Her mouth, left uncovered, was set in a polite smile.

How different she seemed from their stolen moments in the garden. Here, she held herself with practiced grace, but beneath it lay something Sebastian recognized—the careful composure of someone enduring rather than enjoying.

"Mr. Nathaniel Clarke," the steward announced.

Sebastian stepped forward and bowed. "My lord."

"Mr. Clarke, welcome," Wentworth nodded with perfunctory courtesy.

Rose inclined her head. "Welcome to Wentworth Manor, Mr. Clarke."

Sebastian took her gloved hand briefly, bowing over it without the excessive gallantry a younger man might display. "Lady Rose."

He released her hand and continued into the ballroom, where another steward announced his arrival. His borrowed name echoed over the chamber, drawing no particular attention. Precisely as intended.

He was in.

The ballroom had been transformed into an enchanted woodland. Chandeliers overhead were draped with gossamer fabric, casting golden shadows across polished floors. Garlands of ivy and jasmine wound along the columns, while arrangements of roses—his roses, though he must not think of them as such— stood in sculpted vases throughout the space.

Glass orbs hung like stars above the dance floor, casting shifting patterns on the walls. Tables along the edges held floating flowers, moss-covered branches, and delicate golden moths pinned among the greenery. It was dreamlike, otherworldly. Designed to transport guests into fantasy.

Rose had created something beautiful. If only she could take pleasure in it.

Sebastian positioned himself near a column where he could observe while remaining inconspicuous. Several minutes later, Rose entered the ballroom, flanked by three companions. One wore a sleek fox mask that shimmered beneath the chandeliers, another had a cream silk mask painted with delicate fawn spots, and the third was adorned in a striking owl mask, its brown and gold feathers catching the candlelight like burnished bronze.

Now or never. He crossed the room and bowed. "Lady Rose, might I request the honor of a dance, if your card permits?"

Her companions drifted away tactfully, leaving them alone.

"As it happens, there are several openings available, Mr. Clarke." She untied the silk ribbon securing the parchment card at her wrist.

Sebastian glimpsed the card as she opened it. Nearly every line remained blank save one—Baron White's name claimed the supper dance in bold, possessive strokes.

The sight answered questions he hadn't dared ask. Her isolation was not by choice.

"The waltz, if you would honor me," he said, taking the card to write his name.

"The waltz?"

"Unless you prefer another dance?"

She glanced around the room, and he caught her checking for a particular presence. White, no doubt.

"No, it would be my pleasure. Thank you, Mr. Clarke." Her smile seemed genuine this time. "Your mask is quite remarkable. The Green Man, is it not?"

"You have a keen eye for folklore."

"It reminds me of someone." Her voice grew softer. "Someone rather dear to me."

His heart quickened. "Is he here tonight?"

"No. He cannot attend such gatherings."

"Then perhaps I might serve as adequate company in his absence."

"No one could replace him," she murmured, then seemed to

catch herself. "But a pleasant distraction would be most welcome."

Before Sebastian could respond, the woman in the fox mask returned to claim Rose's attention, drawing her away into the crowd.

Sebastian retreated to his observation post, but his attention was soon caught by movement toward the terrace doors. Lord Wentworth and Baron White were making their way outside, and something in their purposeful manner suggested this was no casual stroll.

He waited several moments before following, slipping through the doors and into the cool night air. The men had moved to the far end of the terrace, where they stood lighting cigars near the stone balustrade. Sebastian eased behind a large yew shrub, close enough to hear but hidden by the dense branches.

"The arrangements are proceeding as discussed?" White asked, drawing deeply on his cigar.

"I am a man of my word." Wentworth's tone carried warning beneath its civility. "She will comply, or face the consequences of defiance."

"You're certain she understands the gravity of her situation? The girl has shown more spirit than anticipated."

Sebastian pressed closer to the shrub, his fingers gripping the cool stone of the nearby railing.

"She will do as she is instructed," Wentworth said, exhaling smoke slowly. "Or she may find herself facing circumstances similar to those that befell her mother."

White's low chuckle made Sebastian's skin crawl. "One must sometimes be firm with the gentler sex. They require guidance."

"Rose would be wise not to follow her mother's path of obstinacy. In hindsight, we should never have allowed women to learn to read. It gives them too much power."

"I trust there will be no repetition of past difficulties?" White asked.

"That depends entirely upon Rose's willingness to accept her duty." Wentworth flicked ash from his cigar. "I have made the consequences of rebellion quite clear to her."

"And our other arrangements remain secure?"

"For the moment. Though the situation has become more urgent than anticipated." Wentworth's voice dropped. "Rose has learned things she ought not know. The timeline must be accelerated."

Sebastian's blood turned cold.

"How accelerated?"

"Tomorrow. Before she can act upon her newfound knowledge."

Tomorrow. They meant to marry her off tomorrow.

"That is rather sudden," White said, though he sounded pleased rather than concerned.

"Sudden circumstances require swift action. Eleanor discovered things she ought not have known as well. I will not make the same error twice—allowing sentiment to delay necessary action."

"And if Rose proves as troublesome as her mother?"

"Then she will learn that defying me carries the same price it always has." Wentworth's voice held no emotion whatsoever. "I protected this family's interests then, and I will do so now."

White ground out his cigar against the stone railing. "I understand perfectly, my lord. Rose will present no difficulties once she is properly guided."

"See that she does not. I have worked too long to build what we have to allow one foolish, spoiled girl to destroy it."

They replaced their masks and moved back toward the ballroom doors, leaving Sebastian frozen behind the yew shrub.

Tomorrow. If he did nothing, Rose would be married to Baron White tomorrow, and God only knew what horrors awaited her after that. Worse, if Wentworth discovered Sebastian's true identity before he could act, he might well be the next to meet an "accidental" fate.

Sebastian stumbled to a stone bench just off the terrace, his mind reeling. What could he possibly do to save Rose from this nightmare? If she remained in this house another day, all was lost.

For years, his every thought had been consumed with one goal—exposing the truth about his father's death and reclaiming the Ashford name. He had promised James and Sophia that he would right this wrong, that he would restore their family's honor.

But sitting here in the sweet night air, listening to the distant music from the ballroom where Rose was trapped in a web of her father's making, Sebastian felt something fundamental shift within him.

He thought of his father—gentle, loving, devoted to his children even after losing his beloved wife. Lord Ashford had set aside his own grief to honor his dying wife's final request: to love and protect their children as she would have done.

Perhaps it was time for Sebastian to honor that same spirit of sacrifice.

Rose had never been part of his plans for revenge. He had not anticipated falling in love with the daughter of his enemy. Yet here he was, and the truth was undeniable. He would rather ensure Rose's safety than prove his father's innocence. He would rather protect her than reclaim his birthright.

Even if she could never forgive his deception. Even if she chose to walk away from him once she learned who he truly was.

The realization should have felt devastating—abandoning the promise that had sustained him through years of exile and servitude. Instead, it felt like awakening from a long, bitter dream.

His siblings would understand. They loved him regardless of titles or estates. And perhaps, just perhaps, love was stronger than hatred after all.

Sebastian rose from the bench, his resolve crystallizing. Tomorrow was too late to begin planning Rose's salvation. It had to be tonight.

# CHAPTER SIXTEEN

"LADY ROSE, IS it true?" Daphne asked, adjusting her lavender mask adorned with gauzy butterfly wings. The scent of ladies' perfumes drifted from the ballroom behind them as her friends ushered her onto the moonlit balcony. "You're to marry Baron White tomorrow?"

Lydia, Arabella, and Violet gathered around her like conspirators, their silk skirts rustling against the stone balustrade. The distant sound of violins and laughter seemed to mock Rose's predicament.

Rose nodded, her throat tight with unshed tears. "Yes, he says I have no choice, or he'll see me committed to Bedlam. Or worse."

"What do you mean, worse?" Arabella's voice sharpened behind her fox mask. "Rose, you're frightening us."

"Indeed." Lydia's owl mask bobbed as she leaned closer. "Speak plainly."

Rose glanced toward the ballroom's glowing windows, ensuring they were truly alone. "There's no escape now that I know the truth about his enterprises. They're more determined than ever to keep me silent. One way or the other."

"This is bad," Lydia said under her breath. "What are we to do?"

Arabella stepped forward, her mask making her appear predatory in the moonlight. "We shall spirit you away tonight. After the festivities end, Lydia and I will see you safely hidden."

"Father claims no corner of England exists where he cannot find and punish me."

"Nonsense. I have connections among certain resourceful ladies who excel at such disappearances." Arabella's tone carried the confidence of one accustomed to bending Society to her will. "We could exchange masks during the evening's confusion, create a diversion."

Rose caught sight of the ornate clock visible through the ballroom doors. "I must return. I've promised Mr. Clarke the next dance."

"That towering gentleman?" Violet asked with curiosity. "He cuts quite an imposing figure."

"Indeed, rather substantial," Arabella added with barely concealed amusement.

Rose promised to find them later and hurried back toward the ballroom, her heart already dreading the charade she must perform.

THE MOMENT ROSE entered the glittering ballroom with its crystal chandeliers casting dancing shadows across the polished floor, the air thick with perfume and the heat of hundreds of bodies, she regretted accepting Mr. Clarke's invitation. Couples whirled past in a kaleidoscope of jewel-toned silks and elaborate masks, their laughter piercing her melancholy like shards of glass. She longed only to see Sebastian, yet knew it was impossible. Duty demanded her compliance, even as her heart rebelled.

Mr. Clarke materialized before her like a specter. "Lady Rose?"

Something in his voice made her pulse flutter with recognition, though his elaborate Bauta mask concealed every feature. He stood tall and commanding in emerald evening wear, his presence both unsettling and oddly comforting. Like fragments of a half-remembered dream, familiarity teased at the edges of her consciousness.

"Good evening again, Mr. Clarke."

He stepped closer, executing a perfect bow that spoke of gentle breeding. When she placed her gloved hand in his considerably larger one, his grip proved firm and warm even through the barrier of silk. Her pulse quickened as they assumed position for the waltz.

His movements commanded the floor with confident grace, guiding her as if they'd danced together countless times. How divine it felt to be held in such strong arms, the heat of his palm burning through her stays where it rested at her waist, their breath mingling in the intimate space between them. He made her feel utterly secure, as though he would catch her should she stumble, regardless of what trials awaited.

Ridiculous thoughts. She knew nothing of Mr. Clarke. She could neither see his face nor place his voice with certainty. Yet her treacherous body responded exactly as it did to Sebastian, all fluttering heartbeats and tingling awareness. He possessed Sebastian's height and broad shoulders, his purposeful bearing.

Could he have gotten in somehow? His mask covered his entire face, which was unusual. Most men wore only half-masks.

"Tell me," she murmured, scarcely aware the words had escaped, "have we partnered before? You seem most familiar."

A pause stretched between them, filled only by the orchestra's lilting melody. "Would you recall such an occasion?"

"Would you not?"

"Any gentleman privileged to hold you thus would carry the memory to his grave."

Her breath caught as he spun her expertly, his grip tightening possessively at her waist. Who was this mysterious man? She dared lift her gaze, desperate to glimpse some telling detail, but the mask revealed nothing.

How could it be Sebastian? By what miracle could he have

gained entry?

The music began its final, haunting refrain. He held her motionless in that last beat of silence, the spell of the dance suspended between them like a held breath. Then he leaned close, his voice a whisper that seemed to caress her very soul. "Do not marry him tomorrow. Run."

The words struck her like lightning, sending shock waves through her entire being. Recognition crashed over her with devastating certainty. "Sebastian?"

"Do you know me truly, Lady Rose? With or without this mask?"

"It would seem I do," she breathed, wonder and terror warring in her chest.

Without another word, he turned and strode toward the terrace doors with that distinctive, purposeful gait she'd memorized from her bedroom window. The determined set of his shoulders, the angle of his proud head, the way he moved as though the very world would bend to accommodate his passage.

Sebastian. But how? And why risk everything to be here?

Before she could gather her scattered wits, Baron White appeared at her elbow like a malevolent shadow. "My dear, I believe our dance is next?"

BARON WHITE WORE a heavy, grotesque mask in deep gold and bronze, shaped like a wild boar. How perfect for him. Suddenly, she felt violently ill.

From the moment she placed her hand in his, a cold weight settled in her stomach. His considerable belly pressed against her stays as they moved through the dance, his breath thick with brandy and cigars. Perspiration seeped through his gloves, dampening her own, and she focused on breathing through her mouth, willing herself not to retch.

White led her through the steps with all the grace of a lumbering bear. Where her previous partner had been steady and fluid, White was heavy-handed and oblivious, yanking her too close, moving with jarring, awkward motions that left her stumbling to keep pace. This was the supper dance, meant to be elegant and celebratory—the last before masks came off. But there was nothing elegant about it. There was only dread and the knowledge that if she didn't escape, she would belong to this sweating, panting creature.

He leaned in close, his voice warm with drink and something far more unsettling. "You look quite appetizing in that gown. When we're wed, I'll have different costumes for you each evening. Silk, velvet, perhaps nothing at all. It shall be most delightful."

She stiffened but kept her expression hidden behind her mask, thanking God for the concealment. "I am not a doll to be dressed up for your amusement."

White chuckled indulgently, as if she were a child who hadn't yet learned her proper place. "You say that now, my dear, but you'll learn soon enough. Wives always do. You'll discover how pleasant it feels to be properly guided."

His fingers pressed into the fabric of her sleeve, just hard enough to leave a message without leaving a mark. "You won't need books or contrary opinions. You'll have me to think for you. I shall be everything to you. And should you stray—should you give me even a whisper of reason to believe your affections lie elsewhere? I will ensure no gentleman ever finds you desirable again."

She said nothing. Couldn't. His tone remained soft, conversational, but carried an undercurrent of menace that made her skin crawl.

White leaned closer still, his labored breathing hot against her ear. "We shall have such agreeable times together, you and I. Provided you prove biddable."

Her insides recoiled, but she kept her face carefully blank. She had to escape him. But first, she must survive this dance.

Across the ballroom, she caught sight of Arabella dancing with Lord Ellsworth. She tried desperately to catch her friend's eye, but the masks concealed too much.

"Who was the man you danced the waltz with?" White asked. "You seemed familiar with him."

"Mr. Clarke means nothing to me." She spoke calmly, even though she was a mess of nerves. "I don't truly know him. Whatever you observed was mere politeness. And even if it weren't, what does it signify now? I'm to be your wife on the morrow."

He studied her slowly, as if assessing whether she was sufficiently pliable to mold. His damp fingers slid lower on her waist before she managed to edge away.

"Stop," she whispered. "Someone might observe us."

His smile spread slow and serpentine. "Then behave yourself, my darling. What transpires after we're wed depends entirely upon your conduct. I can prove most generous. Or most unpleasant."

A chill wrapped around her despite the ballroom's stifling heat. She had no choice. Not yet. But if she could find Sebastian, speak to him before the night ended, perhaps she might finally have answers about who he truly was. She scanned the crowd desperately. There! On the far side of the room, near the terrace doors. The gentleman in green.

Sebastian.

He slipped through the doors and vanished.

Panic flared in her chest. She had to reach him. But first, she had to lose White.

As the final notes played, White bowed with exaggerated gallantry, then clasped her fingers in a lingering, possessive grip. "Now I shall escort you to supper."

The supper gong rang out across the ballroom. Guests began removing their masks amid animated chatter and compliments. Rose lowered hers to dangle from its ribbons. When White turned to acknowledge another gentleman's greeting, she saw her opportunity.

"Baron White, might I refresh myself before we dine?" She spoke sweetly, touching his sleeve with what she hoped appeared wifely deference. "I'm rather overheated from dancing, and I shouldn't wish to embarrass you with such a flushed complexion." She smiled, soft, obliging, utterly docile.

His chest swelled with satisfaction. "Very well. Don't tarry."

She curtsied and turned, her stomach already twisting as she hurried across the ballroom floor. The moment she cleared the doorway, she gathered her skirts and ran toward the rose garden, her heart hammering against her ribs.

*Please be there. Please be waiting.*

LANTERNS ILLUMINATED THE garden pathways for guests who might wish to take the evening air, thus she had no trouble finding her way. As she approached the rose arbor, she spotted the shimmer of emerald silk. It was him.

"Hello. Wait, please." Her slippers flew over the gravel as though the devil pursued her. Which, she reflected grimly, he very well might be.

She arrived breathless seconds later. The lanterns cast dancing shadows but couldn't disguise the masked figure who had stopped before the wooden swing. He stood with his back to her, shoulders rising and falling as if he too struggled for breath.

"Please, tell me who you are."

Slowly, he straightened and turned. The intricate details of his mask remained barely visible in the lamplight. He had not yet removed it.

She swallowed hard and stepped closer. "Please. Take off your mask. I must see who you are."

A pause stretched between them, filled only by the distant sound of music and laughter. Finally he spoke: "You already know the answer."

She did know. The way he moved, the way he had touched her during their dance, the way her treacherous body responded to his mere presence. No one but Sebastian had ever stirred such feelings. She suspected no one else ever could.

He hooked his fingers beneath the mask's edge and pulled it away with one fluid motion. Sebastian stood before her, transformed by elegant evening dress yet unmistakably himself. She drank in the sculpted planes of his face, the waves of dark hair, that determined mouth she had dreamed of kissing.

Sebastian had risked everything to infiltrate her ball. But why?

Her temper suddenly blazed. He would tell her the truth, or she would walk away and never look back. "What are you truly doing here? You're no gardener. No man dances as you do without years of proper instruction. You're a gentleman, aren't you?"

"Lady Rose, it's difficult to explain."

Heat, fury, and desperate longing crashed through her in equal measure, leaving her breathless and shaking. "Why are you at the ball in disguise? What game have you been playing with me?" The worst possibility struck her like a physical blow. "Did my father employ you to watch over me?"

"God, no. I want nothing to do with your father's vile enterprises."

"Then what?" Her pulse thundered so loudly she could barely hear her own voice. "Your continued silence only compounds your deceptions. Can't you see that?"

Sebastian's jaw tightened visibly. "I hardly know where to begin."

"Try the truth." Her voice cracked. A reflection of her breaking heart.

Sebastian stepped toward her, regret flickering in his dark eyes. "I came here seeking vengeance. For what your father did to my family."

"What do you mean?" Her mind raced through possibilities

but could settle on none that made complete sense. "What did he do to your family?"

Sebastian exhaled slowly, as if steeling himself for battle. "Forgive my bluntness. I know no gentler way to tell you this. I am Sebastian Ashford. Lord Ashford was my father. Your father orchestrated his execution for your mother's murder—a crime of which he was entirely innocent. Since I was twelve years old and watched Papa hang, I have thought of little else. My sole ambition has been proving what Wentworth did and reclaiming what was stolen from us. Your father murdered your mother, Rose. Then he had Hargrave plant evidence in our gardens. He allowed an innocent man to die for his crime, leaving us orphaned. He stripped us of our titles, our inheritance, our only surviving parent. He destroyed our lives, and I came to destroy his."

At first, she couldn't even process what he'd said. Her heartbeat stuttered, her hands trembling around the fabric of her gown. "You're an Ashford? But why pretend to be a gardener?" Even as she asked, she realized how foolish the question was. They had left him nothing when they found Lord Ashford guilty.

"Where did they send you after...after the execution?"

Sebastian's expression darkened like storm clouds gathering. "We were dispatched to a distant cousin who set me and my brother to work in stables and gardens while my sister scrubbed floors. The Langstons treated us little better than slaves for years. In fact, their cruelty rivals your father's. Lord Wentworth consigned us to hell on earth. You've seen the evidence carved into my back."

Her thoughts tumbled wildly, unable to fully grasp what he was revealing. "You came here to ruin my family?"

"Your father. Not you."

It was too much to comprehend. All these weeks, he had been performing an elaborate charade.

"I came to expose Lord Wentworth, to gather evidence proving my father's innocence."

"You've been lying to me this entire time? Sneaking about, collecting information?"

"Keeping this secret has been eating me alive. I've desperately wanted to tell you, but I was terrified you wouldn't understand. He is your father. I'm merely a stranger seeking to destroy him."

Her shoulders sagged as she exhaled. "You haven't discovered any evidence, have you? It's impossible. My father always prevails."

"I've heard testimony from servants convinced of his guilt, but nothing that would stand in court."

"No magistrate would heed them," Rose said. "Servants' words against a lord's?"

"Precisely. Your father has won. He will escape justice for everything. Murdering your mother, orchestrating my father's death, condemning us to years of abuse. The death of Lizzie." His voice grew heavy with defeat.

Rose crossed her arms, studying him carefully. "How did you gain entry tonight?"

"Hale assisted me. He discovered my true identity and proposed we collaborate. He's known who I am for weeks."

"Because he loved Lizzie." Understanding dawned. "He wanted to help you achieve vengeance."

"Indeed. But it's hopeless. Your father wields too much power."

"Are you certain he committed these crimes?" Rose asked, though something deep within her already knew the answer. "Killed my mother, framed your father—how can we be absolutely sure?"

"Earlier this evening, I followed him and White onto the terrace. I concealed myself behind the shrubbery and heard him speak the words plainly."

"What words?"

"That he's wedding you to White to ensure his silence regarding their illicit business. And that he murdered your mother."

Black spots danced before her eyes. "He confessed outright?"

"He stated in absolute terms that you would suffer your mother's fate should you prove rebellious."

A sob tore from her chest. "How could he? How could he steal my mother from me?"

"I cannot fathom such evil. Nor can I understand how he allowed an innocent man to hang. We may never comprehend his motives, but we must face the truth of who he is and what transpired twelve years past. Everyone in this household knows it, though we cannot prove it." He paused, his voice softening. "But I can choose to live in freedom, releasing these futile desires for justice. I want to do so—for you. I've learned something profound since meeting you. Love proves stronger than hatred. I choose love over vengeance."

She stared at him, certain she must be dreaming.

"I'm desperately in love with you," Sebastian said softly. "My heart has belonged to you since first I saw you. Come away with me. We'll build a new life together."

"But how could we ever manage it?"

"You would have to accept me despite my lack of title or fortune. Abandon all this luxury to live on a working man's wages."

"Is such a thing truly possible?"

"If you wish to be with me, then yes. I can protect you, provide for you."

"No." The word escaped before she could stop it. "It won't succeed. Father will hunt us down." Her father would find them, and they would both suffer his wrath.

"I'll find a way to keep you safe."

But she couldn't focus on his promises. Another voice echoed in her memory. Mrs. Blythe's words from weeks ago.

*They never found her mask. We all thought it peculiar. Lizzie searched the lady's quarters thoroughly, but it had vanished entirely.*

The loose floorboard in her father's study. He had noticed her staring at it and grown defensive. Had he hidden the mask there? Finding it would prove his guilt beyond question. Could there still be hope?

"They never found my mother's mask."

"What?" Sebastian asked, confusion clear in his voice.

"The mask she wore that night. The night he killed her." Yes, she had said it aloud. She knew it was true now. Had known it for weeks, buried beneath layers of desperate denial. "Sebastian, I believe I know where it is. Father concealed it in his study."

"Why would he retain such evidence?" Sebastian asked. "Why not dispose of it with the candlestick?"

She didn't answer immediately because suddenly, without warning, images began flooding her vision—memories long suppressed rushing back with devastating clarity. Her mother on the study floor, blood pooling beneath her golden hair. Lord Wentworth standing over her corpse.

Before that scene, she saw her father reaching for the heavy silver candlestick, moving with terrifying swiftness as her mother tried desperately to flee. The sickening crack as it connected with Lady Wentworth's skull. Her mother crumpling like a broken doll.

Rose whimpered as another memory surfaced. Her father ripping the mask from the lifeless body, holding it aloft like a trophy as he whispered, "You have done this to yourself."

"I remember," Rose whispered, her voice barely audible.

Vertigo seized her, and she could no longer stand. Her knees buckled, sending her tumbling onto the damp grass at Sebastian's feet.

He immediately knelt beside her, his voice urgent with concern. "Rose, what do you remember?"

She clutched desperately at her silk skirts, still trapped in that long-ago night. The study had reeked of candle wax and her father's cigars. "He used the candlestick. She tried to escape, but he was too quick, too strong."

"You witnessed it?"

"Yes. I saw everything." The suppressed memories felt like shards of ice in her chest. Until this moment, she had forgotten.

Her mind had protected her from the unbearable truth.

"Where were you hidden? Why weren't you abed at such an hour?"

Excellent questions. How had she seen them? Why had she been awake? She closed her eyes, forcing herself to return fully to that terrible night.

She had awakened because of noise from the ball below, disoriented and frightened in the darkness. "I woke wanting my mother. I went searching for her and ended up in Father's study. But I heard them approaching down the corridor, arguing violently. I didn't want them to discover me there and face punishment, so I hid in the closet."

Her eyes flew open as the full horror returned. She trembled so violently her teeth chattered together. "Oh, Sebastian, I watched it all happen."

"Tell me," Sebastian said gently. "I'm here with you. He cannot harm you now. I know it's agonizing, but let the memories play out."

She nodded, steeling herself to witness it all again. Through the wardrobe's narrow slats, she had seen her parents before his desk, voices raised in furious argument.

"I know what you've done," Lady Wentworth said, her usually gentle voice sharp as steel.

"What is it you believe you know?" Lord Wentworth replied with deceptive calm.

Lady Wentworth lifted her chin, delicate features drawn tight with righteous fury. "I overheard White tonight, boasting of how vast his wealth has grown and why. You're his partner in this smuggling venture? French brandy? Oh, Richard, how could you? Lord Ashford told me everything he's suspected of you this very night. You've deceived me all these years, used Papa's money to fund criminal enterprises. He would be appalled."

"You've enjoyed a comfortable existence, dearest. Why should you care how I provide it?" His voice turned to flint. "How dare you flaunt Lord Ashford before me."

"It's my inheritance you've squandered, or have you forgotten you were penniless when we wed?"

"Women cannot hold property, you little fool. Everything belongs to me now. You exist to bear me an heir and look decorative. Neither of which you've accomplished satisfactorily."

"Rose should be sufficient. She's perfect in every way."

"She's not a son."

"You're avoiding the subject, as always. What if I were to inform the magistrate of everything I've learned? What then?"

Lord Wentworth sighed, shaking his head as if she were a child throwing a tantrum. "No, you won't risk that. You'd lose everything if I were arrested."

"*You* would lose everything. Not I. I have Rose, and she's all I require. I'd rather live in poverty than with a criminal."

And then he moved, swift as a striking serpent. He reached behind him for the heavy silver candlestick, the one Rose had been warned never to touch lest she drop it on her foot.

She could still hear her father's labored breathing as he stood over the motionless body. He crouched beside her mother for a long moment, tilting his head as if examining a painting, then violently stripped the mask from her neck.

In the wardrobe, Rose's small fingers clamped over her mouth, her tiny chest rising and falling in panicked, silent gasps. *Mummy. Mummy.*

Lord Wentworth pried up the loose floorboard and thrust the mask into the hiding place before replacing the wood. Finally, he walked from the room as casually as if he were merely fetching his evening tea. She heard his footsteps fade down the corridor.

"He concealed the mask beneath a floorboard, then simply left her there," Rose said to Sebastian, tearing herself from the past. "I crept from the wardrobe, desperate to reach Mummy, but Mary appeared. She told me not to touch anything and hurried me upstairs. She rushed me to my chamber and made me promise never to tell anyone what I'd seen. She said I must forget it all, that everything would be well again."

"But it wasn't," Sebastian said softly.

"Mary must have heard the entire confrontation and rushed in to protect me from discovery."

"We were right. She knew more than she admitted," Sebastian said.

"She was only thirteen herself—barely more than a child."

Sebastian took her trembling, gloved hands in his steady ones. "Two children who witnessed something so heinous that at least one of you buried the memory to survive it."

"I remember everything now." The words felt like liberation and condemnation combined.

"If we can locate that mask and convince Mary to accompany us to the constable with your testimony maybe we can finally have justice."

A voice cut through the night air behind them, coldly precise and calculating: "How very touching."

Rose spun around in horror.

Baron White stood at the garden's entrance. His mask had been discarded, revealing a face flushed with exertion and drink. Yet, his eyes were sharp, predatory, entirely sober.

"I must confess, I've been listening for some time," White said conversationally, stepping closer with measured precision. "Such a fascinating tale. Lord Wentworth's confession overheard on the terrace. Your recovered memories of that tragic night twelve years past. The location of crucial evidence." His smile was reptilian. "Most illuminating indeed."

Rose's blood turned to ice as understanding crashed over her. He had heard everything.

"You see, my dear," White continued, his tone almost pleasant, "you've just provided me with the most valuable currency in existence—information that could destroy your father completely. The question now becomes—what shall I do with such power?"

Sebastian stepped protectively in front of Rose, but White merely chuckled.

"No need for heroics, gardener. I'm not here to harm anyone. Quite the contrary. I'm here to make a proposal." His gaze fixed on Rose with calculating intensity. "You see, Lady Rose, I no longer require your father's partnership. With what I've just learned, I can control him entirely. His smuggling operation, his fortune, his very freedom. All mine to command."

"What do you want?" Rose whispered.

"Ah, the pertinent question." White's smile widened. "I want you to marry me tomorrow, exactly as planned. You will be the perfect, dutiful wife. You will never speak of what transpired tonight, what you remember, or where any evidence might be hidden. In return, I will allow your father to live out his days in comfortable ignorance rather than at the end of a rope."

Rose felt the trap closing around her. "And if I refuse?"

"Then I shall present everything I've heard tonight to the proper authorities. Your father hangs for murder, you face charges as an accessory after the fact for concealing evidence, and your precious gardener here meets the same fate as his father. Though this time for the very real crime of trespassing and conspiracy." White's voice remained maddeningly calm. "The choice is entirely yours, my dear. A comfortable marriage to me, or the gallows for everyone you hold dear."

The silence stretched between them, filled only by the distant sound of laughter from the ballroom. Rose realized with growing horror that White had outmaneuvered them all. He didn't need violence or threats. He held their very lives in his calculating hands.

"I'll give you until tomorrow morning to decide," White said pleasantly. "Though I suspect you already know there's truly only one choice, don't you?"

# CHAPTER SEVENTEEN

"INDEED THERE IS." A calm voice from the shadows behind the rose trellis. "Though perhaps not the choice you imagine."

White spun around, as Constable Stephens stepped into the lamplight, his expression grim but unsurprised.

"Constable." White's voice had lost all its calculating smoothness, replaced by something that almost resembled panic. "I… we were just…"

"Discussing blackmail, extortion, and accessory to murder?" Stephens said. "Yes, I heard quite enough." His steady gaze moved to Rose. "Lady Rose, are you unharmed?"

White's mind was clearly racing, searching for an escape route. "This is all a misunderstanding. A lovers' quarrel, nothing more."

"Baron White, you are under arrest for the assaults committed against Lady Margaret Jones, Miss Catherine Mills—maids whose testimonies you no doubt thought would remain buried." He took a step forward, his expression cold and resolute. "And based on what I've just witnessed, I'm adding conspiracy and attempted extortion to the charges. And there's your smuggling operation. I would venture to guess if anyone is to hang, it will be you." He paused, letting the silence stretch. "I came here tonight to take you into custody. I didn't expect you to be so obliging as to confess to additional crimes in front of witnesses."

White staggered backward, his composure cracking visibly. "This is impossible. How long have you been—"

"Long enough." Stephens stepped closer, his hand resting on the pistol at his side. "Mr. Hale brought me compelling evidence this afternoon regarding both your illegal activities and Lord Wentworth's smuggling operation. I've been observing the estate since dusk, waiting for the appropriate moment to act."

"Constable, surely we can discuss this as gentlemen," White said, his voice taking on a wheedling tone completely at odds with his earlier confidence. "I can provide you with information about Lord Wentworth's operations that would prove far more valuable than—"

"Than watching you attempt to blackmail his daughter with threats of false imprisonment and murder?" Stephens's voice turned arctic. "I think not."

White's face contorted with desperate fury as he realized his situation was hopeless. "You have no idea what you're interfering with. The profits from our arrangements could make you a wealthy man—"

"And there's the attempted bribery of a peace officer to add to your charges." Stephens drew his pistol with practiced ease. "Place your hands behind your back, Baron White. You're coming with me."

"This is outrageous!" White's mask of civility finally shattered completely. "I am a peer of the realm! You cannot treat me like a common criminal!"

"You are a common criminal," Rose said quietly, finding her voice at last. "You prey upon women who cannot defend themselves. You threaten and manipulate for your own gain. Your title means nothing when weighed against your actions."

White turned on her with venom. "You self-righteous little chit. Do you think this changes anything? Your father is still a murderer, and without my protection—"

"Your protection?" Stephens interrupted with cold amusement. "The protection of a man who just attempted to extort sexual compliance through threats of false accusation?" He shook his head. "I think Lord Wentworth will find his situation much improved without your particular brand of assistance."

Sebastian stepped forward, his voice carrying years of suppressed rage. "Baron White, you've spent your entire adult life harming innocent people. Tonight, that ends."

"You have no right to speak to me, you worthless—"

"Sebastian Ashford has every right," Stephens said firmly. "As does Lady Rose. As do all the women you've hurt over the years." He gestured with his pistol. "Now turn around and place your hands behind your back, or I will be forced to make this arrest far less comfortable for you."

Faced with no other choice, White slowly complied, his shoulders shaking with impotent rage. "This isn't over. I have connections, influence."

"Had," Stephens corrected as he secured White's wrists with iron shackles. "Past tense. I suspect your connections will quickly distance themselves from you once the truth comes out."

As if summoned by the commotion, footsteps approached through the garden. Tobias Hale emerged from the shadows.

"Constable Stephens," Hale said with evident relief. "Thank God you arrived in time."

"Your information proved invaluable, Mr. Hale," Stephens replied.

"We'll need formal statements from all of you," Stephens said. "But first, we must locate Lord Wentworth and search for the evidence Lady Rose described." He turned to Sebastian. "Mr. Ashford, I believe you deserve to witness your father's name being cleared at last."

Sebastian's voice was thick with emotion. "Twelve years I've waited for this moment."

Rose's heart twisted at the rawness in his voice. So many years, so much weight he'd carried alone. But she no longer questioned his heart. He had told her he loved her. He had been willing to walk away from his revenge—for her.

And in that moment, she knew. He meant it. He still meant it.

"Mr. Hale, would you go inside and have my deputies secure Mr. Hargrave?" Stephens asked.

"Nothing would please me more," Hale said, before tearing across the yard toward the house.

Rose drew a slow breath and stepped forward, her voice steady. "What will happen to my father?"

"Justice, Lady Rose," Stephens said solemnly. "At long last. For your mother. For Lord Ashford. For everyone who suffered because of his actions."

Somewhere inside the house, she heard her father's voice raised in fury, the sound of boots on polished floors. Her stomach clenched, but she did not waver. The man who had killed her mother, who had lied to her, who had nearly sacrificed her future, was about to face the reckoning he never thought would come.

"We should go inside," Rose said. "I need to show you where the mask is hidden. If it's still there."

Sebastian moved closer, his eyes never leaving hers. "Rose, you don't have to do this."

"Yes, I do." She looked up at the man who had come into her life in disguise and shown her the truth. "I need to see this through. For her."

They walked side by side toward the house, the night thick with rose-scented air. Her mother's rose garden, planted with such love, the only thing left of her. No, that wasn't right. *I am here*, Rose thought. *I made it.*

Baron White was in custody. Her father would soon face judgment. And Sebastian—Sebastian had found the justice he came for.

But he had also found her.

She glanced at him. His borrowed finery still clung to his frame, but beneath it, he was still the man who had knelt beside her in a rose garden and wrapped her bleeding hand in his own.

What came next was uncertain.

But those were questions for later. Right now, she had a promise to keep to her mother's memory, and a father to confront with the truth of what he had done.

BY THE TIME they returned to the house, most of the guests had departed or were slipping away in tight-lipped silence, leaving behind a weary, wide-eyed staff to handle the remains of the night. Baron White had been taken into custody by two constables and led out the front door in disgrace, shackled and snarling threats no one took seriously.

Inside, a second group of constables had already detained Lord Wentworth in the study. He stood near the fireplace, arms bound, his expression dark with barely suppressed fury.

Sebastian felt the curious stares of the servants as he and Rose followed Stephens down the corridor, Hale just behind them. Despite everything that had happened, he ached for Rose. She moved with grim purpose, but her pale face and trembling hands betrayed the toll it was all taking.

"I'll need statements from anyone who worked here twelve years ago," Stephens said as they reached the study. "But first, let's find the mask."

He closed the door behind them, sealing out the whispers and curious stares.

Seconds later, a knock came, followed by Hale's swift entrance. His coat was unbuttoned, his hair windblown. "Hargrave's gone. One of the kitchen maids saw him ride off not five minutes ago."

Stephens swore under his breath. "He won't get far. I have men watching the roads."

"We're looking for the mask," Rose said, voice taut. "Then my father can answer for what he's done."

Wentworth didn't speak. His jaw was locked tight, his posture unchanged, as if denial alone could undo what had already begun.

"I'd not noticed the floorboard until today," Rose said. "Because the rug covered it. Someone must have moved it." Mary, she realized. It was her way of helping without getting involved and risking her job or life. Smart.

Stephens nodded toward the hearth. "Go on, Lady Rose."

Deputies flanked the doorway as Rose took a letter opener from the desk and knelt at the spot on the floor where the board was loose. Sebastian watched her hands shake as she worked the metal tool beneath the wood. His chest tightened with anguish. She was so brave, so determined to see this through, but what would this cost her?

For a terrible moment, as her back rose and fell, and she hung her head, Sebastian thought the mask wasn't there. However, seconds later, she lifted it from its hiding place where it had remained concealed for twelve years and held it up for them all to see.

Although faded from time, dark stains still marked the delicate material. Rose's hands trembled as she passed it to the constable. "I was right." Her voice was flat, almost hollow. "It's over."

Wentworth sneered. "She never understood what I sacrificed. She would have thrown it all away."

"She was trying to protect me," Rose said.

"She was trying to unravel everything I'd built. She couldn't see the necessity of it. The cost of power."

Stephens stepped forward. "Are you admitting to the murder of Eleanor Wentworth?"

Wentworth ignored him, eyes fixed on his daughter. "She gave me no choice. She would have gone to the magistrate. She would have destroyed us."

"So you killed her," Rose said.

"I did what was required," he said coolly. "I preserved the

family name."

"And you let an innocent man hang for it," Stephens said.

Wentworth's face darkened with something close to grim pride. "Ashford was hardly innocent. He lived a charmed life. The title. The land. The admiration. He took what should have been mine."

Rose stepped forward. "You mean Lady Ashford? The woman you loved?"

Wentworth's voice dropped, bitter and full of old wounds. "She was meant to be mine. But Ashford had the name. The fortune. She chose him, and I was left with scraps."

"My mother was not a scrap," Rose said. "But that aided in your temper, didn't it? When she mentioned his name? He'd told her about what you were really doing, so you wanted to punish him for it."

"You destroyed him," Sebastian said. "For simply telling the truth to your battered wife about who you really are. Isn't that right?"

Wentworth turned sharply. He stared at Sebastian. His gaze narrowed. "Who are you?"

Sebastian stepped forward. "I'm Sebastian Ashford. Son of the man you murdered. Son of the woman you coveted."

Recognition dawned in Wentworth's eyes, followed by blazing fury. "You?" His voice shook with outrage. "You've been under my roof all this time?"

"Waiting," Sebastian said. "Watching. Doing everything I could to bring you down."

"You dare to judge me?" Wentworth roared. "Your father took everything I ever wanted."

"That's a lie you've told yourself, but we all know the truth," Sebastian said. "Every lie, every cruel act, brought you here. You are to blame for it all."

"You were a child. I should have dealt with you then," Wentworth spat.

"That's enough," Stephens said. "Lord Wentworth, you are

under arrest for the murder of Eleanor Wentworth, the framing of Lord Ashford, the death of Lizzie Morrison, and for criminal smuggling. You will be taken into custody and held until your trial."

Wentworth's eyes flicked toward his desk.

Sebastian tensed. "He's going for something—"

In one violent motion, Wentworth lunged, slammed his shoulder into Stephens, and yanked open the drawer. He seized a pistol, spun, and leveled it.

"I built this life! You think I'll be marched through the streets like a thief? I am Lord Wentworth!"

"Put it down," Stephens ordered.

"I will not swing from the gallows. I choose my end."

Rose met his eyes. "Then choose it. At least be honest in the end."

He stared at her, chest heaving, fury burning bright. "You truly hate me."

"With everything I have," she said. "You took everything from me."

His lips curled, bitter to the last. "I was never sorry. Nor am I now."

Then he turned the pistol on himself and pulled the trigger.

The deafening crack split the air. Rose's knees buckled, and she stumbled backward as Wentworth crumpled to the floor. Sebastian lunged forward instinctively, catching her elbow as the acrid smell of gunpowder filled the room.

"Christ," Hale breathed, his face gone ashen. He pressed his back against the wall, hands shaking.

From the corridor came a woman's scream, followed by running footsteps and frantic voices. Stephens cursed viciously under his breath as he knelt beside the body, then stood with blood on his hands.

"He's gone," he said, fury tight in his voice. "The bastard robbed us of justice."

Rose drew in a sharp, shuddering breath. Her composure

wavered for just a moment—a single tear sliding down her cheek before she wiped it away with trembling fingers. "Good," she whispered, but her voice cracked on the word.

Sebastian's chest constricted as memories of his own father's violent end crashed over him. The relief he'd expected felt hollow, tainted by the horror of witnessing another death. He wanted to pull Rose close, to shield her from all of it, but she stepped away from his steadying touch.

Hale swallowed hard, his voice rough. "Lizzie can rest now."

"Not yet," Rose said. Sebastian noticed her hands clenched so tightly he feared her nails would draw blood in her palms. "Not until we find Hargrave." She lifted her chin, though her face remained deathly pale. "And we will do so, won't we, Constable?"

"We will, my lady." Stephens dipped his chin, still scowling at the body that had denied him his prisoner.

"And now I must care for my staff," Rose said, her voice steadier now but chilling all the same. "They will no doubt be frightened and bewildered."

She turned from the study without a backward glance, stepping carefully around the spreading dark stain on the carpet.

Sebastian watched her go, the woman he had come to love walking away from him without a word. The violence of the moment had shattered something between them—he could see it in the way she held herself apart. A heaviness settled in his chest. She would not want him now. Even if she loved him, he would forever be connected to her mother's and father's deaths.

He'd gotten what he wanted, and yet he felt nothing but an aching, empty sadness.

# CHAPTER EIGHTEEN

Rose STEPPED OUT of the study and into a corridor buzzing with whispers. A few remaining guests were making for the front door, valets scrambling to collect cloaks and hats. Footmen moved through the hall with quiet urgency, guiding people toward the exits with murmured apologies.

Rose kept walking.

As she passed the ballroom, she caught sight of lingering guests craning their necks, murmuring behind gloved fingers, men standing stiffly, pretending not to stare. The orchestra had long since packed up, the tables sat half-cleared, glasses still catching candlelight. A night meant for celebration had curdled into something else entirely.

At the edge of the room Daphne, Lydia, and Arabella huddled together. When Rose entered, they turned to her as one.

Arabella stepped forward first. "Rose, are you all right? We saw them taking Baron White away and then we heard a gunshot."

Rose shook her head gently. "My father's taken his own life. After admitting to everything we already knew, including murdering my mother."

"Oh, Rose, I'm sorry," Arabella said. "What can we do?"

"Nothing tonight. Thank you for your kindness, but I think it best if you return to your rooms. I will need you in the morning."

Daphne reached for her hand, squeezing it briefly. "We'll be here. Whatever you need."

Lydia's eyes were glassy. "We'll stay as long as you want us."

"Do you know where Mrs. Blackwell is?" Rose asked.

"I saw her head upstairs," Daphne said. "After they arrested White. I assumed she was going to her room but who knows with that woman."

"And this was before the gunshot?" Rose asked.

"That's correct," Arabella said. "We feel sure she knew what was coming for your father. The way she scurried away like a black widow proves it."

"I'll deal with her tomorrow then." Rose's voice was quiet but sure. "Now I must speak with Mrs. Blythe and Prudence."

Arabella nodded, understanding. "Of course."

As they turned away, disappearing into the shadows of the corridor, Rose lingered for a moment longer, taking in the ballroom. The flicker of dying candles. The forgotten waltz sheet on the music stand. The scent of roses clinging to the air, stubborn and bittersweet.

Then she turned and made her way toward the servants' stairs and down to the kitchen.

The room still held the heat of the afternoon, and scents of the feast Mrs. Carter and her staff had prepared lingered. At the long wooden table sat Mrs. Blythe, Mrs. Carter, and Prudence, their expressions anxious in the flickering lanternlight.

The leapt to their feet at the sight of her.

"Lady Rose, are you safe?" Mrs. Blythe asked. "When we heard the gunshot we were frightened that something had happened to you."

Rose walked over to stand at the end of the table. "I am fine. Shaken, but fine. My father has taken his own life. After admitting that he murdered my mother." Her hands were still trembling, though she clasped them tightly in front of her. "As I'm sure you know, Baron White has been arrested." She explained as succinctly as she could the nature of his and her father's crimes, even though they probably already knew. "Our gardener,

Sebastian, is the eldest child of Lord Ashford. He came here in the hope of discovering what really happened to my mother and prove his father's innocence. That has been done."

A sharp breath escaped Mrs. Carter's lips. Prudence's eyes brimmed with tears, but she said nothing. Mrs. Blythe simply wrung her hands.

Rose forced herself to say the next part. "And I have remembered everything from that night. I was in the room. I saw him do it."

"The nightmares?" Prudence asked. "They were to help you remember."

"That's right. Mary found me and took me upstairs. She heard it all from the hallway."

"I thought she knew more than she would say," Mrs. Blythe said.

"No one would have listened to her, even if she had come forward," Rose said.

"There has been too much tragedy in this house," Mrs. Blythe said, wiping her eyes with a hanky.

"All of it because of Father," Rose said. "I know there will be further inquiries, and more scandal, and no telling what will happen with the estate. I may no longer have a home here but I will do whatever I can to protect the staff. Constable Stephens wants to speak to anyone who was there the night of my mother's murder. At long last, you will be heard."

"We will answer as best we can," Mrs. Blythe said.

"We're glad to be asked," Prudence said.

"What has been done about the house guests?" Rose asked.

"Unfortunately, many of them witnessed Baron White's arrest and most retired to their rooms," Mrs. Blythe said. "No one will linger tomorrow. I made sure of that."

Prudence, her voice hoarse, asked. "Are we all safe? Tonight, I mean."

Rose nodded. "Yes. Stephens and his men are here. There will be no more violence tonight."

"Lady Rose, do you need anything?" Mrs. Carter asked. "I can make tea."

"No, thank you. Go to bed," Rose said gently. "You've all done more than enough these last few weeks. Sleep in if you can. Tomorrow will have to be faced. It's best we do it after a good night's rest."

"Let me help you to your room, my lady," Prudence said.

"Yes, thank you." Rose gave her a sad smile before turning to head back up the stairs, with her faithful maid behind her.

ONCE THEY WERE safely in her room, she let Prudence unbutton her gown, slide it from her shoulders, and untwist the pins from her hair.

Once she was in her nightgown and her face washed, Rose climbed into bed and curled onto her side, the blankets cool against her skin. Prudence moved quietly around the room, tidying as she always did, as if routine could hold the world together.

"Is there anything I can get you?" Prudence asked.

Rose reached for her hand and gave it a squeeze. "Before you go to bed, please ask Mr. Hale to meet me in my father's study at eleven. I need to understand the legal matters. Once I do, I can begin making plans."

"Yes, my lady."

There was a long pause.

"Did the staff know about Sebastian?" Rose asked at last. "Who he really was?"

"No, my lady. I would have told you if I'd known."

"I knew he was not who he said he was, but I could not have guessed that he was the eldest son of the man my father destroyed."

"How could you?"

Rose nodded, tears brimming but unshed. "At least I know the truth. About everything now. I feel lighter, somehow. Even though there are so many questions about what the future will bring."

"I'll be here by your side, no matter what."

Rose smiled faintly. "Thank you, dear Prudence, for your loyalty and calmness. You provide me great comfort, as you always have."

"It's my pleasure, Lady Rose."

"Please, go rest. I won't need you until after ten."

Prudence curtsied and then left the room.

Rose rolled onto her back, staring at the ceiling, the ache behind her eyes finally giving way to exhaustion.

She thought of Sebastian. Of his deception, yes—but also of his words earlier in the garden. He had been willing to walk away from all of this for her. But would he change his mind? Perhaps she would always be the daughter of the man who wrecked his life. Was there really any way for them to be together or was the past too complicated? Too tragic?

She slipped her hand beneath her pillow and pulled out his handkerchief, breathing in the faint scent of soap. It steadied her, softened her chest just enough to let sleep come.

And it was thus that she finally slept—alone, but no longer lost.

SHE WOKE LATE the next morning to Prudence arriving to help her bathe and dress. While Prudence fixed her hair, she drummed up the courage to ask how the staff was doing. "How did everyone seem this morning?"

"They are fine. Mrs. Blythe brought us all together at breakfast to explain everything to the others. Most already knew, of course, having been on duty as everything unfolded."

"They must be terrified of what happens next," Rose said.

"Yes, they're concerned for the future. As you know, most of us come from the village and have known nothing else. The thought of working elsewhere is overwhelming. Yet, they all declared their loyalty to you, my lady. There's not a servant in this house who thinks ill of you."

"How kind," Rose said softly.

She wanted to ask after Sebastian but didn't have the words to do so. However, she needn't have worried. Prudence brought him up first.

"Everyone's reeling over who Sebastian really is. As you can imagine."

"Yes, they have every right to feel surprised and perhaps duped." Rose's voice wavered. "Prudence, have you guessed how I feel about him?"

"Yes, my lady. I know you well."

"And the others?" Rose asked.

"There have been rumors, Lady Rose. About you and the gardener developing a friendship. Others have seen you bring him books and linger to speak with him."

"Yes, it is true. What are they saying about it?"

"Nothing unkind, my lady. But some noticed. That's all."

"I see."

"This morning Mrs. Blythe said Sebastian will have to make an appeal to the Crown if he is to regain his title. She said perhaps his family's fortune will be restored by the monarchy in compensation for what happened to him and his siblings."

A dart of optimism pierced through Rose's gloom. Could he finally get back everything he'd lost? If so, what would it mean for them?

"Lady Kingsley, Lady Merriweather and Miss Norbury have asked if they might have a word with you before they leave. May I show them into the drawing room after you've had breakfast?"

"Yes, of course."

"Also, Mr. Hale asked for your forgiveness. He cannot meet

this morning, as he and Sebastian departed very early for London. Mr. Hale left a note explaining that time was of the essence. They need to reach the estate's solicitors and begin Sebastian's appeal to the Crown while the events of last night are still fresh in officials' minds."

"This very day?" Rose asked, her heart sinking. Sebastian was gone. He hadn't even said goodbye.

"Mr. Hale said they would return by evening—they're taking the fastest horses and pushing hard to make the journey in one day. Mr. Hale asked if he might call on you tonight to convey the nature of those conversations."

"They'll be back tonight?" Rose tried to keep the hope from her voice but it proved impossible.

"That's right, my lady."

Would Sebastian be with Mr. Hale? Or would he remain in London to pursue his restored future, leaving her and this painful chapter behind?

Rose's stomach fluttered with nerves as the grim reality of her situation settled over her. So much depended on what instructions her father had left regarding the estate. Most likely, some distant male relation would inherit everything she had ever known and loved, while she would be cast out with nothing.

A hollow ache settled in her chest. If she truly had no claim, no inheritance—where would she go?

Perhaps her new friends would help her find a way forward. She could stay with Arabella, maybe attempt another Season in London. Though the very thought of giving her heart to anyone but Sebastian made her sick to her stomach.

For now, she must resign herself to the inevitable truth that her life was about to change drastically. Whether Sebastian would be part of that new life remained to be seen. He had achieved what he came for—justice for his family. Did he still want her, or had learning the full extent of her father's crimes made him reconsider?

After all, she was the daughter of the man who had destroyed his family. That was a burden that might prove too heavy for any love to bear.

"One last thing, my lady. Mrs. Blackwell is in her room, making preparations to leave. If you want to speak to her before she leaves, now would be the time."

Rose thrust back her shoulders. "Yes, I should speak to her. I'll do that before I have breakfast."

"As you wish, my lady."

Sorting through the next steps felt like swimming through mud. But as she'd done for weeks, she drew in a deep breath and prepared to face whatever came next.

ROSE FOUND HONORIA in the blue guest chamber, hastily stuffing gowns into a traveling case with none of her usual grace. Gone was the perfectly coiffed woman who had glided through the ballroom the night before. Her hair hung in disheveled waves, her face was pale and pinched, and her hands shook as she worked.

"Lady Rose." Honoria straightened, attempting to summon her old hauteur, but it rang hollow. "I didn't expect to see you."

"I thought we should speak before you left."

Honoria's laugh was bitter. "Come to gloat, have you?"

"No." Rose stepped into the room, closing the door behind her. "There is nothing of this situation that would give me cause to gloat."

For a moment, Honoria's mask slipped entirely. Rose saw exhaustion there, desperation, and something that might have been pain. "Yes, I suppose not."

Rose moved closer, studying the woman who had tormented her for weeks. "I have to wonder, why? Why were you so cruel to me? You could have simply pursued my father without trying to destroy me."

"Could I?" Honoria whirled around, her composure finally cracking. "Your father made it clear. He wanted you gone. Those were his terms. He would not marry me until you were married."

"I wonder why?" Rose asked. "Do you know?"

For a moment, she thought Honoria wouldn't answer. But after a second, her shoulders sagged and she sat on the edge of the bed, clearly exhausted. "He knew how clever you are. And honorable. Like your mother. He knew it was only a matter of time before you discovered the truth of his operations."

It was as she'd suspected. Father had wanted her out of the way, but it had to be with White. To ensure silence from his only child.

"What about you?" Rose asked. "Did you really want to be married to a criminal? And a murderer?"

"I have to survive." Honoria's voice turned harsh. "You have no idea what it's like to depend entirely on a man's whims for your very existence. To know that one wrong word, one moment of displeasure, could leave you destitute. To smile and charm and debase yourself for the mere hope of security. I did what I had to do."

Rose felt something unexpected—a flicker of sympathy. "Actually, I do know. I was about to be handed to Baron White. It that's not powerless, then I'm not sure what is."

Honoria studied her face. "Your father has left us both with little hope. He's not the first selfish man to leave me with nothing." She turned back to her packing, her movements now mechanical. "I'm sure he won't be the last."

"Where will you go?" Rose asked softly.

"I have a distant relation in Yorkshire. I'll go there and beg her to let me stay until I can find another man who wishes to marry a woman like me." The words came out stilted, clearly painful.

"And Violet?"

"She'll return to her father."

Honoria's hands stilled again. When she spoke, her voice was barely audible. "Think what you want of me, I truly hoped to help her get out of her father's house."

"If I can help her, I will."

"Yes, but as we've agreed, neither of us can," Honoria said. "We're deluding ourselves if we think otherwise."

"I cannot give up. I'll keep trying to do what's right, even though it seems hopeless."

"You're a fighter. Like me."

Rose met her eyes steadily. "I cannot forget what you tried to do—how you wanted me out of the way—helping my father trap me into marrying Baron White. But I can understand why you did it. And I can wish you well despite it all."

Honoria nodded slowly. "That is kind of you."

For a moment, they stood in silence.

Then Honoria returned to her packing with renewed efficiency. "For whatever it's worth, I do hope you find security in the years to come. And that no one can ever take it from you."

"Thank you." Rose moved toward the door, then paused. "Good luck, Mrs. Blackwell. And safe travels."

Rose left without waiting for a response, but as she closed the door, she heard something that might have been a sob.

Walking down the corridor, Rose felt a deep sorrow for the woman who had tormented her. She had looked her in the eye and had seen not a monster, but a woman trying to survive in a world made for rich men. It didn't excuse what Honoria had done. She had acted out of selfishness and cruelty. Regardless, the human instinct to survive perhaps outweighed all else. Compassion and generosity were luxuries for those who had secure futures. Was Rose about to succumb to the same fate? Would her next chapter be one of manipulation and desperation, clinging to whatever or whomever would offer her a warm place to sleep?

LATER, HER FRIENDS gathered around her in the drawing room—Arabella, Daphne, Lydia, and Violet were all there. Rose had decided to tell them the whole truth about her feelings for Sebastian. There was nothing to lose now and she found herself longing for female advice.

"I'm in love with Sebastian." Rose stared down at her hands, fingers twisting in her lap. "And I haven't the faintest idea what's to become of me."

"We figured as much," Arabella said.

"It all feels rather hopeless," Rose said.

Daphne hesitated, then asked quietly, "But what if Sebastian's title is restored? His fortune? Is there a chance you might marry?"

"Dare I even think of such an outcome or is it foolish?" Rose asked. "There is so much uncertainty about both our situations."

"You deserve so much better than what your father left you with," Lydia added, her voice fierce with protectiveness.

"We must never give up hope," Daphne said. "Look at all that's transpired over the last few weeks. Surely there's evidence that somehow things work out as they should."

Arabella reached over and squeezed her hand. "And remember, you can always come to live with me. Write to us the moment you know what your father's left you and we'll plan accordingly."

Rose nodded, her throat tight. "You are a dear friend. I cannot thank you enough. You all are."

"Even though men betray us, we have one another," Daphne said with a rueful smile.

Rose's eyes misted. "You're all far too good to me."

"And what of you, Violet?" She turned to the quietest of their group. "Are you going home to your father?"

Violet's shoulders sagged. "I have nowhere else to go. I shall return and wait for next Season."

"You're not going home to him," Arabella said sharply. "You're coming with me."

Violet's eyes went wide. "Truly?"

"I've already instructed the footmen to put your things in my carriage. I'll look after you from now on." Arabella's tone softened. "And soon, we'll all be together again and all of this will be a distant nightmare. We will all get through this, do you understand?"

"Together," Daphne said.

The others murmured eager agreement just as one of the footmen appeared. "Your carriages are ready, my ladies."

They embraced, and promised letters to keep one another informed. Rose watched from the front steps as her friends departed, their voices calling back to her until the carriages disappeared down the drive.

The house felt impossibly quiet afterward. Rose wandered to the library and settled into her usual chair, but the book in her lap remained unopened. Instead, she gazed out at the bright summer afternoon and thought of her mother—how disappointed she would be to see what had become of everything her father had left her.

A soft knock interrupted her reverie. "Lady Rose?" Mrs. Blythe appeared in the doorway. "Constable Stephens is here to see you."

Rose set aside her book, her stomach clenching. "The drawing room, please."

As Mrs. Blythe turned to go, Rose called after her. "Mrs. Blythe?" The older woman paused. "After Mother died, when I was so grief-stricken, you took care of me. I've never forgotten that kindness."

Mrs. Blythe's eyes grew bright. "It has been my honor." She hesitated at the threshold. "Don't give up hope just yet."

"I won't," Rose promised, though her voice wavered.

Alone again, Rose took a steadying breath and smoothed her skirts. Whatever news the constable brought, she would face it. What other choice did she have?

Rose hesitated just outside the drawing room door, pressing her palms against her skirts to steady herself before stepping inside.

Afternoon sunlight slanted through the tall windows, casting long shadows across the Persian carpet. Constable Stephens stood near the hearth with his hat tucked under his arm, his weathered face grave. He turned at the sound of her entrance, bobbing his head in polite acknowledgment.

"My lady."

She forced a smile, crossing the room on unsteady legs. "Please sit with me. May I offer tea?"

"No, thank you. I wanted to come out as soon as I could, knowing you must be feeling a great sense of uncertainty."

She settled onto the sofa, motioning for him to take the chair opposite. The leather creaked as he sat. "Yes, unfortunately this is true."

"I've taken it upon myself to take care of a few details," Stephens said, his fingers working the brim of his hat. "I hope I've not overstepped."

She clasped her hands tightly in her lap. "Any help is welcome, Constable. I'm quite overwhelmed. Please, go on."

He met her gaze steadily. "Baron White has been transferred to London. He'll stand trial there for his crimes."

A shiver went through her. He was truly gone from her life now, locked away where he could no longer hurt anyone. The relief was so sudden and overwhelming that her vision blurred for a moment.

"How long?" Rose managed.

"Hard to say. Could be months before trial, then…" Stephens shook his head. "Given what we've uncovered, he'll likely never see freedom again."

Rose exhaled slowly, her shoulders sagging as tension she'd carried for months began to ease. He had no more power over her life.

"There is another matter that must be addressed, my lady." The constable's tone grew more serious.

She straightened, wariness creeping back. "Yes?"

He seemed to choose his words carefully. "The investigation into your father's smuggling operation has uncovered the full extent of his crimes. The scale of it is far larger than we suspected."

Rose's stomach dropped. "How much larger?"

Stephens rubbed his jaw, looking suddenly older. "French brandy, arms dealing, counterfeit coinage. The docks down in Hastings have been running shipments for him for years, but we've now identified smaller operations stretching as far as Liverpool and Bristol. He wasn't only smuggling goods but arranging for stolen cargo to be 'laundered' through legitimate businesses."

Her knuckles went white where she gripped the sofa's arm. Each revelation felt like another blow. "What does this mean for the estate?"

The constable's pause stretched too long. When he finally spoke, his voice was gentle but firm. "That depends. If it's discovered that your father funneled his criminal earnings into the estate—if the manor itself was bought or maintained with tainted funds—the Crown could seize portions of it."

The words hit her like a physical force. Rose felt the blood drain from her face, the room tilting sickeningly around her. "Seized?" The word came out as barely a whisper.

"If there's proof that his wealth was gained illegally, yes. But it will take time for the courts to determine. Months, perhaps years. And even then, they may not seek to claim the estate itself—only the profits from it."

Rose pressed a hand to her chest, her breathing shallow. Everything, the only home she'd ever known, her mother's memory embedded in every room, could all be stripped away. She forced herself to focus on the constable's weathered face, using it as an anchor against the panic threatening to pull her under.

"My lady," he said, his voice gentler now. "I tell you this not to frighten you, but to prepare you. There are men who profited from his schemes, men who may yet come forward to try and claim what they believe is theirs."

Rose closed her eyes briefly, summoning what remained of her courage. When she opened them again, her voice was steadier. "So what must be done?"

"For now, you must be cautious. The law will take its course, and those involved in the smuggling operation will be held accountable. But in the meantime, you should have someone you trust overseeing the estate's affairs."

"Mr. Hale has my full trust."

"He's a good man and will do well by you. It was a brave thing—coming to me as he did."

Rose nodded, her throat tight. "You are correct. He will always have a place with me." She paused, the qualifier catching in her throat. "If I have a place, that is."

The constable leaned forward slightly. "I'm sorry it took such a long time for justice, my lady."

She sat quietly for a moment, letting the implications settle over her like dust after an explosion. Then, almost afraid to hope, she asked, "What will happen to Sebastian Ashford? Do you have any idea?"

"It depends on the mercy of the Crown, but I suspect his title will be restored and perhaps some of the wealth. Though it's hard to say for certain." Stephens studied her face. "He means a great deal to you, doesn't he?"

Rose felt heat rise in her cheeks. "He does. Despite how we came together."

"Don't let your father take him from you, my lady. He mustn't win from the grave."

"Thank you for your counsel."

"Indeed. And I must tell you—after asking around and speaking with your servants about the late Lord Ashford—by all accounts, he was a truly noble and benevolent man. Sebastian seems to have inherited the same qualities. All of which bodes well for the Ashford's good name and the restoration of their wealth."

"I hope you're right. He and his siblings have suffered greatly. Because of my father." Her voice caught. "If I were in a position to make it right, I certainly would."

Stephens smiled, his brown eyes warm. "These things have a way of working themselves out, one way or the other. One must not lose faith that good will come to the pure of heart."

Rose blinked back tears, overwhelmed by his kindness. "I'm grateful for everything you've done, including the arrangements about my father. I feel so uncertain about everything."

"I do beg your pardon, my lady, but there's nothing uncertain about your character. Don't let anyone tell you differently."

"You're too kind."

Stephens rose, settling his hat back on his head. "If there is anything further, I will let you know. In the meantime, keep your wits about you."

He turned to leave, pausing just before the door. "And if anyone comes asking questions about what your father left behind, send for me. Do not hesitate. Day or night."

Rose remained on the sofa long after his footsteps faded, watching the afternoon light creep across the floor, and thinking about Sebastian.

ROSE SAT AT the window seat in her room, almost numb. So much had transpired in the last few days it was hard to comprehend how drastically her life was about to change.

A soft knock interrupted her thoughts.

"Come in," she called, expecting Prudence.

Instead, Mary stepped inside, her face pale and her hands twisted in her apron. The young maid had been with the household for years, but Rose had never seen her look so distressed.

"Lady Rose," Mary began, then faltered. "I... I wondered if I might have a word?"

"Of course. What can I do for you?"

Mary perched on the edge of the chair by the window, her back rigid. For a long moment, she stared at her hands before finally meeting Rose's eyes.

"Mrs. Blythe says you remember everything now. About... about that night."

Rose's chest tightened. "Yes."

Mary's face crumpled. "Can you ever forgive me, Lady Rose? I'm the one who told you to forget."

The anguish in Mary's voice made Rose's heart ache. She took Mary's cold hands in hers.

"Mary, we were both children. Very frightened ones at that."

"But I should have done better."

"But how?" Rose asked gently. "Spoken up? Who would have listened to us back then? Not with Constable Morrison in charge."

Mary's eyes filled with tears. "I heard it all. Every terrible sound. And when I found you..." She shuddered. "You were so small, so terrified. I thought if I could just get you to forget, maybe you could heal. Maybe you could be safe."

"You were trying to protect me."

"I was trying to protect myself too," Mary whispered. "I was so afraid he'd come for me if he knew I'd heard."

Rose squeezed her hands. "Of course you were afraid. You were barely older than I was."

"I've carried it all these years, my lady. Knowing what really happened, watching you struggle with those nightmares, wondering if I'd done the right thing." Mary's voice broke. "When Mrs. Blythe said you finally remembered, I thought you'd hate me for making you forget."

"Oh, Mary." Rose felt tears prick her own eyes. "I could never hate you. You tucked me into bed that night when I was falling apart. You stayed with me until I stopped shaking. You showed me kindness when I desperately needed it."

"But if I'd spoken up sooner, maybe everything would be different."

"Then we both might have ended up dead," Rose said firmly. "You made the best choice you could with what you knew then. And now, finally, the truth has come out anyway."

Mary searched Rose's face as if looking for any trace of deception. "You truly don't blame me?"

"Not for a single moment." Rose smiled through her tears. "Thank you for taking care of eight-year-old me. And thank you for finding the courage to speak to Constable Stephens when the time was right. Also, thank you for moving the rug. It was you, wasn't it?"

"Yes. It was all I could think to do." Mary dissolved into quiet sobs, and Rose simply held her hands until the tears subsided.

"It's over now," Rose said softly. "For both of us. We can finally let it go."

Mary nodded, dabbing at her eyes with her apron. "Thank you, my lady. I needed to hear that."

After Mary left, Rose went to her dressing table and examined herself in the mirror. She saw a woman who had not only survived, but one who had been surrounded by love all along. Even in the darkest moments, people had tried to protect her the only way they knew how.

Her father was gone. He could no longer hurt any of the people she loved. For that she felt grateful.

THAT EVENING, MR. Hale arrived just after supper. Rose found him waiting for her in the drawing room in one of the wing-backed chairs, looking weary but calm. The journey to London had clearly taken its toll. His boots were dusty, his coat wrinkled, and his cravat loosened. She'd never seen him so disheveled.

"My lady." He stood, greeting her with a nod. "Please excuse my appearance. I've not been to my cottage. I wanted to speak to you right away."

Rose hurried to the chair opposite him, her hands trembling slightly. "I appreciate it. Please, what did you learn?"

Hale's expression softened as he settled back into his seat. "Your father's will was clear, Lady Rose. Wentworth Manor and all associated properties are yours."

The words didn't seem to register at first. Rose blinked, her mouth opening slightly. "Mine?"

"Entirely. Without condition."

She stared at him, sure she heard him incorrectly. "But that cannot be. Why would Father do that?" Her voice caught. "He despised me."

"Perhaps. But he also wanted to keep the estate intact." Hale leaned forward, his voice gentle. "My instinct is that he intended to protect it from his illegal activities. For you."

Rose's hands gripped the arms of her chair. "What does that mean exactly?"

"The Crown will seize whatever money came from his smuggling. But the estate itself wasn't used as collateral for his crimes." Hale's weathered face brightened. "You own it free and clear, my lady. The manor, the land, the farms—all of it."

The room seemed to tilt around her. Rose pressed a hand to her chest, struggling to breathe. Everything she'd feared losing was all hers. Truly hers.

"I can scarcely believe it." She stood abruptly, pacing to the window. Her reflection stared back, pale and wide-eyed. "No unknown heir will come to claim it?"

"None. No court can strip it from you."

Rose turned back to him, tears streaming down her cheeks. Relief and sorrow warred in her chest. Father had done this for her. How strange, considering everything else. But perhaps there was a part of him that felt guilty and had wanted to protect her. Or, perhaps he'd just not gotten around to changing his will? She would never know. However, she had a future now. She could protect the staff. She could stay in the only home she'd ever known.

Hale watched her carefully. "You can do whatever you like with it. Sell it, lease it or remain here and rebuild."

She sank back into her chair, her mind racing. "Is it possible to make the estate profitable? Without the smuggling, I mean?"

"If you'd like me to stay, we can turn it around together." His confidence was reassuring. "Your father's methods brought in vast sums, yes, but with proper management, we can sustain ourselves quite comfortably."

"Do you want to stay?"

"If you'll have me. I know this place better than anyone. The tenant farms, the ledgers, which servants can be trusted." He paused. "Though I should ask—did you have any idea what your father was doing all these years?"

Rose shook her head. "I never thought about it at all. Isn't that awful? It was Lady Arabella who first told me what everyone else seemed to suspect. I feel like a fool."

"How were you to know, Lady Rose? He kept it all from you. And me, for that matter. I saw enough to know things weren't right, but he was careful to keep his illegal dealings separate from the legitimate estate work." Hale's expression grew thoughtful. "That separation is what will save us now."

She felt herself smiling for the first time in days. "This is wonderful news, though rather daunting."

"You're stronger than you know, Lady Rose. We'll manage it together."

"Thank you, Mr. Hale. For everything." Her voice grew thick with emotion. "None of this would have happened without your courage. Teaming up with Sebastian. Going to the constable."

He shifted uncomfortably. "When I learned of Stephens's

character, I felt it might be my chance to finally voice my suspicions. Though I'll admit, I hedged my bets. If I'd been wrong and word had gotten back to your father?" He shuddered. "I might be the one in prison instead of him."

"But you did it anyway."

"Someone had to."

They sat in comfortable silence for a moment before Rose's thoughts turned inevitably to the one person missing from this conversation. "Mr. Hale, what of Sebastian? Where is he?"

The older man's expression grew cautious. "He's returned to his brother in Brighton. He wanted to tell James what had transpired."

A lump formed in Rose's throat. Why hadn't he come back to see her first? They had so much left unsaid. "Did he learn anything in London about his situation?"

"He's begun his appeal to the Crown. I believe his title will be restored, likely with some compensation, but it may take months. Perhaps even a year."

Warmth bloomed in her chest despite her confusion. "When will he know?"

"In the next several weeks, he hopes."

Rose hesitated, then asked quietly, "Does he know about Father's will? That I've inherited everything?"

Hale's cheeks reddened slightly. "I'm afraid I was quite forthcoming. I was so relieved for you that I couldn't contain myself."

"Don't apologize. I would have told him myself." Her voice grew smaller. "Had he come back to me."

"May I speak plainly, my lady?"

She nodded, bracing herself.

"Sebastian believes you don't share his feelings. He wanted to give you peace, so he decided to step aside and fight the rest of his battles with his family."

Rose stared at him, shocked. "That's what he thinks? That I don't care for him?"

"He said you hadn't confessed otherwise." Hale's tone was

carefully neutral. "Is he wrong?"

She almost laughed at the optimism in his question. Sebastian had clearly won over the estate manager just as thoroughly as he had her. "When we thought I'd have to marry Baron White, Sebastian said we could run away together. Be poor but free. I was so overwhelmed, so frightened, that I didn't know what to say. Then Baron White arrived, having heard it all. And you know the rest." She spread her hands helplessly.

"Understandable. But your hesitation made him uncertain."

Rose stared down at her hands. "I fought my feelings, Mr. Hale. But there's something about him that moves me. He touches my heart in ways I didn't know were possible. I think of him every moment of the day. I couldn't stay away from him despite knowing how dangerous it was." She looked up, tears shimmering in her eyes. "I'm in love with him. Devastatingly so."

Hale leaned forward, his expression earnest. "Despite everything between your families? The history?"

"My father destroyed his family out of greed and jealousy. Should Sebastian and I deny ourselves love because of that?" Her voice grew stronger. "If I let disgust about our past dictate my future, then Father wins, even from his grave."

A slow smile spread across Hale's weathered face. "I couldn't agree more. Sebastian Ashford's a good man, Lady Rose. Courageous and honorable. Now that you can choose your own fate, I humbly suggest you choose love."

Something in his tone made her study his face more carefully. "You speak as if from experience."

His smile faltered. "I would choose love again, if it were ever offered to me. After what happened to Lizzie, I didn't think I'd ever be open to the idea. However, now that so much time has passed, I find myself longing for a love of my own." He trailed off, pain flickering across his features. "I think she would want me to find love again. If Hargrave is found and charged, I can finally move forward."

Rose reached over and squeezed his hand. "I'm so sorry. We

mustn't give up on finding Hargrave."

"Wherever that devil is hiding, his luck will run out eventually."

"The constable won't rest until he's found."

"I know. And when he is, I'll finally have peace."

"May I speak plainly, Mr. Hale, as you have done to me?"

"Please."

"There's a certain housekeeper who looks at you with a glimmer in her eyes. Have you noticed?"

He looked genuinely shocked. "Mrs. Blythe? Are you certain?"

"It's mere conjecture on my part but I've known her a long time. I'm fairly certain."

"I see." He tugged on his ear, gazing behind her for a moment. "She is a fine person. We've been close friends for years. I don't know why I've never considered it."

"Perhaps it's time?"

"Perhaps. And what of you and Sebastian? What do you plan to do?"

Rose drew in a deep breath, decision crystallizing in her mind. "I'm going to Brighton to see him. I must tell him how I feel."

Hale studied her face, then nodded slowly. "Shall I have them prepare a carriage for tomorrow morning?"

"Yes." Her voice wavered slightly. "I want him to come home to me. For good."

"I'll see to the arrangements. But I insist on accompanying you. A woman traveling alone isn't safe, especially with your father's associates still at large."

Rose felt a surge of gratitude for this steady, loyal man. "Thank you. We'll leave at first light."

"And Lady Rose?" Hale's eyes twinkled. "I have a feeling this story will have a much happier ending than either of you expects."

# CHAPTER NINETEEN

SEBASTIAN GUIDED TEMPEST through Brighton's narrow streets as afternoon shadows lengthened across the cobblestones. The familiar sounds and smells of the port city—shouting fishermen, creaking cart wheels, the tang of salt and fish— brought a bittersweet comfort. He'd come to tell James everything that had transpired, to share the miraculous news that their father's name could finally be cleared.

But more than that, he needed his brother to understand what had happened to his heart.

He dismounted outside the Stag & Anchor, his legs unsteady after the long ride. The tavern looked exactly as it had when he left, with its weathered timbers, patched roof, the painted sign swaying in the sea breeze. Through the grimy windows, he could see the familiar dim interior, a few patrons hunched over their ale.

Sebastian pushed through the heavy door, and the conversations faltered as heads turned his way. He'd forgotten for a moment that he was still dressed in the attire from the ball. The fine coat and clean boots marked him as someone who didn't belong in this rough establishment. If they only knew what he'd been through since the last time he'd stepped inside his brother's tavern.

"Brother, is it really you?" James's voice carried across the room, rich with disbelief.

James stood behind the bar, sleeves rolled up, a rag in his hands. He tossed the rag aside and came around the bar in quick strides.

"Sebastian." James gripped his shoulders, searching his face. "You look fine, although tired. What are you doing here? Have you brought good news?"

"I've brought the best news." Sebastian's voice was rougher than he'd expected. "It's good to see you. I've missed you."

James pulled him into a fierce embrace, and Sebastian felt some of the tension leave his shoulders. Whatever else happened, he had his family, his brother and sister who'd stood by him through everything.

"Come with me." James stepped back. "Let's go upstairs where we can talk properly. You look like you have quite a story to tell."

James led him through a narrow door behind the bar and up creaking stairs to the small apartment above. The main room was sparse but clean: a table, two chairs, a narrow bed, and a few books on sagging shelves.

"Please sit." James gestured to one of the chairs before moving to a small cabinet. "You look like you need a drink, and I suspect I will too after whatever you're about to tell me."

"It's been an extraordinary few weeks."

James poured two glasses of whiskey and settled across from him. "You look like Papa. Dressed in such dapper clothing." He gestured at Sebastian's fine clothes.

Sebastian took a sip of whiskey, feeling it burn down his throat. "That's because I am Sebastian Ashford again. Calling myself Doyle will no longer be necessary. Or will be, if the Crown accepts my petition."

James went very still. "You've done it?"

"I have."

"Tell me everything."

So Sebastian did. He told him about Mr. Hale's suspicions, about Rose's recovered memories of that terrible night, about the constable's investigation that had uncovered the full scope of Wentworth's crimes. He explained how Baron White had been arrested and sent to London, how her father had died during the confrontation, how the truth had finally come to light after all these years.

James listened without interruption, his expression cycling through shock, anger, and finally, a deep satisfaction.

"That blackhearted monster," James said when Sebastian finished. "Finally, we know the truth. Not that we doubted Papa's innocence, of course. It is exactly as he explained it to us before he was hanged. This is finally done. We can go forward with our lives."

"The loss remains, but it's easier to accept now that we have justice."

"And this Rose—Lady Rose—she helped you uncover all of this?"

"She did more than help. She risked everything." Sebastian's voice grew intense. "James, when she remembered what really happened that night, she could have stayed silent. She could have protected her father's reputation, maintained her position in Society. Instead, she chose justice. She chose the truth."

James turned back to him, studying Sebastian's face. "You care about her."

"More than care." Sebastian met his brother's eyes directly. "I'm in love with her, James. Desperately, completely in love with her."

James returned to his chair slowly, his expression unreadable.

"Wentworth's daughter," James said quietly. "This is unexpected."

"I know how it sounds."

"Do you?" James leaned forward. "Because it sounds like you've fallen in love with the daughter of the man who destroyed our family."

Sebastian felt his jaw tighten. "She's not her father, James. She's nothing like him."

"Tell me about her."

The simple request caught Sebastian off guard. He'd expected anger, perhaps even accusations of betrayal. Instead, James waited with genuine curiosity.

Sebastian struggled to find words. "She's been virtually imprisoned her entire life, controlled and manipulated by a man who saw her as nothing more than a tool for his ambitions. But instead of becoming bitter or cruel, she remained kind. Compassionate. Everyone who works for her or spends time with her for any amount of time loves her."

"And when you told her who you really were?"

"She was hurt, yes. Confused. But I told her how I felt and that I was willing to walk away and leave it be. For her. For love."

James was quiet for a long moment, turning his whiskey glass in his hands. "What did she say?"

Sebastian's confidence faltered. "That's where I grow uncertain. There have been moments when I was certain she shared my feelings, but I am not so sure."

"Why?"

"I'm not sure she could truly love someone who brought about her father's downfall, even if he deserved it. And no, she has not told me how she feels. In fact, the night it all went down, she left the room without even looking at me. Before I return to her and find out what's in her heart, I needed you to know what had happened and see if you can accept her as my wife. Should she have me, that is. Which is still very much in doubt."

James set down his glass and leaned back in his chair. "What kind of man was our father, Sebastian?"

The question seemed to come from nowhere. "He was good. Honorable. He loved his family. That most of all."

"And if he were here now, knowing everything you've told me about Lady Rose and of your deep feelings for her, what do you think he would say?"

Sebastian considered this carefully. "He would say that a person shouldn't be judged by their parents' sins and that if I love her, then I should pursue her with everything in me."

"Exactly." James's expression softened. "I think Papa would admire her courage."

Relief flooded through Sebastian so suddenly it left him breathless. "You will accept her? If she'll have me?"

"If you love her, then I will too," James said with a slight smile.

Sebastian felt his throat tighten with emotion. "I was afraid you'd see it as a betrayal."

"The only betrayal would be letting fear keep you from happiness." James stood and moved to clasp Sebastian's shoulder. "You've spent years seeking justice for our father. You've cleared his name and brought his killer to account. If you've found love along the way—especially with a woman brave enough to stand against her own father for what's right—then you have my blessing, brother. Completely."

Sebastian covered James's hand with his own. "Thank you. That means more to me than you know."

"So what now? When do you plan to return to her?"

"Tomorrow. I need to know how she truly feels." Sebastian paused, then smiled. "I need to tell her that I love her, not just as Sebastian the gardener, but as Sebastian Ashford. I want to offer her everything I am, everything I might become."

"And if the Crown restores our title and fortune?"

"Then I'll have more to offer her than just my heart." Sebastian's voice grew serious. "Which is what I want. I want to give her everything she deserves."

James grinned. "Then let's hope the Crown helps us."

Before Sebastian could respond, shouts erupted from the tavern below, followed by the sound of chair legs scraping against wood.

James sighed. "I must return. Some of the fishermen get rowdy when they've had too much ale." He moved toward the door, then paused. "Sebastian, whatever happens with Lady Rose, I'm proud of you. You've accomplished something incredible, and if you've found love in the process… well, that's more than either of us dared hope for when this all began."

"I couldn't have done it without your belief in me."

"That's what a brother's for." James smiled. "Now come downstairs. I'll have Mrs. Honeycutt make you some supper. Tomorrow you ride back to claim your future."

The weight that had been pressing on his chest for days was finally gone. James understood. James approved. More than that, his brother had helped him see that their father would have approved too.

Tomorrow, he would return to Wentworth Manor and lay his heart bare. Whatever Rose's answer might be, he would face it knowing he had his family's blessing and his father's memory guiding him forward.

# CHAPTER TWENTY

IT WAS NEARLY noon by the time they reached Brighton, the carriage lurching over uneven cobblestones. Rose's stomach churned, whether from the rough ride or her nerves, she couldn't say.

"Would you like the windows open?" Mr. Hale asked gently. "The sea air might help."

She nodded, and he pulled back the covering. Salt-tinged wind rushed in, carrying the sounds of a bustling port—vendors calling their wares, cart wheels clattering, dockhands shouting. Having spent most of her life in the countryside's quiet embrace, the city's pulse agitated her.

"Are you all right, my lady?"

"It's rather jarring." She pressed her hands together to still their trembling.

He smiled. "We're accustomed to quiet. You'll adjust."

The carriage turned onto a narrower street lined with taverns and boarding houses. Rose's heart hammered against her ribs. "Will we be able to find Sebastian's tavern?"

"It's called the Stag & Anchor," Hale said, peering out the window. "Ah, there it is now."

He rapped against the carriage roof, and they lurched to a stop. Rose stared at the weathered building before them. A tattered wooden sign depicting a rearing stag and anchor hung from a wrought-iron bracket. The tavern's timbers were weathered, its roof patched. Not exactly a gentleman's club. This was Sebastian's world. Thanks to her father.

A group of rough-looking men loitered outside. One spat onto the cobblestones, his eyes narrowing at the sight of her expensive carriage.

Rose's mouth went dry. "I'm suddenly quite nervous."

"I'll be with you every step." Hale's voice was steady, reassuring.

She drew a shaking breath. "I've come this far."

"Indeed you have."

Hale helped her down onto the odorous street. The mingled scents of brine, smoke, and unwashed bodies made her wrinkle her nose, but she lifted her chin and approached the heavy oak door.

A thin boy with unruly brown hair lounged nearby, bare feet dirty against the cobblestones. "Spare a ha'penny, miss? Ain't eaten today."

Rose pressed a coin into his palm without hesitation.

"Bless you, fine lady." He pocketed it and scurried away into the crowd.

Hale opened the tavern door, and Rose stepped inside. Thick air heavy with pipe smoke and cheap ale enveloped her. The few patrons turned to stare at the finely dressed lady who'd appeared in their midst, conversations faltering.

Rose ignored them, her gaze sweeping the dim interior until she found what she sought.

There he was. Sebastian sat at a scarred table near a dust-streaked window, dark hair falling across his brow, sleeves rolled up over strong forearms. Across from him sat a man with honey-colored curls and sharp blue eyes. Was this his brother, James? They were deep in conversation, heads bent close together.

James noticed her first, his body going rigid as he set down his mug. He murmured something to Sebastian, who turned toward the door.

Sebastian shot to his feet so quickly his chair nearly toppled.

His face went pale, then flushed. "Lady Rose?" Her name came out rough, disbelieving. "What are you doing here?"

The familiar sound of his voice made her chest tighten with longing. The smoky air, the curious stares, her racing heart faded into nothing. There was only Sebastian, only this moment, only the truth she'd traveled so far to tell him.

"I'm here to see you." The words rang clear in the sudden quiet.

Sebastian stared at her, his lips parting in shock. James half-rose from his seat, looking between them with keen interest. The other patrons had gone completely silent, sensing drama unfolding.

Rose took a step forward, her hands trembling at her sides. "Mr. Hale has brought me because I could not wait another moment. I had to see you."

# CHAPTER TWENTY-ONE

SEBASTIAN'S PULSE QUICKENED at the sight of the woman he loved. She looked lovely in her dark blue traveling cloak, but there was a lightness, a confidence that made her eyes shine. Justice had been served. She was free to choose her own life.

But had she come for him, or to confront him for his betrayal?

Sebastian nodded, his throat tight. "I'm suddenly without words."

"Perhaps we can start with an introduction," Rose said. "Is this your brother?"

"Yes. James, this is Lady Rose."

James bowed respectfully, his blue eyes taking her in with obvious curiosity. "It's a pleasure to meet you, Lady Rose."

"The pleasure is mine. I imagine the circumstances of Sebastian's and my acquaintance have been most unusual to hear about."

James glanced between them. "Unexpected, certainly. But my father used to say that solace often comes from finding good in even the worst circumstances. Even a kernel can bloom into something beautiful."

"He did say that," Sebastian said with a rueful smile.

Mr. Hale approached. Sebastian held out his hand for the man to shake, before introducing him to James. "This is the courageous Mr. Hale I told you about."

James suggested Mr. Hale come to the bar for an ale. After they were gone, Sebastian turned back to Rose. "Shall we take a walk? Somewhere we can speak privately?"

"Yes, if you think it's safe."

"You're safe with me."

He led her through narrow streets past the hum of taverns until cobbled paths gave way to dunes. The sounds of town faded, replaced by waves crashing gently against the shore. The sea glowed in the late afternoon light, silver and blue stretching to the horizon.

"It's beautiful," Rose said, her voice soft.

"I came here when I needed to think." He paused, then added quietly, "To plan."

She nodded, understanding flickering in her eyes. "I can imagine you here, contemplating your revenge."

There was no bitterness in her tone, but the truth hung between them nonetheless. Sebastian led her to a weathered log near the water's edge. They sat in silence for a moment, waves filling the quiet.

"Mr. Hale told me about your inheritance," he said finally. "Your freedom. I'm glad for you."

"It gives me opportunities I never expected." She turned to face him. "Sebastian, I have something to say, and now that I'm here, I hardly know how to begin."

He braced himself, expecting anger, recrimination.

"I've come to tell you I love you. And that I'd like us to marry."

His mouth fell open. "What?"

"I should have said it that night in the garden, but I was overwhelmed and then chaos ensued."

"I love you too. With everything in me. But are you sure about marriage?"

Her face went pale. "Why wouldn't I be? What else is there to consider now that I'm free?"

"Because I have nothing to offer you. My family is disgraced, my title stripped. And the scandal—marrying the man who brought down your father? Society will shun you. You would have to face that for the rest of your life."

Rose let out a bitter laugh. "I'll be shunned regardless. My father's actions have ensured that. No one will think of me without remembering what he did." She stared out at the water. "But I find I don't care. I'm free to choose what I want. Who I want. I choose you."

"But I'm poor, Rose. You should hate me for the lies and deceit."

"Do you want me or not?" Her voice broke slightly. "Because you seem to have a lot of reasons to reject me."

Sebastian's chest constricted at the tremor in her voice. "God, no. I'm so in love with you I can't think of anything else. I want you by my side, in my bed, building a life together. But I want what's best for you, and I fear I'm not it."

Tears gathered in her eyes. "That's your choice to make. I won't beg." Her voice grew stronger. "I've been at my father's mercy all my life. He took the person I loved most away from me. You can choose to let him do it again, or you can choose differently." She wiped her cheek with the back of her hand. "I've offered myself to you. If you don't want me, I'll go home heartbroken but proud of my courage."

He reached for his handkerchief and pressed it into her hands. "Making you cry is the last thing I want."

"Then don't." She dabbed at her eyes. "Tell me you'll come home with me."

"Will there be a day when you look at me and see only the man who destroyed your father?"

"Sebastian, you didn't destroy him—he did that himself. My God, he killed my mother and was ready to hand me to a monster." Her voice grew fierce. "When I look at you, I see the man who saved me. You offered to give up everything for me. I'll never forget that."

Sebastian reached out, brushing a tear from her cheek. "You saved us, Rose. Your courage, your goodness—that's what made this possible."

"Come home with me," she whispered.

He studied her face, seeing the determination mixed with vulnerability, the love shining in her eyes despite everything they'd endured. How could he refuse her? They belonged together, regardless of how they'd found each other.

"What will we tell our children about how we met?" he asked, a smile tugging at his lips.

Relief flooded her features. "The truth. No good comes from secrets."

"And about our first kiss?"

Her eyes widened. "I don't know."

"Shall we tell them about this afternoon? The sea breeze and the way you looked at me when I asked if I could kiss you at long last?"

"Are you asking?"

"I am."

"If we kiss, you must marry me."

"Yes," he said, grinning. "I surrender completely."

She tilted her face up to his, eyes soft and unafraid. "I'm ready."

Sebastian cupped her cheek, his thumb tracing her jaw. She leaned into his touch, lips parting slightly. He closed the distance slowly, giving her time to pull away. She didn't.

The first brush of his lips was gentle, questioning. When Rose responded by curling her fingers into his coat sleeve and pressing closer, he deepened the kiss, his hand slipping to her waist as the world fell away around them.

When they finally broke apart, both were breathing unsteadily.

"Oh my, that was quite pleasant," Rose said, wonder in her voice.

"Indeed it was."

"Perhaps we should practice more before the wedding."

Sebastian laughed, the sound carrying across the water. "I think that's very wise, Lady Rose. Very wise indeed."

# CHAPTER TWENTY-TWO

THE DAY AFTER her trip to Brighton, Rose stepped into the servants' hall, knowing this conversation was necessary. They deserved to hear directly from her that she and Sebastian were to marry.

The long wooden table was filled with staff taking their morning tea. Mrs. Blythe pouring fresh cups, Finch halfway through a biscuit, Prudence mending one of Rose's gowns. At the sight of her, those sitting stood respectfully.

"Good morning," Rose said, her voice warm but serious. "I hope you don't mind me interrupting your breakfast, but I wanted to speak with you all about something important."

"Of course, Lady Rose," Mrs. Blythe said, though Rose could see the slight tension in her shoulders. The uncertainty of recent days had affected everyone.

Rose looked around at the faces that had been her constant through so many years. "I know you've all witnessed quite a lot these past weeks. You've seen Sebastian's true identity revealed, you've watched constables come and go, and I'm sure you've wondered what all of this means for Wentworth Manor. For your positions here."

A few of the younger staff exchanged worried glances. Even stolid Mrs. Carter seemed to be holding her breath.

"First, I want to thank you for your unwavering loyalty, not just recently, but throughout my entire life. You've been my family when I had no one else." Rose's voice caught slightly. "You protected me, cared for me, and stood by me even when doing so might have put you at risk. I will never forget that. I hope my news will make up for some of the turmoil. My father has left me the estate and everything else, other than the illegal aspects of his business. I can do as I choose now."

Mrs. Blythe dabbed at her eyes, and Rose could see several others looking emotional.

"In addition, Sebastian and I are engaged to be married. As soon as the arrangements can be made, we will marry."

This brought smiles and murmurs of approval, though Rose could tell they were still waiting for the more practical information.

"I know some of you may be wondering what this means for the estate, for your positions. My father's illegal activities are finished forever. Sebastian, Mr. Hale, and I are committed to returning this estate to completely legitimate business. It may take time to rebuild, but we will do it properly."

She saw shoulders relax around the room.

"More importantly, you all have positions here for as long as you want them. This is your home too, and Sebastian understands that. In fact, he's specifically asked me to assure you that he values the kindness you showed him during his time here."

Finch, who had been looking particularly worried, visibly sagged with relief.

"There will be some changes, of course. Finch, Sebastian will need a proper valet—are you interested in the position?"

Finch nearly choked on his tea. "Me, my lady? But I'm no one important. Hargrave always said I was near useless."

"Sebastian and I wholeheartedly disagree," Rose said with a smile. "He appreciates your big, kind heart and your loyalty. We both feel you will shine in this new position."

"I'd be honored, my lady," Finch said, straightening with pride.

"We'll also need to hire a new butler and make other adjustments as we grow the legitimate business. But the point is, we're planning for growth, not reduction."

Mary raised her hand tentatively. "Will Lord Ashford—if his title is restored—will he be bringing his own staff?"

"He has no staff to bring, Mary. His family lost everything years ago. You are his staff now."

The warmth that spread across the gathered faces told Rose everything she needed to know.

"I also want you to understand that while Sebastian will be master of this house, I will still be involved in its daily operations. Mrs. Blythe, I'll still need your guidance. Mrs. Carter, your excellent meals. All of you—your expertise and care. Nothing fundamental changes about how we run this household."

"What about the village, my lady?" asked one of the footmen quietly. "There's been talk."

Rose nodded, having expected this concern. "There will be gossip, certainly. Some may disapprove of our marriage given our families' history. But we're prepared for that. What matters is that we know the truth, and we're committed to rebuilding this estate's reputation through our actions."

She looked around the room one more time. "Are there any other concerns? Questions about what's to come?"

"When might the wedding be, my lady?" Prudence asked shyly.

"Soon. Within the month, if possible. Which means we'll all be quite busy with preparations." Rose smiled. "I hope you'll help me make it a celebration worthy of a new beginning."

The mood in the room had shifted from worried anticipation to genuine excitement.

"We'll make it beautiful, Lady Rose," Mrs. Blythe said firmly. "Won't we, everyone?"

A chorus of agreement filled the room.

"Thank you," Rose said, feeling her throat tighten with emotion. "All of you. For everything you've done, and for everything you'll do."

As the staff began to disperse, chattering about wedding preparations and new arrangements, Mrs. Blythe approached Rose.

"That was well done, my lady. It was good for them to hear it from you directly."

"I couldn't let them wonder about their futures. They've sacrificed too much already."

"Shall we discuss the practical arrangements? There's quite a lot to organize."

Rose nodded, feeling a sense of peace settle over her. "Thank goodness for you, Mrs. Blythe."

"And you, Lady Rose."

A WEEK PASSED before Sebastian returned to the estate. He arrived on Tempest, wearing a well-tailored coat that transformed him from gardener to gentleman. Mrs. Blythe had prepared one of the guest rooms for him until the wedding, though she assured Rose their private quarters would be ready for their wedding night.

The day after his return, they gathered with Mr. Hale in the study to discuss the estate's future. Afternoon light streamed through the tall windows as Hale spread documents across the mahogany desk.

"The estate has always had potential for legitimate profit," Hale began, tapping the papers. "Your father chose smuggling because it was quick and lucrative, but it wasn't the only way."

Rose leaned forward, studying the detailed maps and ledgers. "What do you recommend?"

"Expand the cider orchards, improve the tenant farms, invest in livestock." His weathered finger traced property lines. "The land is fertile. With proper management, we can produce wool, grain, quality cider. Build a reputation as a respectable estate again."

Sebastian nodded thoughtfully. "And the trading connections?"

"Many merchants are eager to distance themselves from the scandal. I've already made inquiries with honest shipping companies in Brighton." Hale's eyes brightened. "They're interested in legitimate partnerships."

Rose felt hope budding in her chest. "How long before we see results?"

"A year, perhaps two for full recovery. But the foundation is solid. There's something else to consider," Hale continued. "The servants and villagers need to see that this manor is no longer a place of secrets. They need visible proof that you both mean to restore its honor."

Rose glanced at Sebastian, an idea forming. "What if we host a wedding feast? Invite everyone from the village, share our plans for the future?"

"I think that's splendid," Hale said warmly. "We haven't had a community celebration since your mother was alive."

"We could make it annual," Rose said, excitement building. "Tie it to the harvest, give everyone something to anticipate." She turned to Sebastian. "What do you think?"

His smile was answer enough. "I am in full agreement. A new tradition for a new beginning."

Rose felt her heart skip at the warmth in his eyes. "Then it is settled." She turned back to Hale. "There is one more thing. Would you walk me down the aisle on my wedding day?"

Hale went very still. His eyes grew bright, and for a long moment he seemed unable to speak. When he finally found his voice, it was rough with emotion. "Me, my lady?"

"You've been our truest ally through everything. There's no one else I'd rather have."

Hale pressed his lips together, blinking rapidly. "It would be my greatest honor."

After the meeting, Sebastian and Rose walked arm in arm to the rose garden. She untied her bonnet to feel the autumn sun on her face, breathing in the crisp air that promised winter's approach.

"I should check on the roses," Sebastian said. "Thorncroft hasn't hired a replacement yet, and I won't let aphids destroy your garden."

Rose smiled. "Do you mean, our garden?"

"I shall forevermore think of it as yours, my love."

They found the swing and Sebastian helped her settle onto the wooden seat before joining her, his thigh warm against hers.

"I'll never forget the first time I saw you here," he said. "You took my breath away."

"You were quite mysterious yourself. The brooding gardener with gentle hands."

He traced a finger along her jaw. "I'm beginning to remember who Sebastian Ashford was. It feels strange, but good."

"And how do you feel now?"

"Like I am exactly where I belong."

They swayed gently, discussing wedding plans and the harvest feast. The more they talked, the more Rose's excitement grew. This would be their fresh start—not just as a couple, but as part of the community.

She did have one niggling worry, however. "I know nothing about… what happens between husband and wife."

His hand stilled on hers. "It is of no consequence."

Heat crept up her neck. "You'll be patient with me?"

"Always." His voice was tender. "I'll take care of you. I promise."

The sincerity in his tone made her chest tight with longing.

Sebastian reached into his jacket pocket. "I have something for you."

He withdrew a delicate chain, sunlight catching on a deep blue sapphire set in tarnished gold.

"It was my mother's," he said, his voice roughening. "Our housekeeper smuggled it out before they seized everything. I've carried it for years, waiting for the right woman to give it to."

Rose's breath caught as he placed the necklace in her palm. The sapphire was deep as midnight, worn smooth with age. "Sebastian, it's beautiful."

"Turn around. Let us see how it looks on your beautiful neck."

She shifted so her back faced him. His fingers were gentle as he fastened the clasp, then brushed the sensitive skin at her nape. The sapphire settled coolly against her collarbone, and she shivered at both the touch of the stone and his hands.

"Perfect." He turned her to face him again. "I wish my parents could have met you."

"I believe they're here with us," Rose said, touching the pendant. "Along with my mother and Lizzie. All of them would want us to be happy."

Sebastian took her hands, his thumbs stroking across her knuckles. "I love you, my beautiful Rose."

"And I love you." She grinned. "I never thought it was possible to be this happy."

The garden was quiet except for the whisper of wind through the roses and the distant call of birds preparing for evening. Rose closed her eyes, memorizing this moment. The weight of the sapphire at her throat, Sebastian's hands warm around hers, the promise of their future stretching bright before them. Nothing could ever be sweeter.

If she had known during her darkest hours that they would lead to this joy, she might not have despaired so deeply. But perhaps those moments of desolation made one all the more grateful for the joyful ones.

ROSE STOOD AT the drawing room window, watching the carriage make its way up the drive. She pressed her dampened palms together and drew in a deep breath to calm her nerves. Sebastian's siblings were arriving for the wedding, and she was eager to welcome them into the family. But what if they were not as keen on the idea as she?

"I must confess to nerves." She turned to Sebastian, who was adjusting his cravat near the fireplace.

"It will all be fine." He came to stand beside her. "Sophia has been looking forward to this since James told her about you."

Rose touched the sapphire at her throat. His mother's necklace had become a treasured comfort. "I do hope we get along well."

"You will," Sebastian assured her. "She's going to adore you."

The sound of voices in the foyer made Rose's heart quicken.

Mrs. Blythe appeared in the doorway moments later, beaming while simultaneously wiping her eyes with a hanky. "Mr. Ashford and Miss Ashford have arrived."

Sebastian took Rose's hand. "Send them in, please."

James entered first, his familiar easy smile warming the room. Behind him came a blonde, petite, young woman with soft blue eyes.

"James, Sophia," Sebastian said, embracing his brother warmly, then opening his arms to his sister. Sophia melted into the embrace, and Rose caught a glimpse of her face relaxing against Sebastian's shoulder. When she pulled back, those blue eyes turned to Rose.

"Sophia, may I present Lady Rose," Sebastian said.

Rose took a careful step forward. "I am pleased to meet you, Miss Ashford."

Sophia's cheeks flushed pink. "I'm pleased to meet you too." She offered a small curtsy, her hands clasped tightly together. "I've been looking forward to getting to know you. And please, call me Sophia. We are to be sisters, after all."

"Only if you will call me Rose."

"I certainly shall," Sophia said.

James stepped forward, kissing Rose's hand. "It is nice to see you again, Lady Rose."

She exchanged a warm smile with James before gesturing toward the sitting area.

"Please, won't you sit?" Rose asked. "I've asked Mrs. Blythe to bring tea."

They settled around the hearth.

Rose drew in another deep breath, knowing this conversation could not be avoided. She must just get on with it. Say the words. Open the wounds. "Sophia, I must say how deeply sorry I am for the pain my father caused your family. I know the truth about what he did now and I'm deeply ashamed for his actions. Your brother has told me about what you endured."

Sophia's eyes filled with tears that she quickly blinked away, but when she spoke, her voice carried a gentle strength that surprised Rose. "You don't need to apologize for your father's actions. I imagine it must be excruciating for you—learning such terrible truths about someone you loved."

The compassionate understanding in her voice made Rose's chest ache. She'd expected anger, or at least coldness. Not this soft wisdom from someone who had every right to hate the Wentworth name.

"My whole life he lied to me," Rose said. "He took my mother from me. And your father from you. It's all too cruel to comprehend."

"I don't suppose we'll ever truly understand why he did what he did," James said gently.

Sophia nodded, her shoulders relaxing somewhat. "James told me you helped uncover the truth. That you chose to believe Sebastian even when it meant facing painful things about your father."

"It was quite clear he was right about everything."

"But it couldn't have been easy." Sophia looked directly at Rose, and there was something wise and knowing in her young face. "I believe you must be very courageous indeed."

Rose felt a kindred spirit in Sophia. "I have not felt courageous. Mostly frightened. I should have had more faith that good would eventually triumph."

Sophia smiled, shaking her head slightly. "It is hard to have faith when everything is difficult. I must acknowledge it is strange, given everything that's happened between our families, that we are to be sisters. But as I told Sebastian in my letter, our best revenge against the evil done to us is to live fully and to love unabashedly." She paused, studying Rose. "You're even lovelier than my brother described. He said you possessed the perfect name to describe your beauty, and I have to agree."

Rose felt her cheeks warm with pleasure. "You're very kind to say so. You are as exquisite as Sebastian said you were."

"If Sebastian was willing to let go of his desire for revenge, then he must truly love you. It has been the only emotion driving him for twelve years. To think that it's all ended with love is quite remarkable, is it not? One might say a miracle, even." Sophia leaned forward slightly, her earlier shyness transformed into earnest enthusiasm. "Your home is absolutely magnificent." Sophia glanced around the drawing room with what appeared to be genuine appreciation.

"Thank you. Now that I've inherited everything, your brother and I plan to make many changes." Rose glanced at Sebastian with a smile. "It might take some time but we intend to bring respect back to the estate."

Sophia's eyes lit up. "My brother is immensely clever, so I believe you'll be successful in no time at all. What will happen to the staff?"

"The staff will all stay, of course," Rose said. "Most of them have been here for years. They're family to me. The only family I've ever had."

Sophia's expression grew thoughtful. "Family is everything."

Rose nodded, understanding passing between them. The shadow of her father's crimes would always be part of their history, but it need not define their future. Together, they could build something beautiful from the ashes of the past.

THE EVE OF her wedding had arrived, and Rose sat in her childhood bedchamber, brushing her hair in the lamplight. Tomorrow she would marry Sebastian, and surprisingly, she felt calm. When one was marrying one's soulmate, there was little to fear.

A soft knock interrupted her thoughts.

"Come in," she called.

Mrs. Blythe entered, followed by Prudence, who was practically vibrating with excitement. The housekeeper carried something wrapped in tissue paper, handling it as carefully as spun glass.

"We have something for you, Lady Rose," Mrs. Blythe said, her voice unusually thick.

Rose set down her brush, curiosity piqued. "How kind. I can hardly wait to see what it is."

Mrs. Blythe placed the bundle on the bed and stepped back. Prudence bounced on her toes, hands clasped behind her back like a child with a secret.

Rose carefully unwrapped the tissue to reveal a wedding veil, delicate and trimmed with lace. Her breath caught. "It's beautiful. Did you make this?"

"I did the sewing," Prudence said, then bit her lip. "But the fabric... well, you might recognize it."

Rose lifted the veil, and something about the fabric's weight and texture made her heart skip. "Is it from Sebastian's handkerchiefs? This is what you wanted them for?" Prudence had asked for them a week or so ago. Rose had not thought much of it, figuring she was merely going to wash them for her. "How clever you are."

"I thought it would be a reminder of how hard you fought for love." Prudence grinned and bounced once again on her toes, making her seem very young for a moment.

"At the time, I knew I shouldn't keep them, but they were all I thought I'd ever have of him." Rose brushed her thumb against the lace.

"Dear Lady Rose," Mrs. Blythe said, her eyes growing bright. "There's nothing wrong with holding onto love, even when it seems impossible."

"My tears are still in these fibers. All those nights I cried into them."

Mrs. Blythe chuckled. "Actually, we washed them thoroughly. But the sentiment remains."

Rose laughed through the tears gathering in her eyes. "Then we'll think of it symbolically." She examined the intricate lacework along the edges. "The lace is extraordinary. Where did it come from?"

Mrs. Blythe's expression grew tender. "That came from your mother, in a way. She saved it for you when you were just a baby."

"She did?" Rose asked.

"It's from your grandmother's wedding gown—your mother's mother. She kept it all these years, waiting for your wedding day." Mrs. Blythe smoothed a finger along the delicate pattern. "She gave it to me for safekeeping, with strict instructions that it was for you and you alone."

Rose sank onto the bed, overwhelmed. "Why didn't Mummy use it for her own wedding?"

Mrs. Blythe's mouth tightened. "Your father's mother had other ideas about what Lady Eleanor should wear. That horrible woman insisted on choosing the veil herself."

"Probably for the best," Rose said quietly. "It would have been tainted, wearing it to marry him."

"My thoughts exactly," Mrs. Blythe said with a sniff.

Rose held the veil up to the lamplight, watching the lace cast intricate shadows on the wall. The handkerchiefs that had comforted her through her darkest hours, now transformed and adorned with lace her mother had lovingly preserved. It was almost too much to bear.

Rose reached for Prudence's hand, squeezing it tight. "I've never seen anything more perfect." Her voice broke. "That you would take something so precious to me and make it even more beautiful. I can't find the words."

"You don't need words." Mrs. Blythe dabbed at her eyes with her apron. "Your face says everything."

Prudence tented her hands under her chin, beaming. "It does."

Mrs. Blythe dabbed at her eyes. "Now then, we should get you to bed. Tomorrow is going to be a very long, very wonderful day."

Rose carefully placed the veil on a chair. Tomorrow she would marry Sebastian wearing the cloth that had absorbed her tears and the lace her mother had saved with such hope. Nothing could be better.

Rose turned to Mrs. Blythe and Prudence as they made for the door.

"Mrs. Blythe, do you think Mother would be happy? About Sebastian and me?"

Mrs. Blythe's smile was radiant. "I know she would be absolutely delighted. She once told me she hoped for a great love match for her daughter."

"I wish she was here," Rose said.

"She is," Mrs. Blythe said.

After they left, Rose sat in the quiet of her room, fingertips touching the sapphire at her throat. Tomorrow she would wear Sebastian's mother's necklace and her own mother's lace, carrying both families' blessings into their new life together.

The pieces of her broken past had somehow arranged themselves into something beautiful. To think how she'd despaired, believing she was doomed to a loveless marriage with a monster. Instead, she was to have her happy ending. From here on out, she would choose to believe that good would triumph over evil, even when the world seemed to challenge the idea at every turn. She promised herself then and there that the home and family she shared with Sebastian would always be one filled with love and compassion.

If so, perhaps Lizzie, her mother and Sebastian's father would not have died totally in vain. Not when their legacy was one of love.

# CHAPTER TWENTY-THREE

SEBASTIAN STOOD BEFORE the tall mirror in what had once been Lord Wentworth's dressing room, his hands shaking as he attempted to fasten his wedding waistcoat. The formal morning dress felt foreign despite weeks of practice, and his fingers seemed to have forgotten how to work the small buttons.

"Blast," he muttered, fumbling with the ivory silk for the third time. His reflection stared back at him. Good God, was that a tinge of green to his complexion? Why had nerves overtaken him?

A soft knock interrupted his struggles. "My lord? It's Finch. May I come in?"

"Please. I'm in desperate need of assistance."

Finch entered, carrying a perfectly pressed shirt and a selection of cravats. He'd grown more confident in his role over the past weeks, though Sebastian could still see traces of nervousness in his bearing. They were both growing accustomed to their new places in a world that had not always been kind to them.

"Good morning, my lord. Are you feeling all right?"

"Not really. In fact, I feel I might be sick." Sebastian gestured helplessly at his half-fastened waistcoat. "My hands won't seem to work properly."

"Wedding nerves, my lord. Perfectly natural. My cousin Billy was sick as a dog on his wedding morning. Couldn't keep his breakfast down."

"That's not particularly reassuring, Finch."

"Ah, but he had a lovely wedding once we got him to the church," Finch said cheerfully, beginning to work on Sebastian's waistcoat with practiced efficiency.

Sebastian watched in the mirror as Finch's capable hands made quick work of the buttons he'd been struggling with. "I knew you were the perfect choice for my valet, Finch. I couldn't be more pleased."

"Thank you, my lord. It's my honor to serve you." Finch stepped back, his gaze sweeping Sebastian from head to toe. "You must look perfect for Lady Rose."

"Yes. I mustn't disappoint her."

"I doubt that would be possible." Finch picked up the cravat they'd chosen for his nuptials. "But half the county will be at that church today, and I'll not have anyone saying Lord Ashford's valet doesn't know his business."

Sebastian smiled at the pride in Finch's voice. "I have no concerns in that regard."

Finch began working on the cravat. "Though I have to say, perhaps you should have a whiskey? To calm your nerves."

"At the moment, I cannot think of anything I would like less." Sebastian closed his eyes as Finch worked. "I didn't expect to be so nervous."

Finch stepped back to examine his work, then made a small adjustment. "You are splendid, my lord. Even if your stomach is slightly queasy. I doubt very much you'll be sick during your vows. It hardly ever happens."

Sebastian laughed. "Again, not terribly comforting."

Finch moved to the wardrobe and selected Sebastian's wedding coat—a deep blue that complemented his eyes. "Now then, let's get you into this. Can't keep your bride waiting."

As Finch helped him into the coat, Sebastian caught sight of himself in the mirror. "I look like my father. Like a gentleman."

"As it should be." Finch paused in his adjustments to Sebastian's collar. He straightened Sebastian's lapels with careful precision. He stepped back to survey his work, then nodded with satisfaction. "There. Perfection."

"Have you talked to Prudence? Is Lady Rose well this morning?"

"Beautiful as an angel, according to Prudence. Though she's a bit nervous too, if that's any comfort."

"It is, actually." Sebastian checked his reflection one final time, surprised to find that his hands had stopped shaking. "I am ready."

"Then let's get you to that church. Your bride is waiting."

As they made their way downstairs, Sebastian's nerves lessened. In fact, he grew more excited with every step toward the door. He was going to marry the most extraordinary woman he'd ever known. She loved him, which frankly, still seemed like an impossibility yet here they were. Choosing each other. A love match for two people who had seemed doomed for lives of misfortune.

At the bottom of the stairs, he squeezed Finch's shoulder. "She chose me. Is that not remarkable?"

"Not to me, my lord."

Mrs. Blythe appeared, slightly out of breath and looking unusually flustered.

"My lord, forgive the interruption, but Constable Stephens has just arrived. He's asking to speak with you and Mr. Hale urgently before you depart for the church."

Sebastian felt his stomach drop. "What's happened? Is Rose all right?"

"Lady Rose is perfectly well, my lord. She's already left for the church with her attendants. The constable seems pleased, if I may say so. Not bearing bad news."

Relief flooded through Sebastian, though he remained puzzled. "Where is he?"

"In the study, my lord. Mr. Hale is with him."

Sebastian exchanged a glance with Finch, who straightened his shoulders with determination. "Go on then, my lord. I'll wait here in case you need anything."

"Thank you." Sebastian made his way to the study, where he found Constable Stephens standing near the window.

Mr. Hale sat in one of the leather chairs but stood when Sebastian entered the room.

Sebastian closed the door behind him. "Mrs. Blythe said you needed to speak with us urgently. I hope there's no trouble—today of all days."

"No trouble for you, Lord Ashford." Stephens turned from the window. "Quite the opposite, in fact. I have news that I felt couldn't wait until after your wedding."

Sebastian took a seat beside Hale, who looked as if he might be holding his breath. "What news?"

"We've found Hargrave."

Hale made a sound somewhere between a gasp and a sob.

"Found him?" Sebastian leaned forward. "Where?"

"Dover," Stephens said. "Trying to board a ship bound for Calais. We'd been watching the ports, and one of my contacts recognized him from the description we'd circulated."

"And?" Hale's voice was barely above a whisper.

Stephens's expression grew grave. "We attempted to arrest him quietly, but he panicked. Ran toward the docks, pushing through crowds, knocking people down. My men gave chase."

Sebastian felt his chest tighten. "What happened?"

"He reached the end of a pier and found himself trapped. When we called for him to surrender, he drew a pistol. We couldn't tell if he meant to use it on us or himself, but he was waving it about wildly, shouting about how he wouldn't hang for what he'd done at the bidding of his employer."

Hale's face had gone pale and he appeared to be holding his breath.

"My sergeant ordered him to drop the weapon. Instead, Hargrave aimed it at us." Stephens's voice grew heavier. "We had no choice. My men fired to protect the innocent."

"Is he dead?" Sebastian began.

Stephens nodded. "Instantly."

Hale covered his face with his hands, his shoulders shaking.

Sebastian reached over to place a comforting hand on the older man's arm.

When Hale looked up, his eyes were wet with tears, but his expression was one of profound relief. "It's over. After all these years, it's finally over. Justice for Lizzie."

"Indeed it is," Stephens said gently.

Hale nodded, pulling out a handkerchief to wipe his eyes. "I'd begun to believe he might escape consequence entirely."

"Evil men often think they're clever enough to evade justice," Stephens replied. "But the truth has a way of catching up with them eventually."

Sebastian felt a weight had been lifted from his shoulders. "Were there any other casualties? Innocent people hurt?"

"None, thankfully. A few scrapes and bruises from when he knocked people down in his flight, but nothing serious." Stephens's expression softened. "I wanted you both to know before the ceremony. Felt you deserved to start your new life, Lord Ashford, with this chapter truly closed."

"Thank you," Sebastian said, meaning it deeply. "This news is everything we could have hoped for."

"Aye," Hale agreed, his voice steadier now. "To know that Lizzie can finally rest in peace? There's no greater gift you could have given me."

Stephens nodded. "She deserved justice. Still, I'm sorry for your grief."

"This lightens it very much, sir." Hale looked between Sebastian and the constable. "Now we can all move forward without looking over our shoulders, worried to see him lurking in the shadows."

Stephens checked his pocket watch. "I should let you gentlemen get to the church. Can't have Lord Ashford keeping his bride waiting on account of police business."

As they all rose, Sebastian extended his hand to the constable.

"Thank you, Stephens. For everything. Your courage and persistence brought justice not just for my father and Rose's mother, but for Lizzie as well."

"Just doing my duty, my lord. Though I'll admit, it's rare to see such a clear victory for the right side." Stephens shook Sebastian's hand firmly. "Now go marry that remarkable young lady of yours. After everything you've both been through, you deserve every happiness."

As Stephens took his leave, Sebastian turned to Hale, who was staring out the window with a peaceful expression Sebastian had never seen on his face before.

"How do you feel?" Sebastian asked.

"Free. For the first time in twelve years, completely free." He turned to Sebastian with a smile. "And on your wedding day, no less. It seems fitting, somehow."

"It does," Sebastian agreed. "All the shadows of the past finally laid to rest."

"Indeed." Hale straightened his cravat and assumed a more formal bearing. "Now then, my lord, we have a wedding to attend. And I have the honor of walking the most beautiful young woman in England down the aisle to marry the finest man I know."

Sebastian felt his throat tighten with emotion. "Thank you, Hale. I couldn't have done any of this without you."

"Nor I without you, my lord. But that's all behind us now. Today is about the future—yours and Lady Rose's."

As they prepared to leave for the church, Sebastian felt a profound sense of completion. The last of his father's enemies was gone, justice had been served for all who had suffered, and in mere minutes, he would marry the woman who had transformed his quest for vengeance into a journey toward love.

The past was finally, truly, at rest. And the future stretched ahead, bright with promise.

THE VILLAGE CHURCH of St. Edmund's sat nestled among ancient yew trees, its weathered stone walls holding centuries of prayers and promises. Inside, afternoon light streamed through tall, narrow windows, illuminating wooden pews polished to a warm glow and adorned with ivy and roses from the estate gardens.

Sebastian stood at the altar, his heart hammering against his ribs. He glanced at the faces filling the pews. His sister Sophia smiled sweetly in the front row while James sat beside her, only the tightness around his eyes betraying his emotion. Behind them, Rose's friends—Arabella, Daphne, Lydia, and Violet— watched with bright anticipation.

The church doors opened with a gentle creak, and Sebastian's breath caught.

Rose appeared on Mr. Hale's arm, radiant in ivory silk that seemed to capture and hold the golden light. Her gown was elegant in its simplicity, fitted through the bodice before flowing into soft folds that whispered across the stone floor.

Her green eyes found his immediately, and he was lost. How had he become so fortunate? This woman who had every reason to hate him had instead chosen to love him.

Rose walked toward him with steady grace, her cheeks flushed with emotion. In the pews, Mrs. Blythe and Mrs. Carter dabbed at their eyes while Finch sat between Mary and Prudence, all three beaming with joy for their beloved Rose.

When she reached him, Hale kissed her cheek tenderly. "Be happy, dear ones." He placed Rose's hand in Sebastian's before taking his seat beside Mrs. Blythe.

Sebastian felt the slight tremor in Rose's fingers as he took her hands. She smiled up at him, and he had to resist the urge to kiss her right then.

The elderly vicar opened his prayer book, his kind face solemn. "Dearly beloved, we are gathered here today in the sight of

God to join together this man and this woman in holy matrimony."

Sebastian barely heard the familiar words, lost in Rose's eyes.

"Sebastian Luke Ashford," the vicar said, "do you take Rose Eleanor Wentworth to be your wedded wife, to have and to hold from this day forward, for better, for worse, for richer, for poorer, in sickness and in health, to love and to cherish, till death do you part?"

Sebastian's voice came out steady despite the emotion threatening to overwhelm him. "I do."

"Rose Eleanor Wentworth, do you take Sebastian Luke Ashford to be your wedded husband, to have and to hold from this day forward, for better, for worse, for richer, for poorer, in sickness and in health, to love and to cherish, till death do you part?"

Rose's voice rang clear in the hushed church. "I do."

James stepped forward with the rings. Sebastian's hands shook slightly as he slipped the golden band onto Rose's finger. "With this ring, I thee wed."

Rose's eyes shimmered as she took his ring in turn, her whispered vows wrapping around his heart.

"Those whom God hath joined together, let no man put asunder," the vicar proclaimed, raising his hands in blessing. "I now pronounce you husband and wife. You may kiss your bride."

Sebastian cupped Rose's face gently and did as instructed.

The church erupted in quiet cheers and applause. When Sebastian and his bride stepped outside of the church, the gathered villagers burst into celebration at the sight of the newlyweds. Rose's hand was warm in Sebastian's as they paused on the church steps, taking in the faces of the people who had chosen to welcome them despite everything.

"Lady Ashford," Sebastian murmured near her ear. "Are you ready for the rest of our life?"

"Lord Ashford, there has never been a bride as keen as I to start a life with the man I love."

Together they raised their joined hands to acknowledge the cheering crowd before stepping toward the carriage that would take them home.

# CHAPTER TWENTY-FOUR

THE ENTIRE VILLAGE had turned out for the wedding feast, transforming the gardens of Wentworth Manor into a tapestry of celebration. Under the golden light of late afternoon, long tables draped with crisp white linens groaned beneath the weight of the harvest—platters of roasted lamb studded with rosemary, golden pastries filled with late summer fruits, wheels of local cheese, and bottles of locally made wine.

The air was perfumed with the mingled scents of honeysuckle and lavender from the nearby borders, roasting meat from the kitchen fires, and the sweet fragrance of roses that climbed the manor's stone walls. A gentle breeze carried the sound of laughter and conversation across the grounds, rustling through the ancient oak trees that provided dappled shade for the guests below.

Farmers in their Sunday best raised pewter tankards filled with local ale, toasting the newlyweds while discussing the promise of the coming harvest. Their weathered faces were animated with good humor and the unaccustomed luxury of leisure on a working day. Children in their finest clothes darted between the tables like bright butterflies, their laughter ringing out as they attempted to snatch sugared almonds and honey cakes when they thought no one was watching.

The blacksmith stood deep in conversation with the baker and the village carpenter, all three men marveling at a master who had thrown open his gates to celebrate alongside his people rather than retreating behind manor walls.

Near the musicians—a cheerful group with fiddle, flute, and drum—young women from the village clustered together, their best ribbons fluttering in the breeze as they stole glances at young men.

Rose felt certain there would be many more love stories that would come from this day of celebration.

Constable Stephens sat at one of the long tables with his wife and children, and Rose felt a warm satisfaction seeing him relaxed and smiling. This man who had risked so much to help them find justice would always possess a piece of her heart. His youngest daughter had fallen asleep against his shoulder, worn out by the excitement and the warmth of the September afternoon.

Sebastian had barely left Rose's side since they'd come from the chapel as husband and wife, but now he stood with Mr. Hale and several tenant farmers near the estate's prize apple trees, already deep in discussions about expanding the orchards for next year's cider production. His animated gestures and the farmers' nodding heads suggested plans taking shape that would benefit them all.

Arabella appeared at Rose's elbow, linking their arms with the easy familiarity of true friendship. "What a day this is. I am delighted for you."

"I never thought it possible to be this happy."

"You deserve every happiness, dear friend," Arabella said.

They wandered toward the fragrant lavender bushes that bordered the formal gardens, their purple spikes heavy with late-season blooms that hummed with the drone of satisfied bees. From this vantage point, they could survey the entire celebration—the swirl of colorful dresses, the gleam of polished boots, the flash of silver serving platters being passed among the guests.

"How is it possible? After all the ugliness, to have a day such as this?" Rose asked.

"It's a reminder that we must never give up hope," Arabella

said.

The late afternoon light was beginning to take on the golden quality that spoke of autumn's approach, casting everything in a warm glow that made even the humblest cottage garden flowers look like treasures. The harvest feast was in full swing now—platters being refilled, wine flowing freely, conversations growing more animated as neighbors who rarely had time to talk at length caught up on months of news.

"Lady Rose?" Prudence hurried over, slightly breathless and flushed with excitement. Her best dress, a soft blue that complemented her eyes, was slightly rumpled from helping in the kitchens, but her smile was radiant. "Sebastian is ready to make the toast."

Rose felt a flutter of nervous anticipation. This would be Sebastian's first public address as Lord Ashford, the moment when he truly claimed his place as master of the estate.

She excused herself from Arabella and made her way to the stone terrace where Sebastian waited, devastatingly handsome in his wedding finery. The crowd began to gather around them, glasses and tankards raised, faces turned expectantly toward their new lord and lady.

"Thank you all for celebrating with us today," Sebastian began, his voice carrying easily across the garden, strong and confident. "Rose and I have great plans for Wentworth Manor. Ones that will bring prosperity to our entire community. Today we celebrate not just our marriage, but a new beginning for all of us."

A great cheer erupted, the sound rolling across the estate grounds like thunder. Tankards clinked together, wine glasses caught the last rays of sunlight, and even those who had initially been skeptical of the former gardener now looked at him with evident respect and approval.

"And now," Rose called out, her voice bright with joy, "please dance!"

The musicians struck up a lively waltz, and Sebastian turned to her with an elegant bow that made her heart race anew. "May I have this honor, Lady Ashford?"

"You may, Lord Ashford."

He drew her into his arms, and they moved in slow, graceful circles on the grass, their steps perfectly matched despite the unconventional dance floor. The earth was soft beneath their feet, still warm from the day's sunshine, and Rose could smell the crushed herbs that released their fragrance with each step.

Around them, other couples joined the dance. Finch boldly asked Prudence, who accepted with a blush that rivaled the sunset, and even some of the older village couples took to the makeshift dance floor with the enthusiasm of newlyweds themselves. Children clapped in time to the music, and those too elderly to dance tapped their feet from their seats at the tables.

"I cannot imagine a more perfect day." Sebastian's breath was warm against her cheek as they swayed together.

Rose looked up at him, this man who had started as her enemy and had become her salvation, her heart so full it felt as though it might burst. "Nor can I."

His eyes darkened with promise as he spun her gently under his arm. "Soon we can slip away and begin our wedding night properly."

Heat bloomed in her cheeks, but she met his gaze boldly. "I have waited long enough to feel you next to me."

As they continued to dance under the deepening September sky, surrounded by the laughter and music of their village, Rose's heart nearly burst with the joy of it all.

"Have I mentioned how much I love and adore you?" Rose asked, gazing up at her husband.

"Yes, but say it again."

And so she did.

# EPILOGUE

T HE DAY BEFORE Christmas, snow fell softly over Wentworth Manor, transforming the gardens into a winter wonderland. Inside the drawing room, a fire crackled in the hearth while the scent of spiced cider and pine filled the air.

Sebastian stood by the mantel, watching his wife with the contentment of a man who had found the center of his universe. Rose sat beside Sophia on the settee, their heads bent together in quiet conversation, while James lounged in an armchair, looking more relaxed than Sebastian had seen him in years. Having his siblings here for Christmas felt like a gift he'd never dared hope for.

Their new butler appeared in the doorway. "Excuse me, my lord, but Constable Stephens is at the door."

Sebastian exchanged a glance with Rose before setting down his glass. In the foyer, Stephens waited with ruddy cheeks and an official-looking letter in his hand.

"Apologies for calling so late, Lord Ashford, but I didn't think this should wait." Stephens handed him the correspondence with a meaningful look.

Sebastian broke the seal with unsteady fingers, Rose appearing at his side as he scanned the words. For a moment, he couldn't breathe. The Crown had officially restored everything—title, wealth, and Ashford Hall. His father's name was completely cleared.

"What is it?" Rose whispered, her hand finding his arm.

"It's all been restored." His voice shook with emotion. "Everything. The Crown has righted the wrong done to our family."

Rose's eyes filled with tears. "Oh, Sebastian." She turned to the constable. "Please, you must join us for a drink. Our family is in the drawing room. They will be overjoyed to hear this news."

Back in the drawing room, Sebastian held up the letter. "The Crown has reinstated our title and returned our estate. With their deepest apologies."

The silence stretched for a heartbeat before James shot to his feet. "You're serious?"

"Completely." Sebastian's voice broke.

Sophia covered her mouth, tears spilling over. "Papa would be so proud and happy. Finally, justice."

James grabbed the letter, scanning it himself. "It's all here. We've won. We've finally won." He looked between his siblings. "It seems impossible, but it's all true."

They all thanked the constable and asked again if he would stay, but he declined. "My family's home waiting for me to begin our celebrations. However, I didn't feel this could wait."

After Constable Stephens left, the four of them sat in contemplative silence.

"Will you return to Ashford Hall?" James asked eventually.

Sebastian looked at Rose, knowing they were of the same mind. "No. Our work is here. The estate, the tenants—they're counting on us. This is our home." He met James's gaze. "It is for you to with it as you please. If you want it. We have the funds now. You can restore it to its former glory."

James grinned, rubbing his hands together. "I accept. There is nothing I like better than a project. We will make it a beautiful home once again."

"Perhaps you can find a bride to share it with?" Rose said.

"Let us not get ahead of ourselves," James said, laughing.

"Sophia, you can finally have your Season," Rose added with enthusiasm.

But Sophia shook her head. "I'm not ready to leave Amelia. She needs me."

Sebastian studied his sister's stubborn expression. "Sophia, you're a lady now, not a governess. You deserve your own life."

"I am all Amelia has. I will not abandon her as we were abandoned."

The pain in her voice made Sebastian's chest tighten.

"Give us one more year," Sophia said. "Let me find someone suitable to replace me first."

He did not believe she would leave in a year. If anything, she would be even more attached. Sebastian wanted to argue, but Rose's gentle touch on his arm stopped him. His wife's wisdom had guided them this far. He would trust her instincts now.

"One year," Sebastian said. "But then you come home to us."

"You won't force me to marry someone I don't love?" Sophia asked.

"Never," Sebastian said.

When they were called to Christmas Eve supper, Sebastian offered Rose his arm. "Our first Christmas as husband and wife."

"The first of many." He looked into her eyes, intoxicated by her beauty and grace, awed that she was truly by his side.

Hours later, Rose lay warm in Sebastian's arms, the manor quiet around them. Just as he was drifting toward sleep, her voice pulled him back.

"Sebastian? Are you awake?"

"Always, for you. What is it, my love?"

She turned in his arms, her eyes bright in the moonlight. "I have news. The most wonderful Christmas gift."

Something in her tone made his heart race. "What kind of news?"

"The kind that arrives in about seven months."

He sat up so quickly he nearly tumbled her from the bed. "Rose, are you saying—?"

"I'm saying we're going to have a baby."

Joy crashed over him like a warm wave. He gathered her

close, one hand coming to rest reverently on her still-flat stomach. "A baby. Our baby."

"If it's a boy, we'll name him after your father. And if it's a girl, after my mother."

Sebastian felt tears prick his eyes. "Nothing would make me happier."

As Rose nestled comfortably into his arms, moonlight spilled gently through the curtains, bathing them both in silvered peace. Sebastian inhaled softly, breathing in the delicate scent of her hair as he gazed upward, awed by the quiet enormity of their blessings. A cleared name, a reclaimed legacy, and now, the promise of new life. But greater than any of these gifts was the woman beside him. Rose was his anchor, his guiding star—his beautiful rose who had blossomed bravely through every thorn in her path. Now, she would be the mother of his child. The first of many, he hoped. Smiling, he decided to keep that thought to himself. No need to overwhelm his wife with his dreams of a large, rambunctious family. Tonight, on this most perfect of nights, he was content to pull her ever closer and fall asleep listening to the beat of her heart.

## The End

## About the Author

Tess Thompson Romance... hometowns and heartstrings.

Tess Thompson is a USA Today Bestselling and award-winning author of clean and wholesome Contemporary and Historical Romance, with over 60 published titles. Her heartfelt stories feature family sagas, romance, a sprinkle of mystery, and all the second chances her characters deserve.

Tess is happily married to Cliff, affectionately known as "Best Husband Ever." Their love story is one for the books—they met on Tinder in their forties after both had endured heartache. Tess was a divorced mom of two girls, and Cliff was a widower raising two teenage boys. Now, their blended family includes two "Bonus Sons" and two daughters, all grown and forging their paths. Tess is incredibly proud of each one, even if she's still puzzled by her daughter's talent for Chemistry, which didn't come from her!

A small-town girl at heart, Tess grew up in a place much like the towns in her novels. After earning her degree from USC's Drama School, she dreamed of acting, but her passion for writing won out, leading to the career she cherishes today. Most days, you'll find her matchmaking fictional characters from her cozy office, often with one of her cats—Midnight, Mac, or Mable—curled up nearby.

Tess loves strong coffee, red wine, reading in bed, and spending lazy afternoons binge-watching TV shows, especially Masterpiece Theatre. She's a Zumba enthusiast, despite occasional knee protests, and has a soft spot for French fries over cookies any day. Cooking isn't her strong suit—her cakes often fall apart, even with a mix—and she's prone to a bit of messiness, especially when she's on a writing deadline. But she blames her forgetfulness on the constant swirl of stories in her head.

Grateful for her readers, Tess pours her heart into every story she writes. With Cliff's unwavering support, she's living her dream of writing full-time from their recently purchased dream house on a small lake—a place she still pinches herself over. Tess's books remind us that no matter how complicated life gets, love and second chances are always possible.